REFUSE

(Recoil Trilogy Book 2)

Joanne Macgregor

OTHER YOUNG ADULT BOOKS BY THIS AUTHOR

Scarred (2015)

Recoil (2016)

Fault Lines (2016, Protea)

Rock Steady (2013, Protea)

Turtle Walk (2011, Protea)

If you would like to receive my author's newsletter, with tips on great books, a behind-the-scenes look at my writing and publishing processes, and advance notice of new books, giveaways and special offers, then sign up at my website, www.joannemacgregor.com.

First published in 2016 by KDP.

ISBN 978-0-620-70291-1
ISBN:978-0-620-70292-8 (e-book)

www.joannemacgregor.com

For Jan and Lorna,
I wish you could be here to read this.

"We must not allow ourselves to become like
the system we oppose."
Archbishop Desmond Tutu

"There comes a time when one must take a position
that is neither safe, nor politic, nor popular, but he must take
it because his conscience tells him it is right."
Martin Luther King Jr.

Part One

Chapter 1

Eyes open

When I open my eyes, I am blindfolded, traveling in a vehicle, with my hands tightly bound together and lying in my lap.

I know that my hands are tied because when I try to rub at the tickle of something trickling down the side of my face, both hands move together. They must be secured to something else as well, because I can only lift them as far as my chest before some restraint kicks in. I yank hard, but it holds firm.

I know that I am in a vehicle of some kind because I hear the engine and feel my body lurch against the seatbelt when it accelerates and brakes.

I know I am blindfolded because I can feel my eyelashes brush against something as I blink, and even though my eyes are open, everything is still dark and unfathomable.

Kind of like my life.

I have never seen clearly, never fully grasped what is actually happening, even when it is happening in full view and all around me. I have been like a mushroom — kept well and truly in the dark and fed a load of crap. About my father, about ASTA, about Quinn.

The tickling sensation continues. It must be blood still oozing from the place where the guard hit my head. The fog clouding my brain begins to dissolve, only to be replaced by a throbbing headache.

"Hullo?" My voice is hoarse in my dry throat.

No answer.

I am not alone in this car or van. I can sense the presence, just about hear the breathing, of someone sitting to my left. I am totally alone, though, in my predicament. I helped Quinn escape, but it came at the price of my own capture, and I suspect that things are about to get rough.

At the thought of what I know must lie ahead, my heart kicks into a faster rhythm, and a flush of adrenalin tingles through my fingers. I am not brave, just an ace with a virtual reality gaming console, and a highly skilled expert with a sniper's rifle. But I have no rifle now. No rifle, no tranquilizer dart gun, not even a freaking pea-shooter. I will need to use my brain to get through the next few hours. Or days. Weeks? I swallow hard. I am thirstier than I can ever remember being.

"Can I have some water?"

More silence.

"Please?" It can't hurt to try the magic word.

"Shut up," says a voice to my left. It is deep, male and completely unfamiliar to me. "We'll let you know when we want you to talk."

A bubble of fear releases itself from somewhere deep in the pit of my stomach and begins to rise up through my chest. I fight against it. I need to stay calm and clearheaded, concentrating on the present moment rather than on some possibly painful near future. And the skill of staying focused is one I have in spades. Accurate marksmanship was not the only skill that we sniping cadets were trained in by our instructors at the Advanced Skills Training Academy of the Southern Sector. I force myself to slow my breathing, pursing my lips as I exhale to allow the air to trickle out gradually. Within a minute, my heart rate steadies.

I shift my attention to my senses, determined to register any details I can about this journey and our destination. The cadets in our unit at ASTA were also trained to be exceptional observers, drilled to notice and memorize details. It's time to kick that aspect of my instruction into gear.

The vehicle slows, turns, moves forward more slowly — down a driveway? — turns again, and then stops. The engine is turned off. Silence. The click of a seatbelt clasp and then I am jerked forward.

"Where are we?" I ask.

"Duck," says the voice.

A hand presses against the top of my head — I guess to prevent me banging it as I stumble out. So they do not want me hurt. Not yet. All pain will be inflicted deliberately and intentionally at the right time and for the purpose of extracting maximum information from me.

I yank my thoughts back to the present, force myself to concentrate on the details of our walk. Gravel crunches underfoot, then my feet are on a more level surface — paving? I scan my senses. I can smell the sharp scent of male aftershave or deodorant coming off my captor, but nothing beyond that. The air is cool on my face, and I don't hear birds calling, so it's probably still night then.

"Four steps up," says the man.

I make out the sound of a big car or truck somewhere not too distant. I reckon we must still be in the city, off the street, perhaps at the back entrance to some building where no one will see or wonder at the appearance of a sixteen-year-old girl with long blond hair tied up in a ponytail; wearing a pink dress, a blindfold and restraints; and being hauled, stumbling, up a set of stairs.

"Where are you taking me? Who are you?"

Aftershave says nothing, just shoves me through what must be a doorway, banging my arms painfully against its narrow frame.

"We need to take her straight up. They're already waiting." A new voice, female.

I distinguish two sets of footsteps, apart from my own, clicking against the floor — marble or tiles, judging from the hard, smooth surface — and echoing through the open space. Are we in a foyer?

It occurs to me that we haven't passed through a decontamination unit. Then I register, belatedly, that I am not wearing a respirator and, judging from the fact that his voice does not sound at all muffled, neither is my escort. According to President Hawke's government, the Rat Fever virus supposedly lies in wait, patient as death, on surfaces and in the air, ready to infect and reduce its human victims to gibbering, hemorrhagic bags of pus and blood. But we are not wearing even the most basic of protective masks.

We cross the open space and wait for a few moments, and then a chime sounds the arrival of an elevator. Three paces inside. The doors swish closed behind us, and I am spun around. Going up, three soft pings for three floors.

Already I am noting our route and committing it to memory, forming a picture in my mind's eye of our course through the building. The doors open, and I am tugged forward. Left on exit, twenty-one paces, right turn, a long walk of fifty paces, another right, seventeen paces, left, thirty paces, and then we halt. I use the pause to memorize the route — L21, R50, R17, L30.

I hear a door open to my left, and I am pushed inside and onto a chair. Something fastens around my waist, securing me in place. With a brief tug of hair at the back of my head, the blindfold is pulled off my eyes.

"Where am I?" I demand, squinching my eyes against the sudden brightness. My only answer is the sound of a slamming door and a clicking lock.

It is several moments before my eyes adjust to the light and

I can look around. It takes only one swift glance for me to know where I am. I have seen a room like this before. Was it just last night that I sat beside Quinn on my bed in my quarters at ASTA — my heart full of hope about the two of us, my head full of doubts about everything he had just told me — and stared with growing horror at the illicitly obtained video footage on the screen of his phone? I watched as a man I had immobilized with a tranquilizer dart was questioned and tortured in a room just like this. Perhaps in this very room.

Now I am the one sitting under a bright light, on a steel chair bolted to the floor, in the center of an interrogation room.

Now I am the one about to be interrogated.

Chapter 2

Firewall

The floor of the interrogation room is made of polished concrete which slopes down towards a small drain in the center of the room. All the better for cleaning up afterwards.

Two walls are blank of anything but a no-smoking sign, and the door is in the wall to my left. Across the width of the fourth wall — the wall I face — is a large mirror. It must be one-way glass, and I wonder who, even now, might be standing behind it, observing me.

Sarge — our tough and demanding drill sergeant and sniper unit instructor, the squad leader who tried to turn me into a cold-hearted angel of death? Roberta Roth — the head of ASTA, the outwardly compassionate woman who showed me footage of my father being infected with the rat fever virus in an attack by bio-terrorists, and dying a gruesome death? Or perhaps Leya, my fellow cadet in the sniper unit and my friend? Correction: the mole in our unit, and the girl I had *thought* was my friend.

Together she and I had suffered through Sarge's brutal boot camp drills, learned to shoot and reconnoiter and camouflage ourselves into near-invisibility. She comforted brokenhearted and miserable me when Quinn dumped me after discovering that I was a sniper, and urged me on when I struggled to shoot the mutant rats that had been genetically engineered to spread the plague, and which had grown resistant to poisons. Leya encouraged me when I recoiled at darting M&Ms — the so-called plague-infected Mike and Marys who were ill with rat fever and posed a risk of infecting others — so that they could be brought in to hospitals. She reassured me when I had doubts about shooting suspected terrorists with tranquilizer darts, so that they could be brought in for debriefing. *Debriefing* — ha! She'd done a great job of keeping me on course, and no wonder, because Leya, I discovered this afternoon, is a spy for Roberta Roth. And God knows who else.

There is nothing else to look at but my reflection in the mirrored glass. I am still wearing the awful pink dress that makes me look like an innocent young girl, and allows me to get close enough to suspects to dart them. No one expects blond, pigtailed little girls to be steady-handed snipers or black-ops agents. It is the perfect disguise and the reason, no doubt, why ASTA chose to train teens rather than adults.

I look like I've gone a few rounds in a fight cage. The shin on my right leg is swollen and blue, the knee scraped and puffy. The right side of my face is swollen and smeared with blood, and my eye is starting to blacken. The cut on my cheek has stopped bleeding, but the shiny wetness of the blood in the hair on the side of my head suggests the wound there still oozes. My forehead and upper lip glint with a sheen of cold sweat.

I am still wearing the pink polka-dotted latex gloves and my steel ID band around my left wrist, but my watch has been removed, probably to make me feel even more disoriented. Mechanical restraints gape open on the arms of the sturdy steel chair, but my hands are still bound together with white plastic zip ties in the front of me. My captors made a mistake there. I am bound to the chair with the metal restraining band around my middle, so they probably think there is no need to take the extra precaution of tying my hands behind my back, since there is no way I can escape. No doubt they are right about that. But having my hands in front of me allows me to raise them and press them against the silver earring looped around my left bra strap.

Quinn gave me that earring, back when he still loved me. Or said he did. It's the twin of the hoop he wears threaded through his left eyebrow. I took it out of my ear when he ditched me, but ever since I've worn it over my heart. I press it now with my thumbs. To the eyes behind the mirror, it must look like I'm praying, but really I'm reminding myself of why I'm here, why I did this.

The zip ties pinch tight over the steel ID band, and it hurts where it's cutting into the flesh of my wrist. It's ridiculous, given what I'm facing, to be bothered by a discomfort as small as this. Soon things will get much worse.

Soon they will begin.

I remember the order of the process from the footage Quinn showed me. First, the unnerving wait. Then the polite, almost gentle, questioning. Next the repetitions, the accusations, demands and commands. The shouting and shaking awake, the denial of food and water and rest. Then the blows, the shocks, the near-drowning.

I must have my story straight before they start. I figure I should either confess immediately, or not at all. There is no point in suffering if I just end up giving them the details anyway. I need to prepare my version of events and tell them the whole of it up front, sticking as closely to the truth as possible.

I close my eyes and visualize stuffing what I'm determined not to tell them into a steel locker, padlocking it shut, and burying it deep inside me. Then I cover it with layers of the story I *will* tell them.

I prepare my account in my mind, peppering it with facts and keeping it simple. Silently, I tell myself the story over and over again, visualizing it, making it so real in my mind's eye that it's like a clear memory. I add images and sounds, amplify certain aspects, minimize others, and skip over a few entirely. My twin brother Robin would be proud of my storytelling abilities. If only he could write one of his elegant pieces of code and program me to say no more than I intend. If only he could implant a torture-resistant firewall around my brain.

I think about what questions they're likely to ask me and formulate my responses. By the time they come into the room, I am as ready as I'll ever be.

Sarge enters first, carrying two folding metal chairs. He places one directly in front of me, and sits on the other in the front left corner of the room, to the side of the mirror. His bald head gleams in the strong light, and his dark eyes glitter with some emotion I can't read. Is it eagerness? Determination? As he makes eye contact with me, a sudden manic grin cleaves his face. I should be used to that habit by now, but here in this room, it's shockingly out of place.

"Look at you, Blue," he says. The blue streaks in my hair have mostly faded, but my nickname from boot camp has stuck.

I don't respond, and beneath his mustache, Sarge's smile vanishes as quickly as it appeared.

A tall, thin man with wispy hair so colorless it's almost transparent enters the room. He's wheeling a stainless steel trolley loaded with the instruments I saw put to nauseating use in that interrogation footage. He positions himself behind me — all the better to unnerve me — and gives a phlegmy clearing of his throat. I shudder.

Last to enter is ASTA chief Roberta Roth. She is smartly dressed, as always, from her crocodile-skin high-heeled shoes to her black business suit, but she removes her jacket, hanging it neatly over the chair back, before she sits down directly in front of me. She unbuttons the cuffs of her white blouse and rolls up the sleeves in neat folds, as if she plans to get busy with some gardening. No doubt she intends digging inside of me. Her stark, asymmetrical bob of sleek, black hair dips as she leans forward to smooth her skirt over her knees, and I get a flash of its iridescent, pokeweed-berry-purple underside.

"Mr. Smith." She nods a greeting to the man behind me and then turns her attention to me. "Well, well, well," she says. Her small mouth, stained with crimson lipstick, pulls into a tight, disapproving line.

"Where am I? What's happening here?"

"You are here, Miss Jinx E. James, to be debriefed on today's events in the presence of these witnesses." She extends her manicured hands in the direction of Sarge and the man who may or may not be called Mr. Smith. Her nails are painted the same poisonous color as the underside of her hair.

"By you? Why not by the authorities?"

"We *are* the official authority. We have been mandated by the Civil Security Command of the Government of the Southern Sector, under President Alex Hawke, to question persons who are suspected of being involved in subversive activities. Especially when such persons are our own assets in our training division."

Did that mean that ASTA had other divisions? What else might they be up to apart from using virtual reality games as a way to recruit talented teens, and then training them to become specialists in spying, intelligence analysis, marksmanship, operations management and who knew what other paramilitary skills?

"Can I have a lawyer?" I ask.

I know what the answer will be, but I want to appear ignorant and birdbrained. I want them to underestimate me.

Sarge gives a sharp bark of laughter, there is a wet sniff from Mr. Smith, and Roth shakes her head.

"In terms of Emergency Ordinance 53.2.1 of the Civil Safety and Protection Act, we are permitted to detain you for a period of twenty-one days, without trial or legal representation, in order to interview you."

Question. Debrief. Interview. They make it sound like a civilized process, but I know better.

"And so, cadet JJ20027, let us commence your interview." She extracts a folded sheet of paper from her jacket pocket, opens it and scans it. "First question: how *precisely* did you wind up here?"

"I was driven here, Ms. Roth. In a van, from the sound of it."

She snaps out a hand and slaps me, hard, across my already bloodied cheek. It happens so fast, I'm stunned — until the sharp stinging confirms that she actually did strike me. My eyes well. Jeez, if I'm reduced to tears by a simple slap, then Mr. Smith won't need to resort to his instruments.

"Don't give me any sass, young lady. I want straight answers."

I wonder if I am now seeing the real Ms. Roth. There is no hint of the compassion or friendliness she's shown me in the last few months. In her dark eyes, I now see only cold, shrewd suspicion.

This tight-lipped woman has misled me about many things — including the way my father actually died — in order to manipulate me into functioning as the best little shooter in the Southern Sector. But she's unaware that I know that truth, that her deceit has made me determined to outwit her.

I rub a shoulder against my burning cheek and ask, "What do you want to know? I don't know why I'm here, I've done nothing wrong."

"We both know that's not true." Roth examines the palm of her hand. Is it stinging, like my face? "Why don't we begin with you telling me all about your relationship with young Mr. Quinn

O'Riley?"

"Him!" I channel all the wounded outrage I am feeling from her humiliating slap into my voice.

"Yes, him."

"I'll tell you all about him. He's a jerk! Here I sit on a chair being slapped in the face and where's he? Tell me that? I hate him!" The emotion comes easily — it's a relief to let out some of the pressure.

"When did you first meet him?"

"He was on the same transport as me on the day we all came to the ASTA compound."

"You didn't know him before that?" Roth narrows her eyes at me as if trying to peer into my brain.

"Huh? What? No." I wasn't expecting that question, but it works to my advantage. My surprise is so genuine that Roth leans back into her chair, relaxing fractionally.

I catch a whiff of her fragrance. It's cloying and sweet, and catches in my throat. If deception had a scent, this is how it would smell.

"Go on," Roth says.

"I thought he was cute, I liked him. I *thought* he felt the same way about me. So we … hooked up."

"With a member of the intel unit, even though you were advised to stick to socializing with members of your own unit?"

From his position at the front of the room, Sarge says, "I did warn you, Blue." He shakes his head at what he once called my pigheadedness.

"You were right, Sarge." I'm tempted to hang my head, as if in shame at my own foolishness, but maybe that would be overdoing it. I settle for pulling my mouth into a sour twist.

"Why couldn't you have *hooked up* with, say, Bruce?" he asks.

Bruce, gung-ho cadet sniper and unthinking patriot, had me in the center of his romantic crosshairs from the first time we met.

But I had eyes only for Quinn, which made Bruce instantly hate him. Even if I had never met Quinn, however, I could never have dated Bruce. I don't know how to respond to Sarge's question, so I just shrug.

"Back to Quinn," says Roth, consulting her list of questions again. "What did he tell you?"

"He told me he loved me! He told me he'd never felt this way about a girl before, that I was beautiful and special and —"

"What did he tell you about the *rebels*?"

Roth, I notice, gets irritated every time I lay on the emo teen angst. I store that byte of information in my brain.

"Nothing," I lie.

"*Nothing*," Roth repeats, and her voice is thin and soft. It raises the hairs on the back of my neck.

She wipes one edge of her mouth with a long, purple nail. Behind me, Smith rattles his trolley. Roth holds up a hand, as if to stay an attack dog, then looks back at me.

"He said nothing about his views on the government and the opposition?"

"Oh, he said lots about *that*. He said that our civil rights were being eroded by the government's new repressive measures, that we no longer had real freedom of speech or movement or reproduction, and that we should protest against our email and phone calls and web activity being monitored — stuff like that. But nothing about any rebels."

"Did he say *how* we should all be protesting against the new measures?"

"No. I just figured he meant to sign web petitions, or maybe go on marches."

"Petitions and marches?" She lets the words, heavy with incredulity, hang in the air. I nod several times, like a pet Robodog responding to a voice command. "And what did he tell you about

Connor O'Riley?"

"He said Connor was his older brother."

She moves suddenly, and I flinch, expecting another slap. But she merely shoves her face so close to mine that I see how her lipstick is bleeding into the lines that rise vertically from her upper lip. "Miss James, do not waste my time or insult my intelligence. You are already in an enormous amount of trouble, and I suggest you do not make matters worse for yourself by playing me for a fool, or by being obstinate to the point of idiocy." She says the words in a rush. Her nostrils flare as she takes a deep breath before continuing more slowly. "Now, what did he say about his brother?" She speaks each word distinctly, as threateningly as if she were planning to rip me apart limb by limb.

Perhaps she is.

Chapter 3

The fight

When I answer Roberta Roth, I try to make my voice sound small and cowed. I try not to let the calculation behind the careful choice of every word show on my face.

"Quinn said his brother was with the civil libs, that he disapproved of how the government was taking away individual liberties. And that we should open the borders again, and fight for our rights of free speech and stuff."

I am sticking faithfully to my prepared lines. These are things I *can* tell them about Connor and his kind, because they must already know at least this much about him.

But there are other things I must not reveal that either the rebels or I know, suspicions I must not voice — such as their belief that rat fever, while lethal, is not nearly as infectious as the government would have us believe, that it's transmitted only by direct contact with bodily fluids, or bites from infected critters. Or people. If they find out I know this, they will probably keep me detained forever to prevent me spreading the stories.

"'*Fight*'? How?" asks Roth.

"Vote for the Civil Libs, I guess, I don't know."

"What else do you know about Connor O'Riley?"

"Nothing. I never spoke to the guy. I never even met him until today" — this much is completely true — "when I shot him with a tranq-dart under duress and at the direct instruction of my Unit Commander." I shoot an accusing glare at Sarge.

"I want to know exactly what happened today, starting with you submitting your resignation to Sarge this morning."

Was that only this morning? It seems like a lifetime has passed in just the few hours since.

"Well, I told Sarge I wanted out."

"Why?"

"Why?"

"Yes, why did you want to leave the sniping unit when you were, by all accounts, its most skilled member?"

"Um …" I stall for time, hoping it looks like I am trying to hide something. I *am* trying to hide something — many things — but this, again, is something I am sure they already know. I will give it to them, but not too easily. "I was never … comfortable … with shooting live creatures."

"Sarge says you overcame your reluctance." Roth glances over her shoulder for verification. Sarge shrugs and nods.

"I wouldn't say that. I mean, I forced myself to shoot them, but I never liked it, I was still reluctant."

Roth stares at me, holding the silence. I lift my bound hands to wipe sweat off my forehead.

"But then when we had to start shooting *people*" — another glance between Roth and Sarge — "suspects and M&Ms — that just freaked me out."

"You weren't shooting them. You were darting them with tranquilizers. That's a big difference."

I nod grudgingly, conceding the point.

"You darted the suspects so that they could be brought in for questioning."

I allow my shoulders to tense up fractionally in response to her last word.

"And," she continues, "you darted the infected persons so that they could be brought in for palliative treatment, allowing them to have a peaceful and pain-free passing, and giving their families a chance to say goodbye."

"I know, I know," I say, sagging in my chair. "But it still freaked me out. I had flashbacks and nightmares, and I felt sick all of the time."

"But you were still coping. Then, all of a sudden this morning, it suddenly becomes too much for you and you just have to quit?"

I drop my head and stare at my lap, ease a finger under the plastic ties around my wrists and try to push them off the steel ID band, but they're too tight to budge.

"Look at me," Roth commands.

When I don't lift my head, she slaps me again. Same side, worse pain. I look up at her, blinking.

"Tell me what, or who, made you change your mind."

"Please," I beg, my eyes brimming. "I can't … I don't want to …"

"Tell me!" she shouts the words.

There's a phlegmy cough from behind me.

"I don't want to betray him."

"Whom?"

"Quinn." My voice is a whisper.

"It's not betrayal when you're being a patriot. What you know is vital for this country and its citizens. You can't remain silent in order to protect insurgents." Her eyes glitter, and she speaks the words fiercely.

When I don't respond, Sarge sighs and says, "Blue, the problem with you is you've always been too soft. People like you live in a dream world where everything is fair and people play nice. You have no idea what's actually going on, the harsh realities of what these terrorists are doing, and planning to do, to our nation. And the rebels are making it easier for them to do that. We have to do what it takes to take care of them."

I can't stop myself from asking, "Take care of who?"

"Whoever stands in the way of us defeating the terrorists. This is a war, not a game. And the ends justify the means, Blue, you got to see that."

I say nothing.

Roth tsks and says, "Such loyalty. I wonder — has Quinn been as loyal to you?"

Ouch. Got me with that one.

Quinn believes the worst of me. He thinks I deceived him about the true nature of my job, that I lulled him into a false sense of security by pretending to love him, and that I then betrayed him and his rebel brother to the authorities.

I pause, then murmur, "Okay. So he showed me some stuff."

"Yes? What?"

"He showed me, on his phone, some video footage. Of a suspect, a guy I'd darted, being interrogated. Being … tortured." I say this like it's the biggest secret I know, but the distress in my voice is not feigned. The video of the man being beaten and shocked and water-boarded was horrific. Those very things might lie ahead for me.

Roth is still leaning forward, still listening intently.

"After I saw that, after I knew what happened to the people I helped bring in, I just couldn't do it anymore." I glance at Sarge, who rolls his eyes at me.

"You always were a bleeding-heart softie, princess," he says with a sigh.

"So I quit."

Roth slumps back into her chair. I can almost hear what she's thinking: *That's it? That's all you've got for me?*

She must be disappointed, because for sure Leya would already have told her that I'd seen that footage. I wipe my eyes on the backs of my hands and stare at the floor, sniffling.

"What happened today, on the takedown?" Roth asks.

"Sarge said I had to go on a mission this afternoon. But when I got there, I saw Quinn. He was walking with his brother, and his brother was the target."

"And?"

"I didn't want to take down Quinn's brother. I felt guilty. I mean" — I let my voice become outraged-teen again — "just last night he told me he loved me! The liar! He actually said he loved me when really he —"

"Spare me the dramatics," Roth snaps. "What happened out on the mission?"

"Bruce threatened to shoot Quinn. He hates Quinn, he's been trying to get into my pants ever since I arrived here! You should be questioning him — *that* can hardly be proper procedure, to threaten murder."

"We will, of course, be speaking to Bruce. Checking to see whether your accounts tally."

Great. Something else to worry about. What spin will Bruce put on proceedings?

"Anyway, so Bruce said he'd kill Quinn — kill them both — unless I dropped Connor. So then I did. See? I did what I was told, I followed orders."

I'd followed my instincts. Given a choice to tranq-dart Connor so that he could be captured by the authorities, or risk having Bruce shoot Quinn with live ammo and possibly even kill him, I'd taken Connor down. So if this is the official detention and interrogation center, then there's a good chance Connor is in this building, possibly even being tortured with "enhanced interrogation techniques" at this very moment.

And that's my fault.

But although neither of them knows it, the fact that both Connor and Quinn are alive, and that Quinn is — I hope — free, is due to me too.

"I just followed orders, and now I sit here being given the third degree."

"This, Miss James," says Roth, with a significant glance to the man behind me, "is very far from the third degree. As you will soon find out."

Chapter 4

Coffee break

I swallow hard. I have no idea how I will find the courage to endure what's coming.

"Please continue," says Roth, pushing her wings of hair behind her ears. All the better to hear me with.

"Well, Connor collapsed on the sidewalk and was hauled off to who-knows-where." I pause, but neither Roth nor Sarge gives any helpful confirmation that he might be in this very building. "And then Quinn tried to run, but Bruce hauled him into the van, and then we were taken back to ASTA. With Quinn shouting at me all the way, and telling me to go to hell, and kicking me!" I stick out my bruised shin to show her, but Roth doesn't spare it a glance. "So I shot him with the dart gun, too, to subdue him." To keep him safe. "See? I shot *him*, too! Then we got to ASTA and Sarge got Bruce and Leya to drag Quinn off to his quarters, to detain him there."

I'm not sure how to speak about Leya. I told Bruce that she's a spy for Roth, but I don't know whether he will have told them that I know. He was really mad, maybe he wants to get back at Leya and will keep the fact that he knows she's a mole to himself. I hope so, but I can't be sure. I decide to say nothing about it.

"And when the fire alarm went off, why didn't you evacuate the building along with everyone else, Blue?" asks Sarge from his corner.

"I was worried about Bruce and Leya. And even Quinn. *Squad before blood*, Sarge — you were the one who taught us that. I couldn't leave squad members behind and maybe in danger."

"So at least some of the stuff I taught you got through your thick skull and into your soft brain," he says, sounding unamused.

"So, disregarding emergency regulations, you proceeded to Mr. O'Riley's quarters?" Roth is determined to keep us on track.

"I did. I still believed that, deep down, he was a good guy, that it was all a misunderstanding and when I explained what had happened out there on the mission, he'd believe me. *He said he loved me!* And you give people you love a chance to explain, don't you? You don't just flip the switch and ignore everything you know about them and decide they're scum. At least, that's what I thought — stupid, gullible me."

I did think it. I think it still. And my anger at Quinn is real, the wound is raw. "Little did I know he'd just been playing me. Maybe he planned to recruit me to the rebels," I say, wide-eyed as if in shock at this new imagined crime against me.

Clearly annoyed, Roth waves an impatient hand for me to continue.

"Quinn opened the door. Bruce was behind him with the gun and he — Quinn, I mean — started yelling at me again, about how I shot him and his brother and how could I and stuff. He didn't even give me a chance to explain!"

Roth's teeth are clenched. She looks like she is only just keeping her temper in check at my broken-hearted bleatings. Good. I hope she buys my version of a silly, naive girl, blindsided and wounded in love, ignorant of anything important.

"And as I came in and closed the door, Quinn snatched the

dart-gun out of my hands, shot Bruce with it, took Bruce's sidearm and turned it on me," I lie.

"Did you just stand there watching him, Blue? It didn't occur to you to intervene, to take him down?" asks Sarge, leaning forward.

"Yes," says Roth. "You expect us to believe Quinn overpowered you so easily? He's an intel cadet, he analyses information, tracks data patterns. He's not a trained fighter."

Roth's face is skeptical. This part of the story was always going to be a hard sell.

"It happened really quickly," I say feebly. "And how could I take him down without a weapon? He's way bigger than me. Besides, I think he may be trained in fighting — he did this kick thing to my wrist. *We're* the ones who haven't been trained in hand-to-hand combat." I send a reproachful glance in Sarge's direction.

Roth swivels to check this with him. He gives a reluctant nod of acknowledgment.

"So then the bast- the jerk held the firearm to my head and ordered me to shoot out the window pane and then the main power line to the compound. Last night he said he loved me, and today he threatened to blow my brains out!" More lies.

"You didn't think to turn the rifle on him?" Roth asks.

"It's a long weapon, ma'am, and he was right up against the back of me, with the sidearm to my head. I was in a fix. And I was scared."

"And yet you managed to shoot a power line at a distance of, if I have it correctly, over 200 yards?"

It *had* been a fantastic shot, but I keep my face neutral. "Well, that's the kind of marksmanship we *were* trained for." I sneak a glance at Sarge. The expression on his face is an odd mix of pride and exasperation. "And it did take me three shots," I admit.

"And when the power to the compound went out?"

"Quinn made me jump out the window. I nearly broke my

neck, and I really hurt my knee! Then he just ran away and left me looking like I did something wrong, like I helped him escape, or something. Because that's what you suspect, isn't it?" I say, forcing outrage and a grating whine into my voice. "And I did nothing wrong. Nothing! I raised the alarm as soon as I could, and I got hit in the head for it!"

I'd caused the distraction to give Quinn time to escape.

"Do you know where he was headed?"

"How should I know? Home, I guess."

Roth's scarlet mouth twists contemptuously at my stupidity in thinking a wanted man would run home, to the first place his pursuers would be certain to check.

No doubt they will soon question Quinn and Connor's parents, if they haven't already. But there is someone else who might know where he is, someone who would be only too vulnerable to Roth and her henchman — Kerry, Quinn's much younger sister, with her missing front tooth and her lisp, and her love of dragging her mother to Freedom Park every afternoon so she can see the lady with the baby. And her secret habit of carrying notes from Quinn to Connor. If Quinn is now hiding out where his brother used to, then she might well know where that is. The thought of Kerry being hauled in here turns my stomach. I refuse to let that happen.

"What do I care where he is anyway? I hate him! I'd like to kick *him* in the shin!"

Again, the emotion in my voice rings true. Quinn gave up on me, on us. He assumed the worst about me — that I betrayed him and his brother out of loyalty to ASTA.

"Bastard! I kissed him. I nearly slept with him, and it turns out I mean nothing to him."

Again I wipe tears from my eyes. This time, they're real.

In the corner, Sarge fidgets and cricks his neck. I guess training marines in the desert wars was nothing like dealing with brokenhearted teen girls. Roth is tapping her nails impatiently on her leg.

"Have you caught him yet?" I ask her.

I need to know if he got away safely. I have to believe he did, that all of this isn't all for nothing.

Roth doesn't reply and her face remains impassive, but I figure if they'd captured him, they'd be taunting me with it, trying to shake my story by making me watch his interrogation, or confronting me with our differing accounts.

"Well I hope you do, I hope you catch him and bring *him* here for questioning instead of me. Because I don't know why I'm here when I just followed orders. I did nothing wrong," I say in a small, stubborn voice. "And my head hurts."

"I think we've learned all we're going to from you, Miss James. And, on the whole, I'm inclined to believe you," says Roth. My heart leaps in relief — I've done it, I've fooled them. But then she stands up and continues, "However, we need to be *sure*."

She hands her list of questions to Mr. Smith and says to Sarge, "Come, Wayne, we can't be present for this next part of the process. Let's go grab a cup of coffee. It's going to be a long night. When we return, we'll discover if our detainee's account has stood up to more … vigorous questioning techniques."

My stomach is an icy pool of dread, my hands start to shake. Smith slides around to the side of my chair and in one swift movement clamps the steel arm-cuff around my right wrist. In another moment, he has sliced through the plastic zip ties with a box cutter and locked my left arm in the restraint on the other armrest.

"Don't! Please," I call after Roth and Sarge. Again there is no need to fake the emotion in my voice. But this time it's not anger, it's panic. "Think about what you're doing — I'm a US citizen, I'm just a sixteen-year-old girl!"

Roth cuts me a hard look. "At best you're a combatant in the war against terror. At worst you're an insurgent. You haven't been 'just a girl' since you signed on and picked up a rifle."

"You can't do this to me!" I struggle against the restraints around my waist and wrists.

"There is *nothing* I wouldn't do to keep this country safe." Roth nods at the man behind me and then exits the room.

"Sarge," I beg, stretching my trembling fingers out towards him, "you can't let them do this!"

Sarge gives me a long look which I can't decipher. Does he pity me or despise me? Maybe he is merely indifferent, because he does nothing to stop what's about to happen to me. The door closes behind them and I am left alone with the tall, thin man with the transparent hair. And the trolley of equipment.

Chapter 5

Pain

I don't know how long it lasts.

The pain, when it begins, is endless. Without limits. Higher than I can scream, deeper than the marrow of my bones, longer than I can endure. It is without beginning or end, an unceasing now of searing agony. It's an acid burn in my mouth, a rigid clench in my throat, a roaring in my ears. A fire which rises to the highest peak. Then rises higher.

It drives the breath from my lungs and the sense from my mind. My skin singes away to raw nerves, my aching bones quiver and melt before the heat of it. My nails want to claw me up the walls, the whole of me shrieks an order to escape. Bolt! Run! Die.

He is good at keeping me just this side of the dark abyss of oblivion which beckons, promising a respite from consciousness and pain. Every time I'm about to go over, he pulls me back.

He batters me with questions, but I can't speak. I can't breathe around the pain, it takes up the whole of me. If he would just stop, I'd tell them what they want to know. I'd tell them anything. But I can't think, can't make sense of the questions through the shattering vice of pain. I'm broken. In fragments.

I black out, wake to find my head slumped on my chest, a trail of bile flecked with blood across the front of my dress. Smith grabs my long ponytail and pulls my head erect. This is it. This is the moment between agonies when I could catch my breath and talk, when I could stop it. If I can remember how to make words rather than screams, I can tell him everything.

But he has me by my hair.

By my *hair*.

For some reason, this strikes me as more offensive, more despicable than anything that has gone before. A grown man has secured a teenage girl to a chair, has tortured her and is now holding her head up by her ponytail. And, somewhere, Roberta Roth, CEO of ASTA, and Sarge, my squad leader, are drinking coffee.

I had been delighted when I was selected to train as a rat-sniper because of my exceptional skills as a virtual-reality gamer. I had been proud to think that I could serve my country and make a real difference in the war against the plague. I'd thought Quinn was paranoid in his suspicions about ASTA's true purpose and the government's real motivations. Until yesterday, I'd suspected that he was exaggerating or misunderstanding what was happening in our society.

But any organization that can torture children, and any government that can mandate them to do it, or even just turn a blind eye to its methods, does not deserve my loyalty.

I wondered, when Quinn first showed me footage of the torture, whether it might be justifiable, whether it might be a fair moral trade if the information it extracted from suspects saved lives in the future.

But now I know that information extracted like this is worthless. It cannot be relied on to be accurate. Under the pressure of this pain, I'd say anything, invent stuff, confess to being the devil himself if it would make the pain stop.

In his faint Irish accent, Quinn had said, "Can't you see, Jinxy? It's not about them, it's about us. It's not just what we're prepared to allow happen to them, it's about what we're prepared to do, who we're prepared to become."

Quinn was right.

I imagine them torturing others like this — not just suspected terrorists, but people like Connor who believe that our nation is capable of better, capable of moral greatness — not merely of superiority of power. I imagine them torturing other young people, fellow cadets like Bruce or nerdy, perceptive Cameron, or friends of Quinn like Sofia Medina. I imagine them torturing little Kerry.

And in that moment, I know, know deeper than the pain can reach, that I will tell them nothing.

Smith pulls my head back by the ponytail and begins again.

More pain.

Excruciating. Unbearable. Endless.

Yet with every new pinnacle of agony, something inside me strengthens. As my body bows and bleeds and bruises, my will solidifies into something dense and unbreakable. Every strike hammers my locker of secrets deeper inside me. With every twist and blow and shock, I hate them more. My determination to thwart them grows. I may not be brave, but I am stubborn. Roth was dead right when she called me *obstinate*.

I find my lips and my tongue, and my voice — rasped almost to silence by my screams — and I speak. But I tell him only what I told Roth. I say, sob, scream the same things over and over again, clinging to the words like they're solid buoys in an unending sea of agony.

The door opens and Sarge comes in. I think he comes in sooner than intended — maybe he has no real appetite for this. I am slumped, panting, shaking and dripping wet. It's from sweat, not water — Smith hasn't yet gotten around to using the water and the sack and the board, and perhaps he's disappointed at being interrupted before he can, because his pale fingers, already on the dial, give an extra twist. My body goes rigid. My wrists bite into their restraints. My back arches against the chair.

My eyes roll, and I drop into a vortex of black.

Chapter 6

Keeping records

There is a soft clicking sound from somewhere to the left of me. Fingers on a keyboard? Then a phone rings.

"Hi, honey," says a man's voice.

A moment of confusion holds me still, then a shudder of terror trembles through my body as I remember. I draw in a ragged breath, cover my mouth with my hand to stop myself crying out, and open my eyes in time to see a short, white-coated man walk out of the room, a cell phone pressed to his ear.

He half-closes the door behind him, but I can still hear his side of the conversation, so he must be just outside — probably no way to escape then. And anyway, I feel exhausted, weak and sore all over, and wouldn't have the strength to fight off a kitten. Plus, I have no idea where I am or which way is out.

"Nothing much, I've just finished stitching a girl's head wound, but she's still out cold, so I've got time to chat."

I raise a hand to my aching head, feel the thick bandage wrapped around it, see the bandages wrapped around both wrists, notice the red welts on my hands, and feel a tug on the inner elbow of my left arm where a needle pierces the skin, connecting me to a tube leading up to an almost-empty drip bag hanging from a stand beside the bed. I want to curl up into a ball and sob. But right now I have to hold it together and figure out what's happening.

It takes me a few seconds to orient myself. I'm lying on an examination table in what I think must be a doctor's office, though it's been years since either Robin or I visited one. There are glass-fronted cabinets storing medicines and equipment and gleaming steel instruments, a large sterilizing unit, and biohazard medical waste disposal bins. A decorative, multicolored hologram of the human nervous system rotates above a projecting pedestal in one corner, and in another, a 3D printer is laying down strata, building up what looks like an anatomical model of a heart. At the far end of the room is a door with a bathroom icon on it.

"But you're up late, honey, what's up?"

To the left of me is a large, paper-strewn desk with a computer monitor and keyboard in the center. The computer is on.

"But he's okay?" I hear the voice beyond the door say.

Trying to ignore the throbbing in my heavy head and the protesting ache in my every muscle, I push myself up so that I'm sitting, then ease myself off the examination table. My legs feel stiff and sore, and my ears are ringing. I have no idea how to unplug myself from the drip without making a mess, but I don't need to — the drip stand is on wheels. Good.

As silently as I can, I move behind the desk, hanging onto the stand to steady myself. There are no pens or pencils on the desk, I guess because these could be snatched up by a detainee and used as weapons.

"I'm not sure, I've still got an examination and some paperwork to do," the voice outside the door says.

Displayed on the computer screen is a logo: "Stapla Inc." But my eyes are drawn immediately to the online form below, which has been partially completed with today's date, the sixth of August, and the title "Medical Chart. Attending physician — Dr. Z. Green,

Detainee: J.E. James (JJ20027)."

That's my ASTA number, the one engraved on my ID bracelet.

I scan the screen quickly, not sure how long I'll have before the chatty doc returns. On the left of the screen is a heading: *Interventions*. Beneath it is a vertical list of items, each with adjacent columns for entries of *date, time* and *notes*. The first two "interventions" on my chart, *intake examination* and *initial questioning*, are blank but the third, *enhanced interrogation*, has today's date entered beside it and some notes have been typed up. This must be what he was busy with when I regained consciousness.

"Yeah, I'm getting too old for these all-nighters." He laughs.

I read the entry. It begins, "*Post-interrogation examination: Shallow laceration on right cheek — disinfected and dressed. Open laceration, approx 2.5 inches, on right upper temporal region of scalp, contusions and swelling, fracture not suspected — 8 sutures.*" It goes on to list my other weals, abrasions, bruises and burns, and their treatment.

My stomach clenches, and a cold sweat breaks out on my top lip when I read the next headings in the intervention list: *enhanced interrogation 2, enhanced interrogation 3, enhanced interrogation 4*. They can do this more than once?

I cannot go through that again. I won't make it. The fracture lines in my mind threaten to crack wide, to let the memories of what happened in that room flow in, but I cannot allow myself to go to pieces now. I must stay focused.

"I should be home in time for breakfast. Any chance of blueberry pancakes?"

He works here, then goes home and eats blueberry pancakes?

I make myself read on. *Polygraph* — that's the next entry. I've watched enough crime movies and episodes of *Lie-dols* on T.V. to know a polygraph is a lie-detector test. And according to the entries in the fields alongside, that's what's on my schedule for tomorrow morning. They must have scheduled it for after my interrogation to double-check the truth of what I've told them. There's nothing else entered on my chart.

"Uh-huh, uh-huh. And what were the rug rats up to today?"

Chuckles from outside the door.

"Sure, put him on, I can chat for a minute."

The doctor's computer looks like a standard PC, so I take a chance and press ALT-TAB. It takes a conscious effort because my fingers feel clumsy, and they tingle with pins and needles. The tip of one is bloody from where the nail is half torn off, so I keep it extended, careful not to let it touch any of the keys. The screen toggles to another medical chart. My heart kicks in my chest like the recoil of a .5 caliber rifle when I read the detainee name at the top of this screen: Connor O'Riley. He *is* here.

I scan the screen rapidly, noting that the fields next to the interrogation and polygraph sub-headings are blank. So they haven't started on him yet. I'm relieved, but also confused. What are they waiting for? Did they want to extract what they could from me first, and then use that to prize more out of him? Judging from the notes beside *intake examination*, Connor was in better shape when he was brought in than I was. More relief — he's still okay, though he won't be once they begin in earnest.

"Hey, buddy, you ought to be sound asleep, not keeping your momma up all the night. What's up?" says the voice in the hallway.

I scroll down the screen — there's only one more completed field. Next to the intervention *Other*, I read the entry: "*Per psych consult, five-day pre-interrogations regimen, incl. restricted fluids and nutrition, administered at minimum levels required to sustain life. Plus sleep-deprivation, hourly disruptions. Med exams 8-hourly.*"

I understand at once. They suspect he won't crack easily, so before they begin interrogations — I didn't miss that plural —

they're going to soften him up, weaken him with thirst and starve him into submission. I, apparently, was considered puny enough in mind, body and will to be interrogated immediately, but Mr. Smith will only be unleashed when Connor is already half-dead.

He's so *not* okay.

"She did, huh? Well that sounds like fun."

On the top of the form, there's a small box, *Main*, lit up blue like a hyperlink. I click on it, trying to remember whether there was one on my chart. Another screen appears. It seems to be a record of all Connor's details with a section for notes. I scan enough of these to discover that he has been a person of interest for some time. He hasn't resided or been seen at his parents' house for the last twenty-nine days, during which time the residence has been under intermittent physical surveillance. No calls from him have been picked up on the monitoring taps on their landline and cellphones. The house has been placed under round-the-clock surveillance since Connor was captured, pending possible contact by "other dissidents or the detainee's brother, Quinn O'Riley".

So Quinn *did* get away, then. Or, at least, there's no mention here of him having been captured.

The most recent entry notes that Connor's parents have been questioned — thank God there is no mention of Kerry — but no useful information has been forthcoming. Connor has been scheduled for "*devitalization and enhanced interrogation*".

"Okay, buddy, Daddy's got to get back to work now. And you've got to get back to sleep. See you later." There are kissy noises from the hallway.

Shit.

/ Chapter 7

For collection

BACK. CTRL-HOME. ALT-TAB. CTRL-HOME.

My fingers fly to get the screen display back to where it was when the doctor was interrupted. There *is* a *Main* link on my screen, but there's no time to check what's written up in the notes for me — the doctor will walk in any second.

"No, that's okay, you can just tell Mom I said goodbye, okay?"

I slip silently back around the desk.

"No, wait —"

I replace the drip stand in its original position and climb up onto the examination table.

"Yeah? He said you wanted to ask me something." The voice is still in the hallway.

Damn. If I'd known he was still going to be on the line for a bit longer, I would have checked my notes. But I can't risk going back now.

As I sit with my legs dangling off the edge of the table, breathing slowly to calm my racing heart, I notice that nearby — on top of a shoulder-high bookcase behind the head of the exam table — is a plastic tray labelled "for collection". Inside is a thick padded envelope, stuck all over with warning labels: *Fragile! Biohazard!*

Medical sample. Stuck square in the middle is a large waybill bearing the familiar logo of Swift-Secure, the same local drone-delivery shipping service used by Mom and my favorite online clothing store. Someone — the doc, probably — has filled in many of the boxes. The patient reference number is JJ20027 — me.

In the section for listing the contents, the box next to *blood sample* has been checked. He must have drawn some blood while I was still unconscious. To check I'm plague-free, or for some other reason? The boxes for sputum, urine and stool samples are mercifully blank.

My gaze moves down the label, and I hit pay dirt: the sender's name and collection address are preprinted on the waybill. Here, in black-and-white type, are the details of where I currently am. Where Connor is. I read the name of the sender.

"I don't know, ask him," says Dr. Zachariah Green of Stapla, Inc. He's still in the hallway.

I read the address on the waybill — floor, building number, street name, city zone — read it and memorize it.

Back in boot camp, we had to do daily exercises to train our skills in observation and memory. Sarge said we needed to be able to reconnoiter a territory and know at once what was out of place — what was new, or missing, or just didn't fit. He taught us how to memorize the array of items spread out on the Kim's Game tray, or the features of an operational arena, and how to remember them in order by making up a rhyme or story incorporating them. I do that now.

Zachariah, a green doctor (I close my eyes and picture a little emerald-green man wearing a stethoscope), stands outside office 303 (I let the green man trace the numbers on the door with his long, alien-like finger), inside building 16-001 (easy — my age, 9/11 year), on Auburn avenue (the street is a wavy line of red-brown hair), in the city's South Downtown zone (I stamp the hair with a glittering *SoDo*). Wait, I've forgotten the organization's name. I'm still trying to figure out a distinctive symbol for it, when the doctor speaks in the unmistakable tones of someone ending a conversation.

"Okay, see you later … Love you, too, honey."

There's just time to stretch back out on the bed before the doc returns, closing the door behind him. I lie still and stare glassily at the ceiling, trying to burn the green doctor scene into my memory.

"Ah, you're awake. How are you feeling?"

I turn my head to study him. The doctor is short and pot-bellied, and he has a surgical mask hanging around his neck. As he walks towards me, he lifts this into place over his nose and mouth. Is this for my benefit — to preserve the myth of airborne transmission of the rat fever virus? Or for his, so his features are mostly disguised?

"Not good. I hurt all over," I say hoarsely. My throat is raw from all the screaming. "From the torture," I add pointedly.

"I think I can help you with the pain," he says, ignoring the accusation in my eyes and words.

He gets a tiny glass vial from the cabinet, draws up the clear liquid into a syringe, and injects it into the line in the crook of my arm. He shines a light into each eye, takes my temperature with an infrared thermometer, and measures my blood pressure with an electronic cuff which inflates around my upper arm, squeezes tight and then deflates. A silicon clamp fitted on one finger feeds more information into a connected monitor. By the time it's captured my vital statistics, the pain is just beginning to ease.

"I need the restroom. Badly."

"A rehydration drip will do that to you," he says, removing the IV needle from my arm.

"And can I shower? I smell."

I smell rank. Sour sweat and blood and vomit. And the taste in my mouth is like the rancid smell made solid.

"No shower, I'm afraid."

He helps me sit up and slide off the bed, then steadies me with a hand under my elbow as I sway, fighting a wave of dizziness. After a moment, the floor seems steady and I walk gingerly across the office to the bathroom. My knee gives a stab of pain on every step.

"But there's a basin in there, and you can wash up. I keep some toiletries on the shelf, for when I work late. You can use them to freshen up if you like." He sounds … kind.

The bathroom is tiny, and everything — the toilet, the basin, the small mirror, soap-dispenser and shelf bolted to the wall — is made of unbreakable stainless steel. The door closes, but there's no latch on the inside. After I've used the toilet, I wash my hands, neck and face with the liquid soap and warm water. The cuts and burns sting, and the water runs pink with blood. The blue eyes in the mirror stare back at me from a bruised and puffy face. I look away, focusing instead on the shelf, where a stack of paper towels and a small assortment of toiletries are neatly laid out. I unzip my dress and let it fall around my waist so that I can clean the crusty rivulets of dried blood off my chest with a clutch of wet, soapy paper towels. My eye falls on the earring around my bra strap. My eyes prick with tears. I must have gotten soap into them.

The tops of both arms sting sharply. Twisting from side to side, I see a pair of adhesive wound dressings covering the spots where the shock-electrodes were applied the longest. I don't want to see what it looks like underneath.

While I scrub under my arms with the paper towels, trying to clean away that acrid odor of fear and adrenalin, I check the toiletries on the high shelf. A toothbrush and whitening toothpaste, dental floss, antiseptic mouthwash and breath-freshening mints — the doc is obsessed with oral hygiene — dry-stick antiperspirant which promises strong cover for twenty-four hours, a comb, a small electric shaver, an economy-sized pump-action bottle of hand sanitizer, and a box of Kleenex. Nothing with the potential to be used as a weapon.

It hurts to lift my arms, but I snag the toothpaste tube, squeeze a worm of white paste onto my finger and give my teeth a thorough rubbing. I rinse with the mouthwash, hissing against the pain when the antiseptic hits the spots where I've bitten my cheeks and lips, then drink as much water as I can, just in case they schedule a "devitalization" regime for me, too. I'm tempted by the comb, but my reflection shows me that my long, blond hair is snarled through with knots and caked with blood. It will have to wait until I can shower. I apply the antiperspirant liberally even though it smells disgusting — like toilet disinfectant — and I'm just zipping my dress back up when there's a knock at the door.

"All right in there?" the doctor asks.

"Almost done."

My hand is reaching for the doorknob when my head turns, as if by itself, back to the shelf. What is it? What does my brain want me to register? My gaze fixes on the dry-stick antiperspirant.

Antiperspirant. Strong 24-hour cover.

Why has my brain fixed my eyes on this? *Think, Jinxy.* What does an antiperspirant do? It stops you sweating. And? So?

Then I gasp as an image pops into my head of a suspect undergoing a polygraph. Frantically I try to recall every movie or T.V. scene I've ever watched that shows a lie-detector test in action. Images flash through my mind. An operator asking questions. A machine with a bank of needles tracing graphs on rolls of paper. Wires connecting the machine to the person being questioned, to sensors in bands around their fingers, arms, chests. And foreheads? Sensors which measure their pulse, their rate of breathing, their blood pressure, and — I'm sure of it! — how much they're sweating.

"Miss James?"

"Coming!"

I snatch the dry-stick and rub it across the backs of my hands and all over my palms, up and down and between my fingers from tip to base, top and bottom. For good measure, I apply it to my forehead and face, blending the white streaks into my skin with my fingertips. In the mirror, I see the door opening, and I thrust the antiperspirant stick under the neckline of my dress so that I'm applying it in the more usual places when the doc sees me.

"Sorry," I say guiltily, replacing the lid on the dry stick and returning it to the shelf. "Hope you don't mind?"

"We're finished up here. It's time for you to go to your cell."

He leads me out of the room into the hallway, where two guards are waiting to escort me. Good thing I didn't try to make a run for it earlier. One of the guards, a cranky-looking woman, makes me face the wall, spread my legs and stretch my arms away from my body. While I'm splayed out like a starfish, she pats down every square inch of me, checking that I haven't got something from the doctor's rooms concealed on my person. I figure they probably patted me down somewhere between ASTA and here, too. The thought of being touched all over, while I was unconscious, creeps me out.

As we walk down the hall, one guard ahead of me and one behind, I wring my hands like I'm frantic with worry. I *am* frantic with worry, but I'm also making sure the antiperspirant covers every last bit of skin, without any telltale white streaks.

This time I don't try to memorize the route. My brain has another sequence of words and images on auto-repeat.

Dr. Zachariah Green, office 303, 16-001, Auburn, Sodo.

Chapter 8

Cat's eyes

"Wake up." A booted toe shoves roughly against my hip. "I'll be back in five minutes for you."

The door slams and locks, and I look around in the suddenly bright light, trying to blink away the nightmarish images still chasing each other across the screen of my mind. I'm still in the small, windowless cell, lying under a worn blanket on a thin mattress on the ground. When they dumped me in here last night, I allowed myself to splinter into pieces and sob out my horror at everything that's happened. Sometime during the bawling, I must have fallen asleep.

On the floor next to me are a Styrofoam cup of water and a wrapped power bar. I sit up, wincing. My head feels swollen and heavy, and every muscle in my body is aching and stiff. I feel like I've been run over by a steamroller.

I grab the cup with unsteady hands and drink the water greedily. I'm so thirsty, I could drink a gallon, but while there's a small, metal toilet in one corner of the cell, there's no basin or tap. I don't feel much like eating, especially when I remember that Connor is being denied food somewhere nearby, but I force myself to eat the Blueberry-Banana flavored protein bar, wincing with every swallow as the food scrapes my sore throat.

Two guards, different from the ones from last night, escort me to the room where my polygraph will be conducted. One comes into the room and stands guard behind my chair. The other must be waiting outside.

The polygraph operator's eyes have yellow irises with black, vertical pupil slits, and impossibly long eyelashes which sweep up and outwards. I know it's just contact lenses and false lashes — one of the ways people accentuate their appearance in these days of masked faces — but the effect of her catlike gaze is unnerving.

She sticks two wireless electrodes onto the palm of my left hand, another around its middle finger and one on each temple. When I try to rub away the twitching tic in my left eye, the operator moves my hand back to my lap. Then she straps a band around my chest and a blood pressure cuff around my upper arm. The restraints feel too much like yesterday, and for a moment I have to fight my body's intense urge to flee.

The operator sits facing a computer screen where I'm guessing graphs and monitors and all kinds of measures are displayed digitally, because there is no wavering needle on an unspooling roll of graph paper. Blinking her feline eyes slowly, she spends ages telling me how super-accurate her test is at detecting deceit and how I had best tell the absolute truth on everything. Or else.

I figure she's trying to scare me. This test may be more hi-tech than anything I've seen on T.V., but surely the basic principles are the same? And I've watched enough polygraph scenes on the small screen to know that they can be beaten. Either I have to be extremely anxious throughout, overreacting to every question so that my 'guilty' lie responses are masked, or I have to stay completely calm throughout.

Well, Sarge did once call me an ice-maiden.

Cat-eyes starts by asking me a bunch of yes-no questions

that have nothing to do with Quinn or the rebels or yesterday's events. Is my name Jinx Emma James? (Yes.) Is today the seventh of August? (Yes, at least I think so.) Am I sixteen years old? (Yes.) Am I a surveillance specialist cadet at ASTA? (No.) Do I have one brother called Robin? (Yes.) Is my father still alive? (No.) She pauses for a few seconds between each question, and marks each answer on her screen with a sensor pen.

Then the questions get more serious.

"Have you ever lied to anyone?"

"Yes, of course."

"Just answer yes or no, please. Have you ever lied to anyone?"

"Yes."

"Have you ever killed anything?"

"Yes." Spiders in the bath. Those damn rats. A rabid coyote.

"Have you ever killed anyone?"

"No."

Is she trying to get a reading on how my body reacts when I tell the truth and when I lie so she can compare my responses to the trickier questions which lie ahead? Maybe there's a third way to pass this test — I can mess with her system a little by tossing her a few lies and allowing myself to get a bit upset about them. Then when I stay calm on the answers that I *am* lying on, it will look like I'm telling the truth.

"Have you ever lied to get out of trouble?"

I pause for a fraction of a second, then say, "No," thinking specifically about the time Robin and I denied drinking half of Dad's bottle of orange liqueur.

"Have you ever deceived a person in authority?"

"No!" I say quickly, remembering the time I switched out my half-face respirator for a lighter E97 mask when Mom couldn't see. I bite down on my tongue until it hurts, figuring this should rev up her graph lines.

"Have you ever cheated on a school test?"

"No." This is the truth. I take a deep breath and relax.

"Have you ever stolen anything?"

"No!" Of course I have. Cookies from the cookie jar after bedtime. Batteries from my mother's secret stash. And once, a beautiful piece of rose quartz as big as my fist, which pretty Linda Langton brought to our first-grade show and tell and left on the nature display table. I'd slipped it into my schoolbag, but once I got it home, I hid it in case Mom or Dad spotted it. When the teacher asked who'd taken it, I sat on my hands and said nothing, though I'm sure now that my face must have been glowing hot with the shame burning inside me. I allow that guilt to rise again now.

"No," I repeat.

Then the questions turn serious and I make a real effort to stay calm. Since I don't know what body language will indicate that I'm lying, I play it safe and sit perfectly still. I use my sniper's tactical breathing methods to keep my heart rate steady and my anxiety at bay. The antiperspirant stops me sweating. I try to find an element of truth in every deceiving answer and focus on that, while making myself believe the lies.

"Do you know Quinn O'Riley well?"

"No." Apparently not. Else I wouldn't have hoped.

"Did you know him before you met him on the transport to ASTA?"

"No." True.

"Do you know what the rebels are planning?"

"No." I don't *know*, not for sure.

"Do you know where Quinn is now?"

"No." Haven't got a clue.

"Did Quinn take Bruce's weapon?"

"Yes." When I handed it to him.

"Did Quinn force you to shoot the power lines?"

"Yes." My hand *was* forced — how else could I have gotten him out of there?

"Do you still care for Quinn?"

"No." This time I allow myself to feel the lie. Her eyebrow lifts a fraction as she watches my reaction on her screen. Ha!

She repeats some of the questions, or comes at them from different angles. It seems to take hours. At the end of all the questions, the operator fixes her yellow gaze on me for a long minute, then gives a tiny shrug and enters something into her system. I reckon I passed the polygraph.

As she removes the bands and electrodes, she gets very friendly and chatty, tells me she's never conducted a test on someone so young before, touches my bandaged head very gently and asks me if I'm feeling okay. I sense a trap.

"You were very calm in that test," she says.

"You told me that if I didn't lie, I had nothing to worry about. I assumed you were speaking the truth."

"Hmm. But I could tell you were lying on some of those items. You can tell me now, you know, we're no longer recording."

Liar. I spotted the tiny fisheye lens in the corner of the room as soon as I entered.

"I mean, I actually think it's wrong to do a test like this on an asset as young as you. You've obviously had a tough time of it, and hell, you're just a kid!"

"Are we finished here?"

She frowns at me. "Take her back," she tells the guard.

Back in my cell, there's nothing to do except repeat the address of this place to myself over and over, and try to ignore my various aches and pains. I bite the ragged fingernail with my teeth until it tears away, and my finger starts bleeding again. I rub at a tickle on my cheeks, and my hand comes away wet. I'm not actually crying,

I don't think, just leaking tears. I can't seem to stop them coming. There's no one to talk to and nothing to read or look at except the walls, which are painted a greenish-yellow color that reminds me of vomit. I have the rest of the day (at least, I think it's a day, I have no actual idea of the time) to sit and think.

And what I think about is how much I hate them. I like that feeling, it dries my eyes and stills my trembling.

I hate them for what they've done to my father, for what they've done to this country, and especially for what they did to me yesterday. For what they'll soon be doing to Quinn's brother.

The last few days have changed me. I am not who I was a week ago. I feel old and grim, as if I screamed out every ounce of trust and joy and optimism while I was in that chair, in that room with the mirror on the wall and the drain in the floor.

I seethe with a cold fury at how they've lied to me and deceived me. Now that I know who they are, what they do, what they're capable of, and how rotten they are at the core, I want something different.

I have a new goal. If there's any way I can bring them down, I will. If there's anything I can do to thwart them, to undermine their power or expose their crimes, I'll do it. Any chance I get to uncover what those other divisions are doing, I'll take it.

My fingers crush the Styrofoam cup and tear it into pieces. I pile them up in a tiny hill of white fragments while I consider what I could do and how. And where.

I don't reckon there's much I can do from home. I'm pretty sure that if I *had* been able to click on the screen of notes on my computerized file, I'd have discovered that I'm to be put under surveillance too. Roth strikes me as a very thorough woman. My every future call, email and internet action will surely be run through intel, and a spook will be on my butt if I leave the house.

Back when I won The Game and was offered a chance to train

at the Academy, I jumped at it because what I wanted most in the world was to be free and away from my mother's smothering overprotectiveness. I thought that leaving home and going to ASTA would bring me that. It didn't. I was less free there than I had been at home, and if I'm sent back there, I'll be subject to even more scrutiny. But at least at the ASTA compound there is stuff to be investigated, people who know things and who may be in a position to help, opportunities to exploit.

Though I dread it with every fiber of my being, I need to go back.

Probably, it will be my next stop anyway. I don't reckon they'll allow me to go straight home from here — they won't want my family to see me all battered and bruised. But I'm guessing the resignation I submitted to Sarge just yesterday morning will be accepted within the next week or two, and they'll send me packing.

They won't easily believe that I want back in, not after what they've done to me, but somehow I need to convince them that is exactly what I want. Somehow I've got to get Sarge and Roth to trust me again. What spin can I put on my about-face so that they buy it?

My hands push the pieces of Styrofoam, smudged with blood from my finger, this way and that, making patterns on the floor, while I weigh up the possibilities. By the time the third energy bar and cup of water of the day is shoved through the cat-flap type opening at the bottom of my cell's door, I've got a rough idea of what I'll say to Sarge.

As I bite into the dense coconut-flavored chewiness, I realize that somewhere in this building, Connor has passed at least twenty-four hours with almost no food, water or sleep. Guilt sits heavy in my chest.

I've got to figure out a way of getting him freed. He's in here because of me, so I need to help get him out. I have a new mission.

Failure, as I have spent the last three months telling myself, is not an option. And I will not quit.

My fingers have arranged the white scraps on the floor into a rough approximation of an eye, with a hooped earring through its brow. I brush them aside.

If I assume that the O'Rileys have a way to get a message to Quinn or the rebels, then I need to get a message to them about where Connor is being held.

And I may just have an idea about how it could be done.

Chapter 9

Back and forward

That night I sleep restlessly. I dream I am sitting beside Quinn on a bed and we're kissing, deeply. He pulls me into his lap, murmuring Irish endearments and touching my face tenderly. I feel safe and cherished. And excited. I push myself tightly against his chest, my fingers knot themselves in his thick, mahogany hair, but he grabs my wrists and pulls my hands away. Then he places his phone into my palms.

"Look who it is!" he says, gray eyes blazing.

I look down at the screen and see it's me, on the metal chair in the torture room. There are real flames in my eyes.

"You see?" he says, shaking his head down at me. "You see?"

I wake up sweating. The antiperspirant's twenty-four-hour power has expired.

After I've had my water and power bar — apri-peach this morning — the cranky guard comes to fetch me.

"You're being released."

"I'm going home?"

She laughs sourly at this. "Not likely."

She tosses a disposable personal protection equipment suit on the floor next to me and instructs me to change. I peel off the stinking pink dress, hissing as it sticks and has to be ripped off a burn on my shoulder, then kick it into the corner. They haven't given me fresh underwear, so I'm stuck in what I'm wearing under the PPE suit, unless I go commando.

The journey back to ASTA is a repeat of the one that brought me to the interrogation center (*green doctor, office 303, 16-001, Auburn, Sodo*). I'm blindfolded and escorted into a van, and accompanied by a silent guard, but this time my hands aren't tied. It's stuffy in the van, and I roll up my sleeves, wishing I could open a window, stick my head out and allow the wind to scour my brain clean of the last few days' memories.

My guard tugs off the blindfold as we pull into transport bay C at ASTA, and the driver tells me, "End of the line, kid." He says it like it's a joke, but it sounds like an ominous prediction.

Sarge is waiting for me. I don't know what I feel towards this man. He won my respect and even a grudging affection during my time in his unit at ASTA, but then he earned my hatred for allowing me to be tortured. Then, too, I feel an unwilling gratitude that he came back to the interrogation room and stopped the pain. My emotions are all mixed up inside me, like tangled clothes in a drier.

"Blue," he says, rubbing a hand over his shaved head.

"Sarge." The tic in my eyelid has started up again.

"I didn't think … I didn't expect them to —" He interrupts himself, clears his throat and looks away. "You've been scheduled for a hearing at oh-eight-hundred tomorrow."

"*Another* one?"

"It's regulation. You are to proceed directly to your quarters and you are not to discuss the last forty-eight hours with anyone, do you understand?"

I nod.

"Dismissed," he says and stalks over to the decon unit.

I trail behind, pressing my fingers against my twitching eyelid, trying to press my anxiety back inside. Waiting for me on the other side of the decon unit, inside the main building, is my unit of cadets. Or what remains of my unit, since there is no sign of Leya. It seems like an age since I've seen them, like the world has changed in just a few days, although really, it's just me who has.

I hear Bruce curse when he sees me, but it's Tae-Hyun — still slim and still wearing his hair in a thin ponytail — who speaks to me first.

"Hey," he says, clicking his tongue-stud against his teeth as he always does, and giving me an elbow bump.

Mitch — tall, dark and built like a brick outhouse — follows suit. "What up, Blue?" he asks. "Are you back?"

"Don't know, I've got a hearing tomorrow. I guess they'll tell me then."

"Good luck," says Mitch.

"Yeah, well, we're off to the range. See you later?" says Tae-Hyun, and they walk off. They clearly aren't eager to hang out with me. Maybe I smell like trouble.

Maybe I just smell.

Quiet Cameron, with his geeky glasses and scarred upper lip, enfolds me in a big, gentle hug. I know he is safe, but my body panics at the contact. I want to push him off me and run away.

"You okay?" he asks softly beside my ear, and for a moment tears threaten at the real concern in his voice.

"Yeah. Yeah, I'm okay." I pull back before I can start blubbering.

"We'll talk later."

He ambles off after the other two cadets, and I am left alone with Bruce. He's a couple of years older but not much taller than me, though his muscled shoulders are about twice as wide as mine. I notice that he's had a new pattern shaved into the buzz-cut hair at his temples.

"Blue," he says, scanning my damaged face, twitching eye, bandaged head, and filthy, tangled hair. "What the hell did they do to you?" He sounds genuinely shocked.

It occurs to me that ASTA has allowed me to return to the compound in this state as a lesson to the other cadets — a kind of show-and-tell of what happens if you don't toe the line.

"I'm not allowed to talk about it," I say.

"I know — they've ordered us not to ask you questions but, damn, you look like … like you've been banged up pretty bad."

"Yeah. Well, you know, they wanted some answers."

He curses, stares down at his boots. "I am so sorry, man. I didn't think they'd go so rough on you."

I shrug. I didn't either.

"You're a cadet, not a mook!" He seems to be struggling to understand how the ASTA he's been so loyal to could have done this to one of their own. Welcome to the club, Bruce.

"Hey, I'm sorry, too," I say, "for you getting darted and stuff."

"That was Quinn?"

"Yeah."

"I figured. Then he took my weapon and made you take out the power lines?"

I nod.

"That was some shot, dude, respect!" he says, grinning widely.

"It wasn't bad," I admit.

My own smile cracks a cut on my lip open again, and I dab at it with the back of my hand.

He stares at the smear of blood, the section of raw nailbed where my fingernail used to be, the angry red welts on my hands and the bandages on my wrists, then his eyes travel up my arms to fix on the spots below my shoulders where the burn wounds have seeped through the dressings and the disposable fabric of the PPE suit.

"Man, this blows big time," he says. "This pisses me off majorly."

I start walking towards the west wing where my quarters are, and Bruce falls in beside me, in the place where Quinn always walked. He opens the fire doors for me just as Quinn always used to. I flinch when they bang shut behind us.

Out of the blue, Bruce says, "I wouldn't have shot him, you know. Quinn, I mean, on the operation. I was just bluffing."

He sounds sincere, but I don't automatically believe what people tell me anymore. I study him for a moment. "Were you? Really? You sure sounded like you meant it."

"No way. I was just angry, and jealous, I guess. But I would never have shot a cadet."

"Good to know." Wish I'd known it then. "So, what are these new symbols?" I brush my hair at the temple where he has a shaved section on his own.

"It's Korean — Tae-Hyun helped me. It means *be cautious*. It's a reminder to myself not to trust things just because they look good, to look a little deeper."

"It reminds me of Leya's tattoo."

She had a tattoo of what looked like a Chinese character at the outer corner of her left eye. I never did find out what it stood for.

"Yeah, well, that's part of the reminder. Effing rat! I'm still bummed about that, man. I didn't hardly believe you, but you were right."

"She's gone?"

"She's gone. Splitsville. Sarge just told us she 'won't be returning' to the unit. Probably been reassigned to spy on someone else. That is just so not okay. We ought to be spying on terrs, man, not each other. I mean, just who are we fighting this war against?"

It's a very good question. I let it hang in the air between us for a while. Before I ask my next question, I check around us, but no one's near.

"Did you tell them? That I knew about Leya?"

"Nah, I figured you were in enough trouble already. Besides, I'm still mad as hell. What happened to loyalty and trust? I dunno, Blue, if they set a rat to spy on us, it makes you wonder what else they've been doing."

I glance at him sharply. Is Bruce starting to question things a bit more? Or is he fishing to find out my feelings?

"Yeah, it does," I say.

Alone in my quarters, I strip off the PPE suit and shove it in the bio-disposal unit, along with the awful hair ribbon and my underwear — once I've carefully removed Quinn's earring from my bra strap. In the bathroom, I remove the bandages in front of the mirror and run my fingers over the shaved band of scalp and the spiky row of stitches beneath. The right-hand side of my face is a swollen blue-and-purple mess intersected by the vivid red scar of the cut, and crowned by a puffy and purple eye. Dark shadows arc beneath my eyes. I look older. I feel ancient — heavy with things no sixteen-year-old should know. The image in the mirror blurs as tears well in my eyes. *Cut it out!* I have to stop this incessant weeping. It's pathetic.

My wounds smart and throb in the hot water of the shower, but it feels good to scrub myself clean from top to toe and to wash the caked blood out of my hair. The adhesive dressings on the tops of my arms come off in the water, and I see that there are two red and angry-looking burns, the size of quarters, beneath. It's like I've been branded by ASTA.

After my shower, I rummage around in the first aid kit Mom packed for me when I left home all those months ago, and find a sealed pack of Band-Aids. I stick one over each burn mark, and another two over my head stitches. They don't stick very well and it looks ridiculous, so I pull them off again. I leave my bruised wrists unbandaged, swallow some Tylenol, then wrap a towel around myself and pass out on the bed.

I wake up suddenly, sitting bolt upright, heart hammering, when someone bangs at the door. It's Bruce, bringing a tray of lunch. The expression on his face shifts from slightly repulsed pity at my injuries, to undisguised interest at the swell of boob rising above the towel when I take the tray, and then to resigned disappointment as I close the door on him.

Later that afternoon, I put on my sweats and running shoes and force myself onto the running track in the giant indoor gymnasium. My knee hurts on every step, and I don't manage more than a sluggish hundred-yard jog, before the pain and stiffness slow me down to a walk. A petite female cadet with dark hair tied in a high ponytail breezes past me on the outer track. When she turns her head to give me a filthy look over her shoulder, I see angry brown eyes surrounded by an intricate filigree pattern of henna tattoos.

It's Sofia Medina — a cadet in the blue intel unit who worked alongside Quinn. I always suspected that she had a real soft spot for him, and now I hope I'm right, because I'll be needing her help.

Chapter 10

Penitent

The next morning's hearing is a fifteen-minute formality held in a large conference room dominated by a long, glass table on which there is recording equipment. Roberta Roth, who chairs the meeting, sits at one end with Sarge on her right and some other man whose name I don't catch on her left. My stomach churns when I see her. As usual, she is wearing a business suit. It's black, like her soul.

I sit alone at the far end of the table, where the whole of one wall is taken up by a large screen on which President Hawke's face smiles broadly above the familiar admonition: *If you see something, say something.*

Oh, I intend to.

"Ms. Roth, before we begin, there's something I want to say."

She looks at me with mild surprise, as if a cog in a machine had suddenly spoken. It makes me even madder.

"I want to say that I think you're scum. No, actually, lower than scum. At least scum doesn't pretend to be anything other than what it is. You and your sick sidekicks like Sarge over there, pretend to be good and noble patriots. But I have seen the real you, and it is despicable!"

That's what I badly *want* to say. In fact, I'd like to add a few slaps to emphasize my point, as she did. But, instead, I force my eyes not to glare, my mouth not to sneer, and my voice not to snarl. I adopt what I hope is a convincingly penitent expression and make my voice sound soft and regretful. I practiced in front of the mirror this morning, but I'm still not sure I've got it right — it doesn't come naturally.

"I want to say that I am truly very sorry about getting mixed up with Cadet O'Riley. I was stupid, and I realize I may have jeopardized my career here at the Academy. I only hope you and Sarge can find it in your hearts to forgive my mistake."

I bow my head and stare down at my hands. Both wrists are circled by bruises from where I wrenched against the restraining cuffs, and a scabbed red line circles my left wrist where my metal ID band cut into my skin.

Roth narrows her eyes at me, but her expression stays impassive — I can't tell whether she's buying this or not. She gets me to speak my statement into the microphone on the table, and then hands me a tablet displaying the automatic transcription. I sign it with a sensor pen and get my retina scanned as proof of identity. Sarge, as a witness, follows suit.

"Your version of events has been confirmed," says Roth.

What exactly does she mean by that? Is she just talking about what came out — and what didn't — in the interrogation and the polygraph test? Or have they started questioning Connor despite it only being day two of his "devitalization regime"?

"You have been cleared of the charge of collusion to assist a subversive, and you may return to your unit."

"I'm cleared for duty? I'm back on the sniper quad?" I ask.

"You may not be a subversive, Miss James, but you have proven yourself to be foolish, careless and gullible in the extreme. I, for one, am not eager to trust you behind a rifle again. You are to meet with your unit commander to clarify your future role and options. And it goes without saying that if you make any mention of your debriefing, it will be considered a breach of security, and we will treat that in a most serious light. Our decision to release you can be revoked at any time."

I will not go back to the detention center. I will never be that powerless again, I vow it.

Roth and the other man leave, and I'm left alone in the conference room with Sarge, who is tapping on the screen of the tablet. Keeping notes? Or, more likely, starting a voice recording of our meeting.

"So, Blue, I'm guessing you'll be wanting to head home as soon as possible?"

"No."

He looks up at that.

"Actually, I want to withdraw my resignation from the unit, sir. I'd like to stay and take up my work again."

He raises both his eyebrows and tucks his chin back in surprise. "This is quite a change of heart."

"When I say 'my work', I don't mean darting M&Ms or suspects, sir, I still never want to do that again. Especially now." I give him a dark look. "But I'd like to start ratting again."

"We ain't putting a weapon back in your hands — you heard what Ms. Roth said. And even if she gave you the all-clear, I'm not sure I would." He gives me a speculative look.

"Sir?"

He hesitates a moment, then says, "It may surprise you to know, Blue, that back when I was a wet-behind-the-ears marine on my first tour of duty, I wasn't exactly keen on killing people either."

"Really?" This *is* a surprise.

"Not at first. Not with all the targets. There was this one who was carrying a bag of mortars. He was young, no more'n a kid really. I figured we could just wound him, hit him in the leg or something. But my team leader set my head straight. He told me that if I didn't end the threat permanently, it would come back and bite me on the ass. 'That person you wound? He's going to get up, get a weapon, come back right at ya, especially now he knows where you're at. Maybe he'll be back in five minutes, maybe in five weeks. Maybe he'll get you, maybe your friend or your brother, but he'll be back. Now put him down!' That's what he said, and he was right."

"So … you think I should have been *put down*?" I ask.

Sarge looks at me for a long moment, then gives that grin that I've grown to loathe. "Nah, I just think you should have been chucked out of the program for good. Maybe sent to Alaska. See, that's what the art of sniping is: it's us picking a time and place to do you harm, before you do harm to us."

"But I don't intend to do you harm, Sarge."

He gives a short bark of laughter. "Now, see, *I* ain't convinced that you're harmless. Not since the day you shot me in the neck!"

He's never going to forget or forgive that.

"Besides" — he leans forward suddenly — "hold out your hands."

I do. They tremble. They do this almost constantly now.

I sigh, as if disappointed. "Okay, so maybe you don't trust me fully, and maybe I'm not steady enough to shoot accurately yet."

"Not steady enough to shoot accurately? Hell, right now you couldn't hit water if you fell out a boat."

"But," I continue, "surely I could go along on the missions as a spotter, or help keep the target area civilian-free?"

Sarge runs a finger over his neat mustache. His expression is doubtful.

"I thought you'd be wanting to head back home, spend some time catching up with your momma and your brother?"

"I'd like to visit them, of course, and I've already put in the paperwork with Personnel for a home-visit next weekend." Every graduated cadet gets one four-day R&R weekend each month, and I need to take mine as soon as possible. "But I don't want to stay there permanently. I know I'll go stir crazy with boredom at home. Also, when I'm not kept busy, I get flashbacks and nightmares." This much, at least, is true.

"I'll be honest, Blue, I did not think you'd want to come back into my unit after … Well, I didn't think you'd ever want to work for us again."

I twist my face into what I hope is an expression of heartbroken anger. "Ms. Roth said I had Quinn O'Riley to thank for all that happened to me in the last week, and she's right. He *used* me. He dropped me in hot water and ran off. After he said he loved me! I'm done with him and all of his kind — they can all go to hell. I've learned my lesson, and now I just want to get my life back. I promise I'll be good and keep my nose clean, Sarge. Maybe one day I can prove to you that I'm worth trusting again."

Sarge stares at me for a long while, then says, "I'll have a talk with Ms. Roth, and we'll let you know."

At least it's not an outright no.

Part Two

Chapter 11

Allies

Once, before the Plague hit, our family went on an outing to a medieval festival. Robin and I were both fascinated by the knights in armor and placed bets on our favorite champions in the jousting contests, but the best part was walking through the living museum. Robin dragged my mother off to watch a blacksmith hammering out a sword on his forge, and I insisted Dad come watch the glassblower with me.

I was spellbound by the way the man scooped up a blob of honey-colored molten glass from the furnace and gathered it onto the end of his long blowpipe. He turned and twisted and swept that pipe through the air, using pincers to tweak out decorative edges and carve grooves into the delicate surface, all the while blowing into the glass, stretching it wider and thinner as if he was inflating a balloon. We held our breaths as the glass stretched finer and finer until it looked as insubstantial and fragile as a soap bubble. Then the blower scored it at the base, tapped it free from the pipe and held it up for the gathered crowd to admire. The applause had not yet ended when he lifted the vase high above his head, then turned and dashed it onto the ground behind him, shattering it into countless sharp shards, and turning our oohs and ahs of admiration into gasps of shock.

"Why did you break it?" I demanded, horrified at the destruction.

"It was flawed, it would have cracked anyway," was his explanation.

Today, I feel like that vase, stretched brittle-thin and pulled into fragile shakiness by anxiety and impatience. I, too, am no doubt flawed and set to crack along my hidden fault lines. Every so often I get a panicky, breathless feeling in my chest. And my hands are still unsteady.

I urgently need to get a message to Quinn about his brother. Since his phone is in fragments somewhere in the city's sewerage system, and since all telephone, email and internet communications with his family are being intercepted and analyzed, I will need to go low-tech.

I spend most of the day in the compound's huge indoor gymnasium, waiting and hoping the person I want to see will show up today. I intentionally take a long time to stretch and warm up my stiff muscles. I'm still sore, but it's only been a few days since I last exercised properly and, thanks to Sarge's intense training sessions over the last months, I am fit and strong. I spend half an hour on the ergometer, rowing slowly on the lowest resistance setting and resting often, while keeping one eye on the gym's entrance. The rest of my unit arrives and comes over to check how the hearing went.

"Okay, I think. But they won't let me near a weapon. Sarge is going to see if I can go on missions with you guys as a spotter."

"Cool," says Mitch.

"Yeah, I'll put in a good word for you," says Bruce, seating himself on the erg next to me and beginning to row. Almost at once, he stops to crank up the resistance on the flywheel to the maximum, and then continues in a smooth rhythm, catch and drive, catch and drive.

Mitch and Tae-Hyun set off running on the track which runs along the outside perimeter of the gym, and Cameron takes the erg on the other side of me as soon as it's vacated.

"You can come out on the range with me, if you like," offers Bruce on the out-breath of a backwards pull. "I'll let you practice with my rifle so you can keep your eye in."

Cameron shakes his head.

"Thanks," I tell Bruce, "but there are cameras out there, and if they caught me shooting when they've forbidden it, then I'd be bounced out and you'd be in trouble."

"There are cameras on the range?"

"There are cameras everywhere." I keep my voice carefully neutral, but his, when he replies, is mad.

"It's seriously beginning to piss me off that we've got no privacy in this place."

I grin at him. "You sound just like Quinn used to."

Cameron laughs, and Bruce snorts derisively, but for once he doesn't insult my ex. He pulls hard on the cables, says, "So he got away, then?"

"Looks like it. Not that they'd tell me if they'd caught him."

"Yeah, they don't tell us much."

Bruce is definitely less blindly loyal to the authorities than he used to be, but he's still as competitive as he ever was, and my slow pace on the erg is driving him crazy.

"Come on, Cameron, I'll race you," he says, jogging over to the track.

"I'll catch you up," says Cameron, then adds in a soft voice to me, "Are you planning something?"

"What do you mean?"

"You can trust me," he says.

I want to, and I kind of do. I like Cameron, for one thing, and for another, he was the one who told me about Leya being a spy. But I no longer feel like I can trust anyone. Who's to say he hasn't replaced Leya as chief rat, that even now he's trying to get me to spill my beans?

"I heard that before, from Quinn," I say. "And it didn't work out so well."

Cameron shrugs and says, "What needs to be done can't be done alone. Just know, when the time comes, I'm on your side. And I'll want in on whatever you're planning."

It's the most I've ever heard him say. I sit, dumbfounded, with the cables loose in my hands, watching as he jogs off to join Bruce. I just had an actual conversation with strong, silent Cameron.

The boys spend the next half hour challenging each other on the track, while I watch, sitting on an exercise mat under the monkey bars, slowly sipping on a bottle of water. They wave goodbye when they leave, and Bruce calls out that he'll catch me later in the rec room. I nod and wave, check my watch and scan the entrance again.

Finally, Sofia Medina comes into the gym, does a few stretches and takes to the track. I follow her, walking, so that she can complete her lap and catch up with me quicker. When she does, she bumps me hard, sending me sprawling onto the track.

She stops and mutters furiously, "You betrayed Quinn!"

Her back is to the nearest surveillance camera. Probably it just looks like she's apologizing for the "accident".

I get up off the ground, noting that I now have *two* scraped knees, and say, "I saved his life. I saved both their lives." I cup a hand in front of my mouth — as if coughing — to hide my lips, just in case someone watching the footage can zoom in and read lips. "They would have shot them with live ammo if I hadn't darted Connor." Would Bruce actually have done it? At the time, I had no doubts, but now I'm not so sure. "And I got Quinn out of here, didn't I?"

Sofia glares at me and sets off running again. I take off after her. Though it still hurts to move, no way is she fitter or faster than me, and soon I catch up.

"Look, I know you hate me. But do you want to help *him*?" I ask, and pass her, then slow a little when I'm several paces ahead.

"What?" she says from behind me.

I allow her to catch up. "Do you want to help Quinn?"

"Do you know where he is?" she asks, without turning her head.

"Go ahead of me." I wait till she's a few strides in front before continuing. "No. But I do know where his brother is, where they're holding him. And I know that they plan to start torturing him any day now."

If they haven't already begun.

I pick up the pace and overtake her. If anyone is watching, it will look like we're racing each other. She peels off to the side of the track to catch her breath and, I guess, to think about whether she can trust me, whether she wants to help. I keep running. When I approach to lap her for the second time, she steps back on the track and starts running again. I slow my stride so that she can keep pace just behind me.

"Okay, yes. I want to help. But how?"

"There's a chance I could get a message to him about his brother, but to do that I need to get out of the compound."

"I don't see how I could help with that," Sofia pants as we change leads again.

"If intel said there were reports of sightings of rats or M&Ms, they'd have to send out ratting squads."

"When? Where?"

I still remember what Kerry, Quinn's little sister, told me on our ASTA graduation day — that her mother takes her to the local park every weekday at four after they finish homeschooling lessons. Kerry likes to visit with the lady who regularly brings her baby.

"Freedom Park, around 4pm on a weekday. In the section where the play park is."

Sofia is silent for a while as she runs ahead of me.

"Well?" I urge as I pass her slowly.

"I could probably do it. Those reports come in all the time, and Brescia and I collate the lists. I could just add it to the list on Monday."

Today is Saturday. That means another two days will go by before anything happens. But I only know times for weekdays.

"Thanks," I say, then repeat, "Freedom Park, 4pm, weekdays."

"I got it," she snaps.

I allow her to run ahead, taking a few minutes to bend over my knees and rest. When she passes by on the next lap, I begin running again.

"We need a way to exchange messages," Sofia says.

I fall into place beside her, keeping pace with her stride, and ask, "Is there someplace out of sight of the cameras?" The old secret spot under the stairwell where Quinn and I used to meet is now under the beady eye of a new camera installed after someone — me — set off a false fire alarm.

"The girl's restroom, northeast wing, on the ground floor. Last toilet cubicle. We could leave notes in the S-bend of the outlet pipe. On the outside of the pipe, obviously."

"What about the camera?"

All restrooms here have a camera in the corner which covers the basins and cubicle doors, even if they don't record what goes on inside the actual stalls. Anyone analyzing the footage would be suspicious if the same two girls repeatedly used the last toilet when other stalls were empty.

"No, the angle at which it's mounted is off. It only captures the basins and the first cubicle door. The rest are out of range." She's getting out of breath now. She'll need to stop soon.

I know the restroom she means. I call an image of it into my mind, trying to visualize the sight-lines, like a sniper looking for ways she might get spotted by the enemy.

"What about the mirrors? Wouldn't they show the reflections?"

"Camera's aimed too low. Trust me, alright?"

I don't want to, but I'm going to have to.

"Okay. Thanks," I say and pull off down the straight section of the track when she collapses onto the AstroTurf.

When I finally call it quits, it's because of a rapid fluttering of my heart that has nothing to do with exercise and everything to do with rising panic. Seventy-two hours have passed since Connor was captured. He has only two days left, at best, before they begin torturing him in earnest.

Chapter 12

Hand-to-hand

Late Monday morning, I visit the last toilet cubicle in the female restrooms on the ground floor of the northeast wing. I latch the door closed, sit on the lid of the toilet and feel along the outside length of the S-bend with my hand, trying not to think about the source of the dirt I can feel under my fingertips. Tucked into the inside bend of the pipe is a small, folded piece of paper. I open it, read the message, "Done," and then tear the paper into tiny scraps which I throw into the toilet pan. It takes several flushes until they've all disappeared.

Done. Good.

The rest of the day drags by slowly as I wait for Sarge to summon us for a mission to Freedom Park. My head is full of doubts. What if he's decided that I shouldn't go? What if I get to go but *they* aren't there? What if we go at the wrong time?

Four o'clock comes and goes, and the only gathering of the sniper unit is in front of the darts board and PlayState virtual reality game consoles in the rec room. Damn. Connor's five days are up. If they hold to their plan, his interrogation will start tonight. Time is running out fast.

I leave a message of my own in the S-bend: *Nothing yet. Can you ping the park again?*

Tuesday morning lasts a century. Finally — finally! — after the lunch-hour, Sarge sends a message that we're all to be in his office at 14h30.

There's more elbow room in the small office without the presence of Leya, but it's still a squash. Next to Sarge stands a tall person of around thirty years, with short brown hair, bulky muscles bulging out from a camo vest, and some kind of strange scar on one forearm. Since I left home, I've seen many of the ways people try to make their appearance stand out when they're so often disguised behind their masks — weirdly colored contact lenses, tattoos, bizarre hairstyles, and all kinds of piercings, but this raised, white pattern of skin is a new one for me.

A swift glance to either side confirms that Mitch, Tae-Hyun, Cameron and Bruce are all staring with puzzled expressions at the stranger. They're probably wondering the same thing I am: is this a man or a woman? There's no softness to the features, no fullness to the lips, but I don't see any stubble on the jaw either.

"Right, piglets, this here is Charlie."

Male, I think. Then immediately remember that one of the girls in my online study group called herself Charlie — short for Charlotte.

"It has been brought to my attention that there is a deficit in your training, a gap in your skills." Sarge gives me a hard look. "Apparently, overpowering someone in this specialist unit and taking their weapon is easier'n taking candy from a baby. So Charlie here is going to be spending time with you over the next few weeks, teaching you the skills of hand-to-hand combat."

"Cool!" says Mitch, fist-bumping with Bruce.

"Awesome," says Tae-Hyun.

Cameron, as usual, says nothing.

I'm not enthusiastic. I expect I will soon be sporting even

more bruises. Also, I'm disappointed — I was hoping we had been summoned to go on a ratting mission.

It strikes me that Charlie is not wearing a mask or gloves. Is this due to macho bravado, or insider knowledge?

"Interrupting an attack, disarming and disabling an opponent, protecting yourself and your unit members — these are the skills you will learn," says Charlie in a deep, gruff voice.

"Will we be doing knife work?" asks Bruce.

"I will show you how to turn your *hands* into lethal weapons."

On the last word, Charlie pulls a fist back to waist height then strikes out with an open-handed blow, like a karate chop, which stops a millimeter short of Bruce's throat. I see that what I thought was a scar on the forearm is actually a pattern of cuts and scratches etched into the skin like a raised white tattoo. It's of a clenched fist with flames rising from the knuckles. Male or female, this is not someone I want to mess with. Neither does Bruce, judging from the hard swallow he gives.

Tae-Hyun laughs a little nervously, but the rest of us stay silent. Sarge grins his mad smile, thanks Charlie and says we'll attend our first training session at 20h00 this evening.

"Right, item two on our agenda, we're going ratting this afternoon."

Excellent. As long as I'm included.

There are murmurs of appreciation from the boys. I guess this is the first mission since the disaster with Quinn and Connor last Wednesday.

"Bruce, Mitch, and Tae-Hyun on point. Cameron, you can spot if it's necessary — I don't know the distances."

"Sir?" I look my question.

"You, Blue, will not be on point. You will not even be spotting. But Ms. Roth has given permission for you to clear the area of civilians. And I'll be coming along to keep my eye on you."

So far so good. "Thanks, Sarge," I say, all enthusiasm.

Bruce asks the question I desperately want answered. "Where are we going, Sarge?"

"Freedom Park, this afternoon."

Yes!

"We've received multiple reports of a rat infestation there. Suit up and get your weapons and ammo from the armory. We leave from bay C at oh-fifteen-hundred precisely. Damndest thing — the varmints seem to come out every afternoon at four when some folks bring their kiddies to the play park on the southern side. Don't look at me like that, Mitch, there are still some people who like to get out of the house. I guess kids bring snacks and the rats are looking for food, but we can't risk someone getting bit."

"Plague rats or ordinary rats, sir?" says Mitch.

"The report didn't specify, son, but we need to be prepared for both. Dismissed."

On the way to the armory, the boys argue about whether Charlie is a man or a woman. I've already made up my mind on this one.

"He's a man, definitely. Did you see those biceps?" says Mitch.

"Dude!" agrees Bruce. "And did you see that scarification on his arm? My older brother wanted to get one. He told me they cut it with scalpels and peel off the skin, or sandpaper it. And then they rub crap into the wounds — iodine or toothpaste or lemon juice — to make the scar worse. That's pain, man, Pain! With a capital P that rhymes with T that stands for testosterone. No way a woman could handle that."

"Charlie is a woman," I say, firmly. "Not only can we handle as much or more pain than you bozos, but we also don't have Adam's apples."

After a moment's silence, Tae-Hyun says, "Hey, Jinx is right, I didn't see one on her."

Cameron nods. He's real observant. He would have noticed, too.

"Huh," says Bruce.

"She's hardcore — the real deal," says Tae-Hyun.

Mitch elbows Tae-Hyun in the ribs and mocks, "Hey, Tae-Hyun's in luurrve!"

Tae-Hyun cuffs Mitch behind the head, and the two scuffle the entire way to the armory.

"Hey guys? Guys! Why do you think she wasn't wearing a mask or gloves?"

"Maybe they tested her before allowing her in," says Bruce.

But that can't be right. The results would take twelve days to come back, and it's been less than a week since I raised the issue of hand-to-hand combat.

"Nah, she's too badass for any virus. Any microbe that lands on her will just check her out and fly the other way," says Tae-Hyun, aiming a blow at Mitch, who is making kissing noises.

If the rebels are right, that's wrong, too. The Rat fever virus isn't airborne.

We pass through the decon units to transport bay C and troop noisily into the armory, where Juan is on duty behind the counter.

Juan asks, "What are we hunting today, boys — rabids? Or rats, or terrs?" Juan gestures behind him to a different shelf of ammunition as he names each target type. Rabids, or M&Ms, are people who are so far gone with the rat fever plague that they've gone "rabid". "Terrs" are terrorists, the creators and spreaders of the plague.

"Just the rodents," says Mitch.

"Right you are, rifles first," says Juan.

He begins issuing Bruce, Mitch and Tae-Hyun their weapons. Cameron leans up against a wall while I hop up to perch on the counter and begin fiddling with a high-power scope I find lying there. I put it to my eye and squint out the doors to where our transport, a black, unmarked Hummer van, is parked. Through the scope, I can see every detail, including the mud splattered on the bumper, and a scratch above one wheel well. I can even make out the tiny date stamp on the registration plate.

I turn and peer inside the armory. Through the scope, the boys appear so close that I'm overwhelmed with the detail of stubble, pores and pimples. I twist around and peer at the racks of weapons and the shelves of ammunition. On the shelf Juan indicated when he said "rabids", there's a Plexiglas ammunition canister. Inside are the special cartridges — each filled with instant-tranquilizing drug — packed upright in molded foam. There's a tiny sticker on the outside of the box, and I focus the scope until I can read it. *1000 x bi-fill cartridges (C11H17N2NAO2S + KCl).*

I have no idea what this is, but in my new, unofficial role as spook-on-the-inside, I want to know everything, so I try to take a mental snapshot. Most likely, it's nothing important, just a product code or something, but I create a quick mnemonic to help remember it. *Cats 11, Hats 17, New 2, Now Attempt Olympics 2 Sing + Kick Crappy lovers.*

Once the boys have had their thumbs scanned to acknowledge receipt of their rifles and ammo, and Sarge has arrived, we leave. Bruce and Mitch are singing, tunelessly, a ditty they've just made up about rodent annihilation, Tae-Hyun is clicking his tongue-stud against his teeth, and Cameron, as usual, is silent. Me? I'm silently chanting the mnemonic while picturing the hatted cats (two of them shiny and new) kicking the shins of a lover who looks a lot like Quinn.

The Hummer carries us in air-conditioned comfort out of the compound and through the largely empty streets of the city. Most folks are like my mother, preferring to stay safe inside at home, but we do pass a rare jogger apparently determined to run on the roads rather than on a treadmill, a band of leather-clad bikers gathered under an overpass and an ancient black station-wagon with a coffin fitted on top of the roof. The warning "*Turn or Burn*" is stenciled on the sides, "*Repent or Lament*" on the blackened rear window, and a strident man's voice broadcasts Bible verses out of a hood-mounted loudspeaker as it rolls slowly down the deserted suburban streets.

As soon as we arrive at Freedom Park and clamber out, we're hit full-force with the sweltering mid-August heat and humidity. We dump our gear at the base of a sign reading: *Caution! Premises and facilities used at own risk. The City accepts no responsibility for injuries or illnesses incurred on these premises. Report any sightings of rats, infected animals or persons to 1-800-RAT-REPORT.*

"Man, this is hot. It's going to be like trying to shoot inside a sauna," Bruce complains, wiping a sleeve across his face.

"Suck it up, cupcake. If you think this is bad, try marching through the desert carrying 120 pounds of gear in temperatures in excess of 46° Celsius. That's over 114° Fahrenheit, my sweaty little hogs," says Sarge.

I am definitely sweating like a pig. The thick cotton boiler suits which are the standard uniform of the sniper unit aren't ideal gear for weather such as this, and the fabric rubs painfully up against my sores and scabs, but I'm not complaining. The suits also have a number of pockets and webbed pouches which are useful for stashing extra clips of ammo, bottles of water or packs of gum.

Or something else you might wish to hide.

"Listen up, soldiers. Put your comms in now, so we can stay in contact with each other."

We all insert the tiny earpieces which are both speakers and microphones, and do a sound-check.

"That clump of dogwoods down there must be the trees where, according to the reports, the rats are hiding out. We can probably get quite close — I don't think you boys will need a spotter. Up there are the civilians that need clearing," says Sarge.

I look up the grassy rise to our right, and a surge of adrenalin fizzes through my veins. At the top of the sloped embankment is a play park. A woman in a yellow dress is sitting on a bench beside a baby stroller, and a few feet to her right, another woman in jeans is pushing a child on the swings.

Can it really be them?

Chapter 13

In the palm of my hand

Please, please let it be them. If it isn't them, then I have no idea how to get a message to Quinn.

"I'll go," says Cameron and begins walking.

"No! No, it's okay, I'll do it," I say quickly. "They might freak out if they're approached by a big, strange man. I'm less threatening."

If Cameron thinks that they might be equally freaked by my Technicolor face, he doesn't mention it.

"Haul ass, then, Blue. I want them cleared out of the park, stat."

"On it, Sarge."

As I walk off and climb the embankment, I hear, through the earpiece, the sounds of the boys loading ammo clips into their rifles and discussing where best to set up their firing positions.

Climbing higher, I notice a man to the rear of the play park, several meters behind the woman in yellow. He's wearing a respirator and is leaning up against a large boulder, his eyes on the two figures at the swings. His face turns to me as I draw nearer. This must be one of the spooks tailing the O'Riley family members. Crap. I should've anticipated this. If the spooks find out who this cadet is, or if Sarge figures out who the mother and daughter are, they'll guess that the contact can't be coincidental. I'll be toast.

The mother on the bench has neon-yellow hair and also wears a respirator. Has she fitted one on her baby, too?

I'm close enough to make out features now, and I see that it definitely is Quinn's mother pushing his little sister on the swings. Mrs. O'Riley is not wearing a respirator. Her face is as pale as the small piece of paper tucked inside my front breast pocket. She looks tired and her features are tight with worry. I reckon she has been getting as little sleep as her eldest son.

Kerry — also mask-free — is the first to recognize me. She is high in the air on an upswing when she smiles widely, showing me the gap of her missing front tooth.

"Mom, look! That's —"

"Excuse me for interrupting you, ladies," I cut in quickly, all too aware that everything I say, and maybe even what they say, is being carried to Sarge's ears. I have to be careful with hand gestures too, because of the presence of the spook and the other civilian. I can't have him see or hear anything he might regard as suspicious, and I can't have her reporting the odd behavior of a cadet to someone later. Some people take the "If you see something, say something" warning all too seriously.

"But —" begins Kerry, looking puzzled.

"Listen up now, folks," I interrupt, before she can say anything more, and then I raise a finger to my lips in a silent shushing gesture.

I hope that the spook just thinks I'm telling the kid to be quiet and pay attention. My back is square to the rest of the team down below, so they won't see it. As Mrs. O'Riley pulls the swing back, she whispers into Kerry's ear. Kerry gives a small nod, and then her face is clear of any recognition and she keeps swinging, pumping herself higher into the air with her legs.

"I have an important message for you." I say this, loudly and clearly, while staring directly into Mrs. O'Riley's accusing eyes. It's clear that she's aware of my role in Connor's capture.

"If you'll all look down there, you'll see a bunch of men with weapons."

As expected, all of them, including the spook, look down the hill to where the sniper unit is gathered, and I use the moment's distraction. Keeping the elbow of my right arm close to my side, I reach with the hand into the breast pocket and remove the folded note, on which I have written, in tiny print, details of the plan to weaken and interrogate Connor. Although I've forgotten the name of the detention center, I still remember the address, and I've written that down, too. I keep the note in the palm of my hand, pressed against my midriff, to still the shaking which has started up again.

Mrs. O'Riley, looks back from the armed team to me, her expression is now alert.

"Now I don't want you to worry about them. We're just an infected-animal eradication team. We've had reports of rats in this area, and we're about to begin an extermination operation."

"Oh my!" says the mother with the pram, beginning to gather blankets and stuffed toys to pack into a large bag.

"So I'm afraid you'll need to stop swinging, young lady." I hold up my hand in a "stop" sign, angling it away from the blonde woman and the man on the right. The note is against my palm, and I'm holding it in place with my thumb. "And I'm going to have to ask all of you ladies, and you too, sir, to clear the park."

"We're not in anyone's way," says Mrs. O'Riley with a scowl. Her Irish accent is way stronger than Quinn's.

Kerry keeps her eyes on the note as I lower my hand in front of me. I take a few paces closer to them.

"It's for your own safety, ma'am. I just want to make sure *everyone* gets away safe and sound, understand? We can't let people stay … where it might be dangerous to their health." Does

Quinn's mother understand that I'm talking about Connor? "So it's important and urgent that you get the message" — I pause for a fraction of a second, widening my eyes at Kerry — "to leave the park."

"A little less conversation, a little more action, Blue," Sarge's voice barks in my ear.

"Yes, sir. They're leaving now, sir." I speak loudly and press my other hand against the ear with the comms, hoping that the O'Rileys have understood that our interaction is being monitored.

The blonde woman stands up, says goodbye to Kerry and her mother, and walks off, pushing the stroller. At the same time, Kerry jumps off the swing and appears to stumble to the ground, losing a shoe in the process.

"Here, let me help you," I say, hurrying forward. I fetch the shoe and slip the note inside before I hand it to Kerry with a wink. She winks back, but to my relief, says nothing as she slips the shoe back on.

"Come on, sweet pea. We need to go now," says Mrs. O'Riley, laying a hand on Kerry's shoulder.

"I'm so sorry." I keep my tone merely polite, but I try to convey my deep regret in the apologetic look I give Quinn's mother.

"That's okay," says Kerry. Her voice is friendly. "We can come back tomorrow, can't we, Mom?"

"We could, but should we? We generally like to come every afternoon this time, and on weekend mornings at ten, but not if it's not safe. Not if there are … dangerous things out to get us," says Mrs. O'Riley and I know she's not asking about rats, know also that she's giving me specific information of when else she would be in the park for possible messages.

"You can come any day and every day, ma'am." I'd like to keep this channel of communication open for possible future messages. "Just not today. Of course, if ever you see a mutant rat or other plague-spreader, or any suspicious activity, you should be sure to report it to the proper authorities. If you see something, say something!"

"Of course," says Mrs. O'Riley. She takes her daughter's hand and pulls her away from me.

"Goodbye," says Kerry with a wave.

I wave back and wait until they, and the spook who follows them, have reached the parking lot and then head back down the hill. Sarge is waiting for me, shaking his head in disgust.

"Hell, Princess, you may not be cleared to shoot, but if we ever need a rat or rabid *talked* to death, remind me to enlist you."

Two sweltering hours later, we're on our way back to ASTA. Sarge theorizes that the boys made too much noise and scared away the rats, and warns us that we'll have to come back another day. The boys talk about sniping, comparing their longest successful shots to the best on record. Cameron watches me silently.

I gaze out the tinted window, wondering if somewhere, somehow, someone is getting the message about Connor to the rebels.

There's a new piece of graffiti spray-painted on the side of a deserted overpass before the turnoff to the ASTA road: *Respect existence or expect resistance.*

Chapter 14

Old wounds, new bruises

That night, before dinner, I duck into the restroom to post another note. In it, I tell Sofia that I delivered the message this afternoon, and ask her to try find out what the code on the M&M bullet box means. I don't dare do it myself because I'm sure my internet activity is being monitored. Unfortunately, although I still clearly remember the eleven cats and seventeen hats and the rest of it, I can't remember whether the letters or the numbers came first. With an apology to Sofia for the confusion, I write down both permutations and tell her where I read the code.

The door to the restroom bangs as someone shoves it open, and I nearly levitate with fright. I sit as still as a sniper, except for my trembling hands, listening as some other female goes about her business. There's the sound of a flush, the stall opening, a faucet running, and then the whoosh of the door closing. I bend over to stash my tiny note in the toilet's S-bend, then stop at the basin to wash the cold sweat off my hands and face.

At dinner, after I get my meal scanned at the cafeteria's nutritional analysis checkout, I deliberately bypass Sofia's table on the way to our unit's usual spot. I cough loudly to get her attention, then give her a speaking look and a tiny nod. I hope she knows that means to check for a new message.

After dinner, our unit heads to the gymnasium for our first hand-to-hand combat training session. Charlie, who is already waiting on the training mats, gives us a gruff greeting, and then it's straight to the business of how to disarm an opponent wielding a knife, Taser or firearm.

I guess Sarge told her I was the babe who had my candy taken by a mere intel cadet, because she demonstrates the moves on me. I point a realistic-looking toy gun at her, and she holds her hands up in the air in a submissive gesture. But an instant later she smashes her hand into my forearm, bats the weapon away, twists my arm behind my back and yanks it up painfully between my shoulders. In the next exercise, she comes in close as if to kiss me — "Disarm your opponent's mental defenses, not just his weapons!" — then strikes my gun hand hard above the wrist and forces my hand inwards until I yelp in pain and drop the weapon, certain that my wrist is broken. Next, she shows us how to "bring a perp to the ground and make him beg for mercy," by sweeping my feet out from under me and slamming me to the floor, pinning me down with a hand at my throat and a knee at my ribs.

"Mercy!" I whimper.

Mitch and Tae-Hyun laugh, and even Cameron smiles. But Bruce, to his credit, looks a little worried for my welfare and helps me up afterwards. I refuse his offer to dust down the seat of my pants.

"You're bleeding," he says, pointing to one of the short sleeves of my T-shirt. I can feel the electrode sore stinging beneath.

"Don't worry about it." I press the soft cotton of my T against it and apply pressure while watching Mitch and Cameron square off.

"You okay, kid?" Charlie asks me kindly.

Define okay.

After some practice, we move on to offensive moves, and I'm

at a height and strength disadvantage again. Can't I just pick on someone my own size? Charlie takes us through the theory and practice of hitting the opponent upside the head with the butt of a gun or the handle of a knife, the fine art of breaking kneecaps and fingers, the knack of punching throats and kidneys, and throws in a side of eye-gouging and eardrum-bursting "just for fun".

After two hours, I'm done. Flat-out exhausted. My head is throbbing, my muscles are aching, and my injured knee won't take my full weight again. Back in my quarters I discover that I have a whole new collection of reddish-purple bruises to complement the week-old set which are now a sickly mix of plum and mustard yellow with webby green borders. It's like I'm wearing camouflage-patterned skin.

I pull off my T-shirt and carefully peel back the bloody Band-Aid on my right upper arm. Underneath, the sore is bleeding on one edge where the thick, soft scab has wrenched free from the raw skin beneath. I figure these burns might heal quicker if I left them uncovered to dry out, so I pull off the Band-Aid on my other arm, too. That sore is oozing a pale-pink, watery substance. I dab them dry with toilet paper, figure they'll stain my bed sheets tonight, realize I don't give a rat's ass.

I poke gingerly at the stitches in my scalp — now surrounded by a patch of stubble where my hair is just beginning to make a reappearance. They're due to be removed in two days' time. At least *they* are healing like they're supposed to.

At 11h00 I fall into bed, worries stinging my tired mind like a swarm of bees. Connor is into his second day of torture. How many sessions would that be? What have they done to him? Have the O'Rileys managed to get my message to Quinn or the other rebels yet? My last thought, selfishly, is for myself: will I survive another combat training session at the hands of Charlie?

I very nearly don't.

I am freshly stiff and sore at 08h30 the next morning when Charlie teaches us more ways to remove an opponent's gun or deflect knife thrusts, how to break wrist- and choke-holds, and get out of headlocks. None of this comes naturally to me — I don't like pain, especially on my already battered body, and I'm neither physically strong nor very well coordinated when it comes to these big, powerful movements. Worse, every time someone grabs me around the wrist or waist, images of the detention center flash through my mind and panic temporarily immobilizes my body. I do excel at getting out of a full nelson, which involves throwing my arms up in the air, going limp and simply sliding out of the attacker's arms and down his front. This much I *can* do. It turns out that not having huge biceps comes in useful sometimes.

Though I wish I was big enough to put the boys in their place, because they're in full frat-boy mode today. When we learn how to defend against an attacker coming from the front, Mitch and Tae-Hyun crack all sorts of jokes about how to deal with a "full frontal". When we progress to defending against an attack coming from the rear, and have to split into pairs to practice, Mitch quips, "Hey Blue, can I try to take you from behind?"

"Shut up, asshole," says Bruce, surprising me. It's the kind of thing *he* might once have said to me.

Charlie sets the boys to working in pairs and pulls me aside.

"You're not holding your own," she accuses.

"They're taller than me. And much stronger."

"If you're shorter, that only means you have a lower center of gravity. That's an *advantage* because it makes you more stable, and more able to topple *them*. But what you really need to understand is this: women are stronger than men."

I guess my disbelief is evident in my expression, because she continues, "They are! Women have greater capacity for endurance and stamina, and are more resistant to pain and fatigue."

I look back at Mitch and Cameron's height and assess Bruce's bulging muscles. No way. Even Tae-Hyun's wiry strength beats mine.

"I've never even won an arm-wrestling contest with any of them."

"Lucky thing you won't be arm-wrestling any opponents in a fight, then," she says, smiling. "Okay, they have greater upper body strength, no question, so your power needs to come from your hips, not your biceps. Look." She demonstrates throwing a punch, an open-handed strike and a high kick, and each time she swivels her hips, driving the momentum of her whole body into the motion. "See? The hips give power to the punch, strength to the strike. Boys have narrower hips, and their arm strength makes them complacent, lazy. You can use that against them. Come, let's practice."

We do, and after a while, I get it. I stop trying to attack or disable using just my arms, and start using my whole body — pivoting at the hip and throwing Charlie off balance.

"There you go. I knew you could do it," she says approvingly, and pushes me in the direction of the boys, saying softly, "Your final advantage as a female? Males will always underestimate you."

"Hey, Mitch?" I call. "You still want a one-on-one?"

"Any time, any place — I'm yours!" he says. "Seems like you're a sucker for punishment, Blue. Should we call the infirmary to pre-book a bed?"

"Sure. You could check they have an extra-length one — I don't think you'll fit in the regular size."

"Ha-ha. Funny — not. You ready?"

"Bring it."

Chapter 15

Blood, sweat and tears

Mitch bends his knees and holds his hands wide, circling me on the gym mat, looking for a good opening. Then he comes at me, brandishing the toy Bowie knife we practice with, and I move in, swiveling my hips, knocking him off-balance and flipping him to the floor, with the knife at his neck and my knee at his nut-purse. There's a WTF expression on his face that brings a smile to my own.

Charlie nods proudly, the guys hoot and whistle, and I raise my arms above my head like a boxing champ. I've beaten the boys regularly in marksmanship, and often in memory and observation, but today is the first time I feel *strong*. It's a glorious feeling.

In the afternoon session, we work hard on throws and take-downs, Bruce volunteers to be my partner, but Charlie, perhaps suspecting he'll go easy on me, insists on working with me herself. In a move which involves her restraining me with a meaty forearm around my throat and yanking my head back by the hair, she somehow manages to rip open my nearly-healed head wound. I cry out in pain.

"Huh," Charlie grunts from behind me. "You're bleeding. Again."

I suppress a groan while she inspects the wound, then says almost gently, "You'd better get yourself off to the infirmary, kid, looks like you'll need more stitches. Here." She pulls off her T-shirt, wads it up and presses it to the cut.

"You'll need to maintain pressure on that. Scalp wounds bleed like a bitch."

Beneath her top, she sports a training bra and a six-pack of abs which seems to have Tae-Hyun near swooning in admiration. Beside him, Mitch has gone gray. His eyes are fixed on the blood I can feel warmly trickling down my ear and neck, and he looks ready to swoon too. Bruce, unaffected by the blood, volunteers to accompany me to the infirmary, in case I faint.

"I'm not going to faint," I say, disgusted at the assumption. "But perhaps you should volunteer to help Mitch — it looks like *he* might."

At the infirmary, the doctor gives me a shot to numb the pain, removes the old stitches, cleans and disinfects the wound, and considers the merits of closing it with superglue or staples. In the end, though, he settles for a new row of traditional stitches, after shaving the strip of hair again. At this rate, I'll be lucky if it ever grows back.

By the time I return to the gym, the combat training session is already over and there's no sign of Charlie or the boys, so I head back to my quarters, taking the route that leads past the message toilet. The note I left is gone, but there's no reply from Sofia. Back in my quarters, my computer flashes a message from Personnel. My long weekend visit home has been approved. On Friday, the day after tomorrow, I'll be going home. It will be so good to see Robin and Mom again — I could do with some serious hugs and loving. Also, it'll be really good to miss a few sessions of Charlie's torture.

In the morning, Bruce, Mitch, Tae-Hyun and Cameron get to

go shooting on the long-distance range out back of the compound, and I'm ordered to work on my strength and fitness in the gym. When I arrive, Sofia is already running around the track, and as she passes, she mutters, "I need to talk to you, urgently." Something has clearly upset her.

I'm too tired to face another session of running, so I go to the bank of stationary bikes, all of which are riderless, and begin pedaling on the lowest resistance. After a few minutes, Sofia heads over and stations herself on a bike behind and to the side of me.

"I've got good news and bad news."

"Bad first," I say. I always like to get the worst over with.

She ignores my request and says, "The good news is that Connor O'Riley was rescued last night."

"Yes!" Elation and relief flood me.

"There was a raid on the detention center in the small hours of this morning, three prisoners were liberated, and they think an insurgent was injured in the attack."

Not Quinn, please not Quinn. Or Connor. Let it be one of the other nameless, faceless rebels, I think callously. I've got enough O'Riley guilt on my conscience.

"But they all escaped and no one has been recaptured," Sofia continues. "All of the spooks and intel are on full red-alert."

"It's fantastic news, thank you." I feel buzzed and light with joy, like a helium balloon filled with happy gas.

"One of the guards was killed in the raid."

Damn. Suddenly the idea of a resistance movement just got real.

"Is that the bad news?" I ask.

"I wish. No, I've found out something." She speaks softly, but even above the whirr of the machines, I can hear that she has found out something significant. Something bad.

"I checked out that code you gave me. It wasn't easy, because I knew it might be a phrase listed to ping on our intel systems when researched. And also because I had to check it in the different alpha-numeric sequences. But I got there in the end."

For the benefit of the cameras, I lean forward, give a burst of pedaling at top speed, as if I'm not listening intently to every word she's saying.

"And?" I prompt.

"It's not a code, it's a chemical formula. The first part is $C_{11}H_{17}N_2NaO_2S$."

I try to remember my school chemistry modules, try to picture the periodic table with its chemical formulas for different elements.

"Sodium? Oxygen?" I venture.

"It's the chemical formula for a substance called sodium thiopental. It's a rapid-onset general anesthetic. Knocks you out immediately."

That fits. I would expect there to be a strong anesthetic for rendering the M&Ms unconscious as quickly as possible.

"Yeah, and?" I'm guessing there's more, else why would she look so concerned?

"It's usually the first of three drugs administered in lethal injection executions."

"It's just an anesthetic, though, right?"

Something like panic is tightening my chest, as if my body knows something that my mind hasn't yet realized.

"Yeah," she says. "Although at high doses it can slow or even stop the person breathing. In executions, they usually administer a muscle relaxant after the anesthetic, not that it's necessary because the person is already unconscious. Then they give the third drug, potassium chloride, which stops the heart, causing cardiac arrest and death within minutes. Combined with the general anesthetic, it's a silent killer — no convulsions, no foaming at the mouth."

My legs slow on the pedals. My hands, suddenly sweaty, slip on the handlebars.

"And" — she blows out a slow breath before continuing — "the chemical formula for Potassium Chloride is KCl."

KCl. *Kick Crappy lovers.*

"The combination of the two drugs would drop a person instantly and kill them in minutes," she says.

"What are you saying?" I turn around to see her face.

"Face the front!" she orders. "I'm saying that those cartridges are a lethal injection in bullet form. They're poison."

I'm gasping now, as if I've just sprinted a mile.

"We've been shooting them with poison?"

No! Just no. It's not possible. We haven't. I haven't. I *couldn't.*

"You've been executing them, yes," says Sofia.

"I don't believe it! They said we were just shooting them with a dissolving cartridge containing anesthetic, just to get them unconscious, so they could be brought in for treatment."

"They lied. I'm guessing the only *treatment* they'd get is incineration." She pauses, then says, "It's appalling. They've been killing people. This place, man, these people!"

I've been killing people. My stomach is cold, my head is dizzy.

"What are you going to do now, Jinx?"

I *want* to throw up. I want to run away and hide in a dark cupboard somewhere. I want to go break Sarge's eardrums and kneecaps, to steal a rifle from the armory and put an "anesthetizing" round into Roberta Roth.

But what *am* I going to do now?

Chapter 16

Dead meat

I'm a killer.

I have killed people.

I have killed people in cold blood. People who were weak and sick and who weren't attacking me. Who weren't attacking anyone.

I've killed at least half a dozen people in the same way as my father was killed. Shot them in the same way I've shot infected rats and dogs. I try to remember the individuals. The woman with the red shoe in the alley — she was my first. The man in the road, with the dreadlocks and bleeding arms — he was my second; the little boy — ah, God, just a kid! — cowering in the shallows of a deserted pond, his shorts stained with the liquefied remains of his insides. There were more, I must remember them. I must never forget.

Am I a murderer?

I hide in my room, gnawing at my damaged nail, my mind swirling with questions.

Quinn called me a killer. Did he suspect all along that this was what our unit was doing? Is that part of why he was so angry when he discovered I was in the sniping unit? On that last night, when he showed me the interrogation footage, he'd said there was more

I had to know. Was this what he wanted to tell me? I hadn't wanted to hear, and he said he needed to get evidence or else I wouldn't believe. Then the next day all hell broke loose, and he never got a chance to tell me.

Why don't they just use ordinary special forces snipers? Why have they recruited a bunch of kids to do their dirty work for them?

But I already know the answer.

They used us kids because we could be inserted into parks and streets and neighborhoods without anyone suspecting what we were. Kid snipers? Nobody would believe it. A memory from one of my online history tutorials flashes into my mind, a quote by Hitler, "If you tell a big enough lie and tell it frequently enough, it will be believed." Killer kids — that was a lie big enough and absurd enough that no one would believe it. And our unit was lied to as well, told over and over that we were helping, that the cartridges contained mere anesthetic, that the M&Ms would be taken in to hospitals for treatment which would give them a dignified death. Dignified!

Roth and Sarge had shown me a biohazard hospital ward where a family was being given a chance to say goodbye to their loved one, had stated that this was what lay in store for all the M&Ms we brought down. Lies! Lies and deceit and euphemisms from day one. Had they even bothered to identify the victims we'd killed, to trace their families and notify them of their relative's passing?

We could have used the same short-range dart-guns and tranquilizer darts on M&Ms that we used on suspects, only filled with the lethal cocktail, but I reckon they were telling the truth, for once, when they said they didn't want us getting within attack range of an infected person. They obviously didn't want to risk their valuable, highly trained and incredibly useful "assets".

But why did they use the filled cartridges instead of regular live rounds if they intended to kill the M&Ms anyway? I think I know the answer to that question, too. In order to ensure an instantaneous kill, the shooter would need to use a normal to high-caliber round. But any cadet sniper armed with a scoped rifle would see how it ripped flesh open and left a gaping, bleeding wound. No way would they believe they were just darting with a minimally penetrating dissolving round.

Also, members of the public might see things they shouldn't. There would be blood at the entry site, and possible spatter of infectious blood and body tissue. A round might go through and through, lodging in a nearby wall or hitting someone else, or coming to land where someone could retrieve it and use it as evidence.

If the sniper's aim was just slightly off, the first shot might not be a kill-shot, and the vic would move, groan, call for help. That wouldn't fit with the story of instant anesthesia. Bottom-line, it would be clear to the sniper and any witnesses that the M&Ms were being put to death.

With the specially designed cartridges, on the other hand, there would be no twitching or moaning, no ballistic or biological evidence left on the scene, no sign that a sick civilian had just been executed by a black ops asset. The poison bullets would leave minimal blood, penetrate only shallowly, and immediately bring down the targets. The victims, dammit! I will no longer think of innocent people as targets, tangos, mooks. They are people, human beings.

Another horrible thought occurs. How can I be sure that we *haven't* been killing the terrorist suspects, too? The footage of the interrogation proves that at least one survived the takedown long enough to be tortured, but there's no proof that they all did. Those "tranq-darts" could just as easily be filled with the same lethal cocktail as the special bullets.

I feel like a scared little girl. How have I gone from computer-gaming kid to executioner in three months?

Quinn was right. I wish with every fiber of my being that he was here. I could fall into his arms and tell him everything. Maybe he would forgive me, tell me he still loved me, and reassure me that things will work out. Right now, I'd even settle for a hug from my mother. My mother! I'm supposed to be going home for a visit tomorrow. How will I get through the rest of today and tonight without revealing what I know?

What am I going to do? The question keeps firing in my brain, and I can think of no good plan.

Should I tell someone? I care for the guys in my unit — it's unthinkable to let them continue killing, blindly ignorant of what they're actually doing. And yet, I don't know how they might react if I tell them. I remember the first time I met Bruce on the transport into PlayState. When our Hummer was accosted by an M&M in the final stages of the disease, Bruce had said that victims like him should be put down, in the same way as rabid animals were. Would he have changed his mind in the last months? Unlikely. But how would he feel if he found out that he had been turned into a killer without his knowledge or consent?

Bottom line, I'm still not sure that I can trust the guys. If any of them are rats for Roth, I'll be screwed. And if they aren't, then by telling them I'll be *putting* them in jeopardy. What Sofia and I now know is enough to get a person permanently detained, perhaps even taken out. On our sort of missions, a friendly-fire "accident" could happen all too easily.

It would be unforgivably dangerous to tell Mom or Robin, too. Oh God, what *am* I going to do?

I still don't know by that afternoon's combat skills session. I'm so distracted that I take a real beating. I'm lifted up, thrown down, and flung around like a rag doll. When I get the crap knocked out of me for the umpteenth time, Charlie says, "What is the matter with you, kiddo? Where's your head at? Come into an armed fight so unfocused in the real world out there, you'll be dead meat."

Dead. The word ricochets around my brain. I remember another victim, a large woman with rolls of fat under the neck and blood streaming from her eyes, banging her head over and over again on the rusted wreck of an old Chevy pickup.

"Cadet James!"

Charlie has me by the shoulders and is shaking me gently. There is real concern in her eyes as she looks into mine. The rest of the unit has stopped their fighting and are staring at me. I mustn't raise suspicion. If I behave oddly, it will get reported. They might check the surveillance footage, see I've been in the vicinity of Sofia and perhaps start investigating her.

I lift a hand to my head. "I've got a terrible headache, Charlie. I banged my head hard in yesterday's session, and it still hurts."

"You, cadet, are craptastically feeble. We can't lay a hand on you without you bleeding or aching or coming apart at the seams."

"Sorry," I say lamely.

Unexpectedly, she gives me a quick, consoling hug, and for a moment I hover on the brink of tears. Then she lets me go with an order to "Go and sit on the bench there, see what you can learn by observing us."

"Yes, ma'am."

I park my butt on the bench, rest my elbows on my knees and my head in my hands, and stare in their direction. But I'm not watching. I'm thinking.

After my capture and torture, I decided to come back to ASTA and find out more about what they were up to. Well, I can put a check in the block next to that item on my to-do list. I wanted to get back into the system and work from within to bring them down. That's no longer possible. Somehow, sometime, they'll discover what I know. I'll slip up and make some comment that will give me away, I'll pull a face when the boys get sent out on an M&M mission, or recoil and refuse when one day they try to send me again.

Now I want out of here, as soon as possible. I've got to escape and do everything I can to expose the system that turned me into a murderer. I want to fight Sarge and Roth and whoever they're serving, fight them properly, directly, and honestly from within the heart of the rebels.

And if there's a way to reunite with Quinn, to convince him I'm on his side, then I'm going to find it and do that, too.

Chapter 17

Keeping secrets

That night I take a turn past the rec room, where Dasha, one of the intel recruits, hangs out every evening selling prepaid cash cards. Using my credit card, into which my allowance and cadet stipend are paid, I buy as many as I think I can without raising an alert on my account. Dasha's got her bootleg business down to a fine art. Using apps on her phone, she processes my purchase across three different business fronts: *Book Bazaar*, *Unlimited Airtime*, and *Candy-Apple Treats*.

"Pleasure doing business with you," she says, handing over the loaded cards. With these, I'll be able to pay for what I need without leaving an online trace.

Back in my room, I tuck them into a side-zipper of my already stuffed bag. I've packed most of my belongings, but not all — just in case. I don't want to tip off any prying eyes that I'm planning to leave for good.

In the morning, when I'm due to go home, Bruce and Cameron are sent out on an M&M mission. I want to scream the truth, but I tell them nothing about what they're about to do.

I give Cameron a hug and tell him, "Stay safe."

"Good luck," he says. Cameron always knows more than I

think he does.

Bruce wants a hug, too. It's tighter and lasts longer than I'm comfortable with, but hugging him doesn't bug me like it used to. Is that because I've changed, or because he has?

"See you on Monday afternoon," Bruce says.

"See you," I say.

Our house has a porch, but no one is waiting to greet me when the ASTA transport drops me off. My welcome will be on the other side of the domestic decon unit. A dark-brown sedan is parked a little way down and over the road from our house, under an oak tree. It's hard to make out because of the dappled shade, but I think there's a figure sitting in the driver's seat. Sofia warned me that a spook has been assigned to keep tabs on my movements during my weekend away from the compound, so I guess this is him. Also, according to her, my internet activity and phone calls are being monitored, but no direct audio surveillance has been ordered. They consider me low risk, but still want to keep an eye on me.

I push into the decon unit and, sure enough, Mom is on the other side of the tinted glass door, her face shifting from joy at seeing me, to concern when she spots the bruises, to anxiety when it looks like I'll come into the house without going through the full decontamination process.

She holds a dressing gown open to receive me and gestures to the disposal bin whose contents Robin has to regularly toss, along with all our bio-waste, into the household incinerator in our basement. She wants me to toss what I'm wearing before I come into her sanitized domain. Why not? If things go according to plan, I won't be needing them again. I peel off my black jumpsuit and the latex gloves and face mask I donned before leaving ASTA and stuff them into the bin, but I shove my running shoes onto the high mesh shelf directly below the disinfecting UV lights. Then, just to please Mom, I strap on a pair of protective goggles and press the GO-button on the decon bath.

For fifteen seconds, I have to stand still in my underwear while I'm sprayed with a disinfectant mist and bathed in low-intensity UV light. Then the door pops open.

"Goggles on the rack," says Mom, wrapping me in the gown.

I replace them in the decon unit. As the door swings shut, the unit goes hot-box, flooding the cubicle with sterilizing ozone and strong UV light.

"Hey, Jinxy," says Robin, giving me a quick hug.

"Hands," says Mom, pushing Robin aside. I stretch out my hands and she sprays them with sanitizer.

"Open wide."

I open my mouth and stick out my tongue so Mom can spritz my throat with oral disinfectant. This is all unnecessary — I know that now, but she doesn't, and it's easier not to argue. Besides, I have no intention of endangering what remains of my family by telling them the truth about how rat fever is, and isn't, spread. Or by telling them what happened to me. Mom would have a freak-out of tsunamic proportions and would probably try to report what happened to me and what I discovered to the authorities. And no way can I risk that — I have no idea how deep the rot goes, what government agencies might be involved in the plot to keep us all ignorant of the truth.

"There," says Mom, finally satisfied that she has done what she can to rid me of any microscopic cooties. "Now I can give you a proper welcome!"

She hugs me tight, and I wince at the pressure on my bruises and arm sores, one of which I think might be infected. Then she stands back to examine me.

"Lord above, Jinxy! What has happened to you?" She can

see only the scabbed cut and fading bruises on my face, and the stitches in my stubbly strip of scalp, but it's enough to alarm her.

"It's nothing," I say. "We've been training in hand-to-hand combat, and I got a bit banged up, is all. Those boys in my unit are strong."

Robin, who saw my wince over Mom's shoulder and now watches how I tug the sleeves of my gown down over my wrists, tilts his head and gives me an "Oh, yeah?" look.

I ignore him.

"But what about your head!" Mom protests.

I duck as she tries to touch the stitches. I had tried to hide them by combing my hair over, but the strands hooked and tugged at the stitches, and it was just too uncomfortable.

"It's nothing, just a little accident. None of my brains spilled out, promise. Hey, are those brownies I smell?"

"I made them especially for you!" says Mom, happily distracted. "Come into the kitchen and tell me *everything*."

I follow her into the kitchen and spend the next while telling her everything about nothing, snowing her with details about how our daily intake of food and fluids is scanned at the cafeteria "register" and analyzed to check we're getting enough nutrition, what my utilitarian quarters look like, how I can outshoot all the boys on the shooting range, and reassuring her that my unit is making a real difference in the war against the rats.

I don't tell her that we also shoot humans, let alone that we kill them.

She's busy bustling about, and I don't think she notices how I jump when she bangs a pot, or how the *bzzzt* of the blender makes me wince and swallow hard.

After we've caught up and I've guzzled two glasses of ice-cold milk and three brownies, I leave her to preparing lunch — she's making my favorite, chili. Upstairs I change into my jeans and a long-sleeved T. It's a hot August day, and I'd rather be wearing shorts and a tank, but I need to cover as much skin as possible.

Robin comes into my room and flops on my bed.

"Time to dish the dirt, Jinxy."

"What?"

"What really happened?"

"What do you mean?" I say, all innocence.

"I mean, it looks like you've been hit upside the head, you've got bruises around your wrists and judging from your pained expression when Mom hugged you, you've got more injuries under all that." He gestures to my clothes.

I hesitate. Everything that's happened to me, everything that I've discovered, is bottled up tight inside me, and the cork is ready to pop. I'm desperate to share, but I mustn't.

"C'mon," says Robin, "it's *me*."

I know what he means. Robin has always been the one person I trust implicitly. Even when we were kids — fighting over toys or what we watched on T.V., or arguing about who was responsible for leaving the door on the hamster cage open — we never ratted each other out to our parents. And when Dad died, and Mom kind of went dark, it was us against the world.

"You can't tell Mom — not a word!" I warn.

"As if I would."

"Okay, well, you remember that guy I told you about in my emails — Quinn?"

"The guy you fell in love with, then ditched?"

"He ditched me." Still hurts.

"Details," says Robin, waving a dismissive hand. "What about him?"

"I kinda shot his brother. I mean, not really shot," I say quickly. "I darted him. With a tranquilizer."

Robin packs my pillows up against the headboard and then

flops back into them, sending a white feather into the air. He catches it and hands it to me — he knows I like to fiddle with things.

"Perhaps you'd better start at the beginning," he says.

I do. Slowly, at first, tentatively. Then it all comes spilling out, like a stream overflowing its banks. I tell him about what happened with Quinn and Connor.

At first I play with the feather, stroking it lightly over the pink, wrinkled skin of my exposed nailbed. But as I offload, as I get to the really hard parts, my hand sneaks under the neck of my T and picks at the sore near my shoulder. It's become a horrible habit.

I tell Robin how I was detained, and that I was tortured, though I don't give him all the graphic details.

"They did *what*?" He comes off the pillows, looking ready to attack. "What exactly did they do to you?"

"They gave me a lie-detector test, can you believe that? Me — hooked up to a polygraph! They wanted to be sure about what I knew, and whether I knew anything about the rebels' plans."

"Do you?" Robin asks, intently.

"Not much." I shrug.

I tell him about how Connor was probably tortured and how I helped get the message to his rescuers. I explain how I chose to go back to ASTA, to fight them from within. I tell him I've found out a couple of things the rebels might find useful, but I stop myself from telling him exactly what I discovered — that we really are snipers, not ratters. That we've been killing people. It's not safe for him to know.

"Does anyone there know you're sniffing around?"

"There's another girl at ASTA. She's in the intel unit, so she sees stuff and can research things. She helped me get the note about Connor to the O'Rileys. I think I can trust her."

To force myself to stop picking at my arms, I sit on my hands.

"And, Robin?" The time has come to tell him. "There's something I need to tell you about Dad. His death."

"What?" Robin's blue eyes, so like mine, are round with alarm.

"He …" There's no easy way to say this. I take a deep breath and plunge on. "He didn't die from a heart attack. He was taken hostage by terrorists in a bank, and they injected him with the plague."

"*What?* No. No, that can't be right."

"It's true. I saw video footage of the attack, from the bank's security cameras and from what the terrorists released."

The images come back in a series of rapid flashes — the young woman with the strawberry-shaped birthmark holding the big poster, the security glass slamming down between the tellers and the bank floor as the attackers stormed inside, Dad's face as he was injected, as he succumbed to the ravages of the plague.

"Then when he became …" Became what — something less than human? "When he got really sick, they turned him outdoors to become a human viral bomb, and some special ops forces shot him. In the street."

Robin remains pressed back into the pillows, as if felled. His face is as white as the feather resting on the bedspread, his arms are limp, his eyes brim with tears. I sit down next to him and hug him, comforting him as he goes through the same shock and outrage that I experienced when I found out the truth.

"Do you think Mom knows?" he asks eventually.

I shrug. I have no idea. "Maybe she knew and she wanted to protect us from the horror of it." I realize I'm shielding Robin from the full awfulness of it, too. "Or maybe they never told her. They're very careful about what they reveal. They manipulate everything for their benefit."

"Why? Why wouldn't they tell the truth?"

"It's only on the surface that the war is against the plague,

Robin." I tell him everything Quinn told me. "The other war is a battle to extend power and profit for the lucky few."

"That's what all wars are ultimately about." His voice is harsh with bitterness.

"And all the hype and measures to protect against the plague? That's part of the propaganda to keep us scared so we toe the line and give up our freedoms uncomplainingly. The rebels even believe that the only way rat fever is transmitted is via bodily fluids and bites."

Robin narrows his eyes and looks at me long and hard. "What are you going to do?"

It's the same question Sofia asked. This time I have an answer.

"I'm going to join the rebels."

"And just how do you intend to do that?" he demands, his face a mixture of shock and admiration.

I smile for what feels like the first time in years.

"Funny you should ask that."

Chapter 18

No show

Dear Quinn,

I scrunch up the paper, cut another small section out of the sheet, and begin again.

Q,

I found out something terrible about ASTA and have to leave. If they discover what I know, I'm toast. I want to join the rebels and help in the fight, if you'll have me? At 9am on Monday morning, I'll be waiting in the drive-through around the back of the old Taco Bell on the corner of Thirteenth and Peach, Seventh West Zone. If you decide not to come, I'll understand.

J

I hope your brother is okay.

I want to add so much more — explanations and apologies, plus a few sharp comments — but there's no room. I fold the piece of paper into a tiny square, write a big Q on the outside, enclose it in a layer of cling-wrap, and then tuck it inside a medium-sized bag of salt and vinegar chips, resealing the top with paper glue.

Over my shorts and T-shirt, I pull on a white disposable PPE suit, which is a lot like my ASTA jumpsuits, except that it's made of a thinner synthetic material and has a hood. I tie my long hair up into a ponytail, strap on a red backpack with integrated water hydration-pack, and grab my mask and sunglasses. Robin and I plied Mom with wine at lunch, encouraging her to toast my visit home again and again, until she'd finished off the better part of a bottle. Now she's upstairs, sleeping it off.

Robin, waiting for me at the front door, stows one of my prepaid cash cards in a specially designed pocket in his zip-up jacket. No one uses wallets anymore — what's the point when no one accepts cash? On his phone's screen is the electronic business card Mom sent us both, in case we ever need to get to the hospital in an emergency: *Hygeiney-Rides, sterilized and sealed driverless transport for your safe journey!*

"It's 3.15 pm. Time to blow this popsicle stand," he says.

"Are you sure you know what to do?" I ask, handing him the packet of chips, which he tucks inside his jacket.

"Yes!" He sounds impatient.

We've been through the plan a dozen times, trying to anticipate possible outcomes and potential problems, and figure out how we should handle them. Now it's time to go. Robin opens the Hygeiney App on his phone and orders a cab. Ten minutes later, I step into the decon unit — it's an irritating delay, but it's the only way to get out the house.

I stride down the garden path and do a few bends and stretches on the sidewalk, being sure to give the person in the parked car a good look at my face and ponytail before I pull on the mask, put on the glasses, and tug the hood of the PPE suit over my head. Then I set off, running away from our house in a westerly direction, hoping that I look like I'm just out for a training run, with a weighted pack on my back for resistance training. When I turn the corner, I see out of the corner of my eye that the brown car is following behind me at a slow crawl. In a few minutes, the cab will arrive to take Robin to Freedom Park.

I run a long circuit of about ten miles, passing the abandoned Taco Bell on 13th and the long-deserted library on 22nd. What did they do with the books? Are they all still neatly filed on their shelves, waiting for a time after the plague when everyone thinks it's safe enough to come out and go to public places, to handle objects that others have touched? If Quinn is right, then that won't be anytime soon. The companies selling us masks and disinfectants and hot-boxes and immunity-boosting super-vitamins, and the people snooping on our communications, building our armies, stocking our arsenals, and manipulating our votes with fear, would lose big money if we resumed our old lives. They won't be in any hurry to question what we've all been told.

There's profit in war, not in peace.

At the halfway mark, I stop and rest, have a drink of water and stretch some more — buying time for Robin to complete his side of the mission. I check my watch. I've been gone almost an hour. It's time to start heading back.

As planned, Robin is already home by the time I get there. Not as planned, he didn't make contact with Kerry or Mrs. O'Riley.

"They weren't there. There was a woman with a baby —"

"Neon-yellow hair?"

"Yeah, but nobody else. I felt like a creeper sitting on the swings doing nothing. I think I made her nervous, too, because she got up and hurried off after a few minutes."

"Did you wait a while — maybe they were just late?"

"I waited until after 4.30 pm, then I got worried that you'd get home before me, and your tail would see me coming home and order up another spook to keep an eye on me too in the future. So I came home."

I kick at the sofa in frustration and feel the pain reverberate in my knee. "We'll have to try again tomorrow — in the morning. That time I passed the note to Kerry, Mrs. O'Riley made a point of saying how they went on weekend mornings at 10 am. We'll try then. Same plan."

"Let's hope they're there," says Robin.

But when I get back from my Saturday morning spook-tailed run — in a northerly direction this time — I can tell even before Robin opens his mouth that once again they didn't show up.

"Damn! Why aren't they there? Maybe they've been detained. Maybe Quinn's been captured. Maybe … maybe Connor's dead!"

"Hey now, that's crazy talk. They don't want Connor dead, they want to capture him alive so they can squeeze more information out of him."

"What if he cracked under questioning? They went at him for at least two and a half days. You don't know how bad it is. I don't know that anyone could survive that and not crack. What if they've found out everything he knows? Then he'd be disposable."

"Nah, they'd use him as leverage against his brother or the other rebels. Dead, he'd just become a martyr. Alive, he's a hostage that they can use, that they could trade for something or someone else."

What he's saying makes sense, and I calm down a little.

"I'm sure they'll be there tomorrow," I say, but my voice sounds like a question. We're running out of time. My weekend's leave ends tomorrow.

"And if they aren't? Will you go back to ASTA?"

I sigh. "I can't go back, Robin. I can't keep up the pretense. I can't risk them putting me back on active duty and ordering me to shoot someone." I can't risk them finding out I know about the poison bullets.

"So you'll resign?"

I shake my head. "Can't do that either. Not after I asked Sarge to ignore my resignation and begged to be allowed back in. He'll know immediately that something's up, and they'll take me back in for questioning. And I can't go back *there*, ever." I whisper the last words through the tightness in my throat. "I'd have to run away."

"Run away? Where to?"

"I have no idea. Not a freaking clue."

"There's always Aunt Ida in Chattanooga," says Robin with a grin.

In spite of myself, I smile. Aunt Ida is our great-aunt on Mom's side and our sole surviving relative in the States. She is eighty-two years old, bedridden and lives in a care home in Chattanooga because she is, as my father used to say, out with the pixies. She's had Alzheimer's disease for the last decade, and could no more help or shelter a runaway teen than fly to the moon. Uncle Bob, my father's younger brother, would help me if he could, but he was in Stockholm when the plague broke out and the borders were sealed, and he decided to remain there with his new Swedish bride instead of coming home.

"They'll be there tomorrow," I insist, not sure if it's Robin I'm trying to convince, or myself. "They've got to be."

Chapter 19

Dangerous games

On Sunday, I set off at the same time, wearing the same gear as on the previous two runs, and drawing the spook off in a new direction. I keep my fingers crossed the whole way. When I get back home, Mom is waiting to chide me, but I have eyes only for Robin, who gives me the thumbs-up.

"Jinx Emma James" — Mom always uses my full name when she's angry — "I insist that you stop sneaking off outside! It's not safe, and it's not necessary. We have a perfectly good mini-gym in the basement. Robin has been training there all morning, why can't you work out with him?"

Because he wasn't there. Robin had cranked the volume on the music system down there up to maximum — a sure mom-deterrent — and sneaked out when she was in her study.

"I was wearing a mask, Mom, it was safe enough."

"But what if a rat attacks you?"

"I run faster than a rat. You worry too much." I give her a tender kiss on the cheek. I know she loves me — that's why she worries.

"Come on, Jinxy, I want to show you something new on The Game." Robin tugs me to the stairs.

"You kids and that game!"

We run up to Robin's room, shutting the door behind us.

"Mission accomplished!" Robin says proudly, flopping onto his bed. Mounted on the wall over his head, like a monument to the time before the plague, is the skateboard he hasn't been able to use in over three years.

"They were there? You gave them the message?" I perch myself on the end of his bed.

"They were and I did. Well, I got there first and hung out on the swings, facing the parking lot. Then Mrs. O'Riley and the kid —"

"Kerry."

"— Kerry, arrived. With a tall guy just behind them."

"Their spook."

"Yeah, their spook. He leaned up against a big rock a few feet back and just stared at us. The kid was coughing. I reckon she's been sick and that's why they didn't come the last few days. Anyway, she came and sat on the swings, and her mother stared at me suspiciously like I might be some paedo, especially when I opened the bag of chips and offered her kid some."

"But she didn't stop you?"

"Will you stop interrupting? No, the kid —"

"Kerry."

Robin gives me a look.

"Sorry," I say, "go on."

"*Kerry*, took a few chips before her mother could stop her. I ate a few more then asked her if she'd like the rest of the packet, but I tilted it so that she'd be able to see the note inside. Her mother said no, but the kid just snatched the packet. But then the spook straightened up and started walking over."

"No!"

"Yes! I figured he wanted to check the packet, so I got off the swing and stepped in front of him to ask him the time, kinda blocking him when he tried to step around me. If that kid's as smart as you say she is —"

"She is."

"— then she would've used the couple of seconds to get the note out and hide it somewhere. Then the guy shoved me aside, and I headed back up to the parking lot and requested my cab."

"Thank you, Robin, really. You did great!"

I'm so relieved that I relax for fully a minute before the next worry starts gripping me tight — will Quinn come to fetch me tomorrow? Will anyone?

"I kinda enjoyed it," says Robin, grinning widely. "After what they've done, I felt like I was sticking it to them, you know?"

I nod, smiling at my brother — daydreaming computer geek turned secret agent.

"It was great to have a little excitement in my life."

"Have you been bored?"

Stupid question. Life in the James household is routine, predictable, dull. It's part of why I was so desperate to get away in the first place.

"After you left, it got insanely boring," Robin says. "It pains me to say it, but I missed you."

I throw a cushion at his head.

"And Mom was driving me crazy. She kept interrupting and nagging and checking. So I started playing The Game again."

This is surprising. I'd played The Game compulsively in the months and years after Dad died — initially because it helped me escape the pain of the loss of him, but later because I kind of became addicted. You can play any of a variety of roles — as a code-breaker, intelligence analyst, spy or soldier — but I'd only ever wanted to play as a specialist sniper. I hadn't known at the time that my performance was being measured and monitored by ASTA, only that it was fun and challenging to pit my skills against other players, and to try take down the Alien Axis Army in spectacularly detailed virtual reality.

Robin, who had always been less interested in The Game, had accused me of being obsessed and a fanatic, so how come he's so into it now?

"Still as a programmer?" I ask.

"Yeah. I played it 24/7, until I got too good."

"*Too good*?" When had that happened?

"I saw what happened to you when you won, and I didn't want to ping on their system and get recruited to that place."

"ASTA?"

Robin nods. "It was way too much like an army base. It gave me the creeps. And that was before I knew what they did to you. So I intentionally struck out on a few program challenges and lowered my score. But *The Game* is not the only game in town. In fact, there are some games and some challenges which are way more fun."

"What about your schoolwork?"

"I hacked into your laptop and copied your assignments and tests, so I've officially met all requirements and passed eleventh grade," says Robin with an evil grin.

"But that's cheating!"

"Nah, it's honing my skills."

"What skills?"

"Well, I decided if I couldn't go out," he gestures beyond the window, the place where you have to get through mom if you want to set foot, "I'd go *in*. So I learned to hack."

"You're a *hacker*?" What the hell!

"You say that like it's a bad thing," Robin says, sounding wounded.

"It is!"

"You sound like Mom, always worrying that something bad will happen."

"You're not paranoid if they *are* out to get you," I point out. Sofia had once said that, back when I still believed ASTA's motives were noble and their methods pure.

Robin points a finger at me. "*You're* living proof that playing it safe and doing exactly as you're told doesn't necessarily keep you out of harm's way."

He has a point.

"Where did you learn how to do it?"

"Here and there. Mostly I'm self-taught." I swear there's a note of pride in his voice. "But now I'm part of a community of like-minded alternative-entry programmers —"

"You mean hackers," I interrupt.

"— who get together and exchange tips and targets, so we can improve our skills."

Targets. That word again. My brother has been targeting computer systems; I've been targeting humans. I guess I'm not in any position to judge.

"Where do you meet?"

"Online. There's a game called War Galaxy — it's awesome — and you're an anonymous character, and you can talk privately with other gamers, in hacker jargon or even computer code. It's like an underground community, really cool. We've all given our avatars names beginning with H — Harry, Hank, Houdini. I'm Hector. I've learned so much."

"And what do you hack?"

"Everything, anything. I got into the school system — gave you an A⁺ for US Gov."

"Robin!"

"Pity you didn't also get one for chemistry, like I did. Gotta say it — I did remarkably well on my finals."

I throw another cushion at him.

"Cheat." I'm laughing — amazed at his nerve. Kind of

impressed, to be honest.

"But the most interesting site I like to sneak into is The Game."

"*The* Game?"

"There's some interesting stuff in there, it's incredibly complex with all these interconnecting matrices. And a bunch of some dual-track architecture I haven't been able to figure out … yet."

Robin loses me in a barrage of jargon and confusing details. I'm sure my eyes glaze over, but I when I hear him say, "I discussed it with my online group. Those peeps have got some interesting theories about it, too," I sit up straight and pay attention.

I'm not laughing any more.

"What theories?" I demand.

"The less you know, the better. It's safer that way."

"I told *you* everything!" Almost.

"It's very technical and complex. You wouldn't understand, anyway."

"Robin, please be careful. ASTA and The Game are the same crowd, practically on the same premises. ASTA uses The Game to identify the talent, and then recruits, trains and employs them. You can't trust anything they say."

"Huh."

"What 'huh'?"

"You've changed. You used to always believe what you were told, do what Mom said. Now you're much less trusting, much more cynical."

"I learned the hard way. I told you what they're capable of."

"Even more reason they need to be investigated. Maybe even stopped."

"Are you crazy? They'll see you snooping around inside."

"Haven't so far." Robin is looking mulish.

"They will eventually. They've got incredibly bright people working for them — they only select the best."

"Like you?" He grins, but I ignore his attempt to divert me.

"They'll catch you sooner or later, and then you'll be in such trouble. Promise me you'll quit?"

"I promise I'll be careful. I hide the secret stuff in a locked safe inside my P.C." He's smiling again. He thinks I'm overreacting.

"I'm not kidding, Robin! They watch and track everything. They'll pick up any intrusions for sure. Maybe they already have and they're monitoring your every move to see what you're up to. For all you know, Hank or Houdini might be moles."

He twists his face into an exaggerated expression of disbelief. "That's a little far-fetched."

"There was a mole in our unit!" I bang a fist on the bed, desperate to make him understand how dangerous his "games" are. "She was planted there by the bosses to spy on us. She ratted Quinn and me out. You think they don't have spies and moles everywhere? Please, Robin, you don't know — there are some things I haven't told you, but please believe me when I tell you they're up to some seriously bad stuff."

"Like what?"

"The less you know, the better. It's safer that way." I throw his own words back at him.

"Very funny, Jinxy."

"It's *not* funny, that's what I'm trying to tell you. It's not a game. What I know could get me detained indefinitely or maybe even … worse. Please promise me you'll stop this crazy-dangerous behavior."

"Don't blow a motherboard. I'll be careful, I promise. Very, very careful. Nothing will go wrong, you'll see."

Chapter 20

Bait and switch

Monday morning is cloudy and cool, with a forecast of rain. Robin checks the weather and announces, "It's a good day for some bait and switch, mother-truckers!"

I laugh, still amazed at how my brother has changed. If I had stayed at home, would he still have changed? Or did the absence of me give him room to unfold? It's something to think about.

Wearing latex gloves, Robin helps me cut off my ID bracelet and stows it in his pocket. When he's back from his run, he'll put it in my bedroom.

I stick my head into my mother's study, where she's working on the design of a new website for an online dating service. It's a service after Mom's own heart, because not only do you find potential dates on the site rather than in the real world, but the actual dates themselves are safely and hygienically online. You meet your date at a virtual restaurant and chat on voice-over IP, or simultaneously watch a new movie release while sitting "together" in a virtual cinema. She's told me that the service plans on introducing program-connected sensor gloves, so online lovers will able to hold hands virtually too. What's next — an implant in your head that fools you into thinking you're tasting buttered popcorn? I miss the old Cineplex with its bubblegum-crusted armrests, massive screen, and excited crowds of teen girls screaming whenever the abtastic hero took off his shirt. The sooner we get our bizarre society back on track, the better.

I'm loathe to disturb Mom — it would be so much easier to slip out unannounced — but I have to say goodbye.

"I'm going for a run, Mom. Bye."

"I wish you wouldn't, Jinxy." Her hands hover over the keyboard. Her eyes are filled with concern.

"I'll be fine, please don't worry about me." I hope she remembers these words afterwards.

"Be quick," she pleads.

I'm tempted to say, "I am just going outside and may be some time," like that Antarctic explorer who left the tent and was never seen again. But I say only, "Goodbye. Love you," and close the door again.

Today, I'm wearing jeans, a long-sleeved T-shirt and a zip-up canvas jacket with multiple pockets, and I'm carrying Dad's old hiking backpack stuffed with my essentials. Today Robin is the one dressed in shorts and a T under a white disposable PPE suit, and he's carrying my small red backpack.

"When I'm not here for this afternoon's transport back to ASTA, they'll send a team to come ask questions," I warn, pulling the PPE hood up over his head and securing it in place with a bobby pin.

"You went for a run this morning, and afterwards you disappeared. No, I have no idea where you might be — that's true — and I'm mad at you because you've caused our mother great concern."

I wince, because that will also be true. But unavoidable.

"And all I know is what you said in the note you left in my room — which is to say: nothing."

In the note, I'd said I was running away because I was unhappy at ASTA and wanted to be with my boyfriend. That I hadn't told either Robin or my mother any details because it was better if they didn't know, and I didn't want them to try come fetch me.

I hope that it will be enough to protect them from more than a basic questioning from ASTA. I think it will. Sarge and Roth will know that I would never share any dangerous details with my mom and Robin, because that would put them in danger of being interrogated. So it would be a futile exercise to grill them.

I hug Robin tightly, make him promise to take care of himself and Mom, and to be ultra-careful online. He makes me swear to try to keep myself safe too.

"Good luck," we both say at the same time.

Robin exits via the decon unit. In the PPE suit and sunglasses, and disguised by the facemask and hood, he looks indistinguishable from me. Almost. His feet are a size larger than mine, and his running shoes are a dark blue while mine are black, but the spook apparently doesn't notice because when Robin sets off running in an easterly direction, the brown sedan trails behind.

I put on a respirator and pull a PPE suit over my clothes, because it will be less likely to attract attention than going out exposed. I force myself to wait ten minutes, then head out, westbound, checking over my shoulder that I'm not being followed. The PPE suit fabric doesn't breathe, so I start sweating almost immediately, even though the soft drizzle of rain is cool on my face. The combination of hot and cold and nerves makes me feel sick, and a little faint, but I run fast — spurred on by my anxiety — and I'm at the old drive-through ten minutes before time.

I shelter under the roof overhang, slouching up against the wall beside the cracked order window, and I wait, telling myself he'll be here, he's coming, he won't leave me here.

Minutes drag by like hours.

I can't stand still. I push off from the wall and pace up and down the weed-choked drive, sidestepping rusted soda cans and kicking an abandoned kiddies' meal toy robot into some nearby weeds. A plastic sign hangs lopsidedly off what was once an illuminated menu pole. I read through the menu slowly, to burn through a few more minutes. *Burritos, quesadillas, tostadas, empanadas.*

I check my watch again. Are the hands even moving?

I'm out of sight of the main road — we still call it that, even though these days it carries almost no traffic — but I still feel exposed, like someone's watching me, waiting to pounce. What if there was another spook tailing me, and I just didn't see him?

09h06. He's not going to come, I know it. No one is — it's too dangerous and, besides, they won't want me. He won't want me.

I should just go.

I'll wait until 09h15 before giving up.

09h13. I hear the noisy exhaust of a nearing car and run to the corner of the drive-through, braced to sprint if it slows and opens a door, but it merely turns the corner, rattles over a pothole, and keeps going. Shoulders slumped, I slide down against the wall and sit, eyes fixed on my watch, on the hands which creep around, lurch by tiny lurch.

09h15 comes and goes. I'll wait until 09h20, 09h25, 09h30.

It's over half an hour after the time I said in the note, and still I sit, head in my hands, staring at the ground where a tiny black ant staggers under the weight of tear-splash. Time passes, but I can't make myself move. What will I do now?

I yelp as I'm nearly run over by the white panel van that swings into the drive-through. A door slides open. A hand reaches out, seizes my wrist and yanks me inside, shoving me onto the floor. It belongs to a girl wearing a black T-shirt and jeans.

"Go-go-go!" she urges the driver and then turns back to face me.

She braces herself against the metal grid behind the driver, crosses her arms, and studies me from top to toe.

"So," she says, and her brown eyes are anything but welcoming, "you're her. The girl who kills."

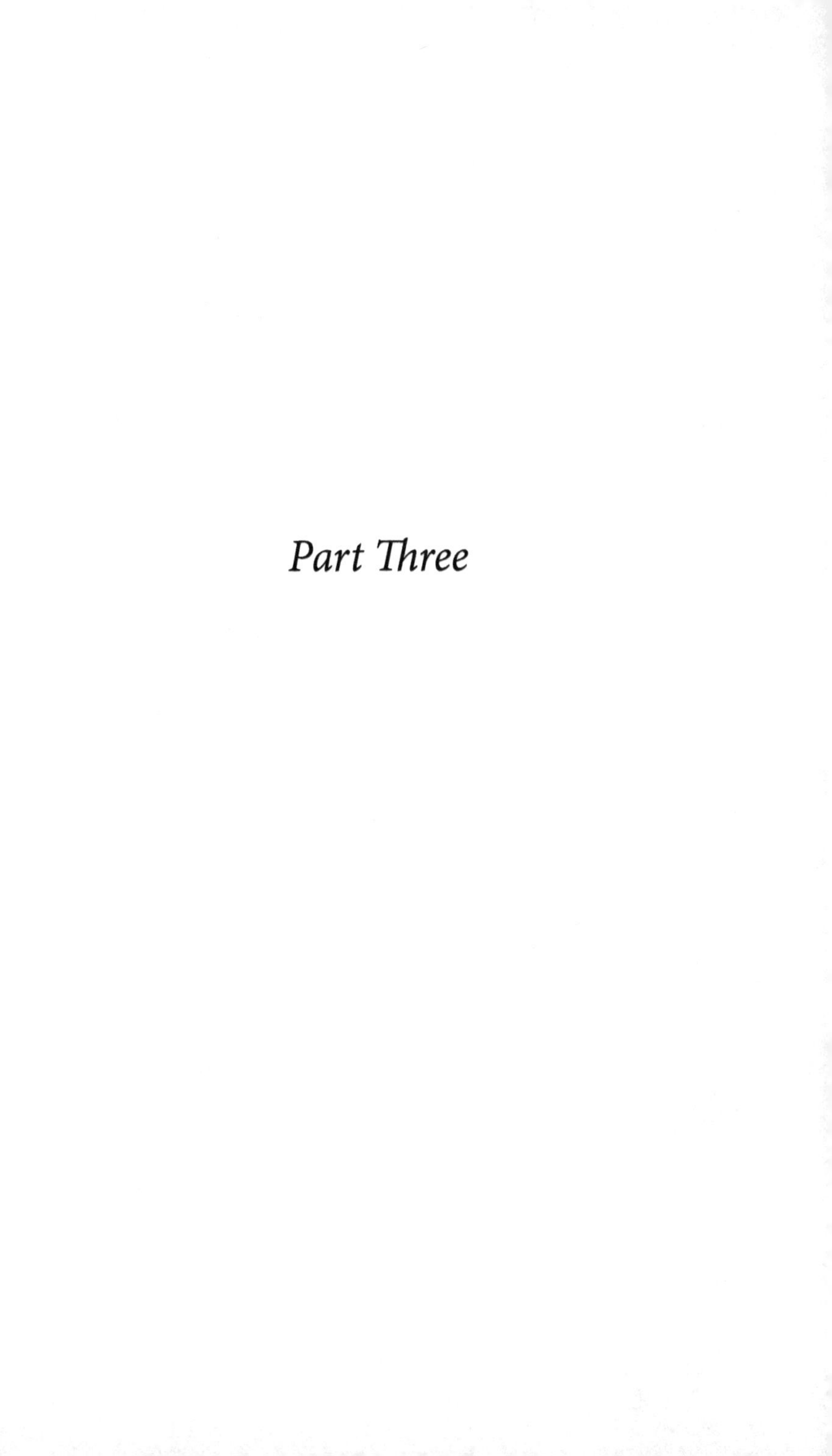

Part Three

Chapter 21

Patdown

"I'm Evyan," says the girl in the back of the van.

"Like the water?"

"It's with a Y — E.V.Y.A.N.!" she snaps.

"I'm Jinx."

"I know who you are. We all do."

"Right."

We say nothing more during the long drive to wherever it is the rebels are hiding out, wherever it is Quinn may be. My hands sneak inside my jacket and pick at my scabs while I covertly study Evyan. She's taller than me, older, skinnier, with jet-black hair shaved close on one side of her head and worn long on the other. The entire outer edge of the one ear I can see is pierced with at least a dozen studs and rings, and there's another through one nostril. She's dressed in Gothic black from head to Doc-Martined toe. She looks tough and mean, though maybe that's just the effect of the sneer that twists her lips every time she looks in my direction.

So much for the welcome wagon.

We travel in silence for hours. The old van rattles and bounces over the last thirty minutes of our journey and then judders to a stop. For a few moments, absolute silence presses against my ears, then with a grating noise, the rusty door slides open, flooding the gloomy interior with light. Silhouetted in the doorway, stooping to climb into the van, is a tall, lean figure. Even before I can make out the thick mahogany hair, the slate-gray eyes or the olive-toned skin, I know it's him by the black-and-white checkerboard-patterned sneakers.

"Quinn!" I breathe out in a whoosh of relief.

Until this moment, I wasn't sure he was safe. But he's alive and well. And apparently unperforated by any bullets.

"And?" Quinn says. He is speaking to the Goth-girl; he hasn't even looked in my direction yet.

"We were there half an hour before she arrived."

They were? Where were they hiding? Some sniper I am, that I didn't spot them. Didn't even think to look because I was so busy checking I wasn't followed.

"And we waited half an hour after. Didn't spot any tail or watchers. Pretty sure we weren't tailed coming back here."

"Pretty sure?"

"I'm sure."

Quinn nods approvingly, and Goth-girl grins.

I feel small and stupid sitting on the floor of the van while they speak over my head, like a child at an adult's meeting, so I clamber to my feet.

"You thought I wouldn't lose my tail before getting to the meeting place?" I ask, offended.

For the first time, Quinn turns to look at me. He's not as handsome as I remember. He's more so. His face looks harder, leaner, sharper, even though it's been less than two weeks since I last saw him. And he still wears the silver ring through his left brow, looking more like a pirate than ever.

His eyes are stony as he studies my face — the faint trace of bruise which lingers, the red scar on my cheek where I've scratched off the scab — and then looks away.

It's Goth-girl who replies. "No. We thought you might *bring* a tail."

"Why would I br— ... Oh, you thought I was leading you into a trap?" I ask Quinn. "You thought that — after I helped you escape?"

"You might have changed your mind. Or they might have gotten to you. Or ... your helping me escape might all have been a setup so that I could be followed, and lead the spooks to the rebels." His voice is still deep and traced with that faint, musical Irish lilt, but it's as cold as a blast of winter wind.

"I don't think you *did* help Quinn escape," says Goth-girl. "Sounds to me like you were all, 'Help, help!' calling for reinforcements to come catch him."

I ignore her and speak directly to Quinn. "Wow." My voice is flat. "You don't trust me at all, do you?"

"After what you've done? With the information you possess?" Quinn snaps. "How did you even know where Connor was being held, if they didn't tell you?"

"Because I was held there, too! That's where they took me for ... for questioning, after you got away." I swallow hard, pushing away the memories that threaten to surface. "I saw Connor's file there."

Goth-girl gives me a deeply skeptical look.

"Quinn, I thought you understood I was on your side, I thought you would want to know what I've found out, that I could help you in the fight, that you —"

"You thought we would just welcome you with open arms?"

I glance from one to the other of them. Goth-girl has her arms folded across her chest again, and she's taken a step closer to Quinn. He has his hands shoved deep into the pockets of his jeans — no chance of open arms there — and there's no warmth in his flat gaze. I want to lift my chin, leap out of this van, and stride off out of here — wherever the heck *here* is — but I swallow my pride.

"Quinn," I say softly. "I've got nowhere else to go. Nowhere."

The silence resonates for long seconds. Then Quinn makes a sound somewhere between a sigh and a growl of irritation.

"Evyan," he says, "can you give us a few minutes in private?"

She cuts me a long, hard stare, then says to Quinn, "Don't forget to check her."

She swings out of the van and stalks off with the driver, who has been standing at the door, curious to get a look at the new arrival.

"*Are* you working for them?" Quinn asks quietly.

"No."

He shouldn't have to ask.

He reaches out an arm to me, and I sag in relief, because I know that he's going to hug me. He was just acting cold and suspicious for the benefit of Evyan, but now that we're alone he'll pull me into an embrace. My own arms begin to move upwards, but Quinn merely pushes my shoulder to turn me around, and pulls my backpack off. He squats down on the corrugated floor of the van and upends the bag, shaking out the contents of every section and zippered pouch, opening my toiletry bag and dumping shampoo and mascara and tampons on top of the pile of clothes and underwear. I can feel my face burning hot with embarrassment and anger.

"Looking for anything in particular?" I snap.

"A gun."

"I don't own one."

"Your phone."

"I didn't bring it — do you think I'm stupid?"

Quinn shrugs. "Any type of weapon, tranquilizer shots, a camera or recording devices." He turns the bag inside out and checks the seams, feels along the lining. "Bugs."

No, he doesn't think I'm stupid. He thinks I'm not to be trusted, that I might still be working for them.

I blink fiercely at the tears which burn hot against my eyes. I don't know what sort of a welcome I expected, but I sure didn't expect this — to be treated like a suspected mole. Is this how they greet every new arrival? Or just me?

"You know what this reminds me of? The inspection of our stuff when we arrived at ASTA. I see you learned from the best," I say, deliberately needling him, using anger to crowd out the other feelings.

No answer.

"Oh, look — you missed this." I snag a mini multi-tool which I pinched from Robin, and wave it in the air. "A contraband weapon which I might use to slaughter the forces of rebellion."

"I have to check," he says.

"Fine. Whatever."

When he's satisfied himself that my belongings are free from any enemy device, he sits back, and I gather them up and stuff them back into the backpack. Boots on top of bras on top of lip balm.

"I have to be sure," Quinn says, standing.

Those are the words Roth used. Suddenly I'm cringing, back in that room with the mirror and the steel chair and the wrist restraints.

And the pain.

An involuntary shudder passes through me. I try to wipe the flashbacks from my mind, try to breathe past the spasm in my solar plexus. Breathe in, and slowly out. And again.

Quinn must notice my reaction, because he asks, "Jinxy? Are you okay?" It's the first time he's said my name.

I stand and shove the bag at him. "You want to go through it all again because you have to be sure? Knock yourself out."

"No, I mean" — he hesitates — "I need to check you, too."

"Huh. Just like the guards at the detention center." I unzip my jacket and hand it to him so he can inspect it thoroughly. "You guys have a surprising amount in common."

"We're nothing like them!"

"Do I need to take my pants and top off, too?" I ask past gritted teeth.

"Just your shoes."

I kick off my running shoes, peel off my socks and then stand, legs apart, holding my arms away from my sides. He runs a handheld metal detector over my body, almost — but not quite — touching my skin. It buzzes when it passes over the chest area just below my left collar-bone. Quinn pauses, jerks his chin at it. I know what's caused the buzz, and right now I would rather run naked through a field of mutant rats than show him, but he's waiting, head tilted, eyes narrowed.

Mortified, I yank the neck of my top down and to the side to show him the silver earring — the one he gave me — looped over my bra strap. An expression I can't read ripples across his face when he sees and recognizes it. I turn my head away to stare resolutely over his shoulder while he finishes scanning.

When he tosses the scanner onto one of the front seats, I turn around to lean up against the side of the van opposite the open door. I know that he must know that not all bugs and weapons are made of metal. My forehead and hands are pressed against the cold metal. My arms are stretched away from my sides, and my legs are spread apart.

I can feel the heat of Quinn close behind me, and then his hands are on me, patting me down to check for hidden objects made of plastic or ceramic or silicone. He crouches down, starts at my right ankle and moves up, briskly patting against my tight jeans, one hand on the outside of my leg, and the other on my inside. Up my calf and over my knee and up to the top of my thigh. My breath catches in my throat, but his hands don't hesitate in their efficient pat-down and he moves to my other leg.

For me at least, there is something charged in the air now, something which divides time into fractions of seconds, and sucks my breath and my anger out of me. His hands, big and warm, feel along my hips and around my waist, and slide up my ribs. I draw in a ragged breath. I may be pissed off at his less-than-friendly welcome, but my body responds to his touch as it always has. When his hands move over my spine, up the back of my shoulders and neck, and dig into my hair, I shiver and only just stop myself from leaning back into his hands.

His fingers stop moving when they touch the line of stitches, the strip of emerging stubble that I'd hidden with a comb-over of long hair.

"What the hell?"

"It's nothing."

I tilt my head so that my hair falls back over the stitches, not wanting him to ask questions, not wanting to remember. After that last flashback, I'm only just managing to keep the memories at bay. Besides, I'm not there anymore. I'm here now, with Quinn. That's all that matters.

"Quinn," I breathe.

He spins me around, and I look up into his blazing silver eyes. There's a heat in his gaze which pulls me closer to him. He may be angry and suspicious, but I can tell he still desires me.

He swallows hard. "What happened —" he begins.

But I don't feel like talking. I'm not going there now — the past will only come between us. My hands slide up his arms to his shoulders, around the back of his neck, into his hair. If we can touch, if we can hold each other, he'll remember me — the *me* he knows and trusts and cares for.

"Jinxy."

He leans closer, his eyes still locked on mine. His hands slide around my waist to pull me in against his body. His lips lower — are just touching mine, when there's a shout from outside.

"Quinn? Quinn!" Someone is coming to the van.

He pulls away, gives his head a quick shake as if to knock the desire for me out of it, and takes a step back. His gaze is wary again. I feel cold, empty, confused.

"Quinn? Is she clean?" It's the damned Goth-girl again, checking up on us.

"Yeah. Yeah, she's good," Quinn answers, his voice a little rough. Then to me he says, "Follow me, I'll introduce you to the rest of us rebels."

Quinn grabs my backpack and steps out into the light.

Chapter 22

Violent energies

The band of rebel outlaws have set up camp in the clearing of a long-abandoned campground which lies in the depths of a thickly forested state park, a few hours beyond the outer boundary of the city metropole.

Water drips off leaves and splashes onto my head as we hike through the trees and underbrush, following an overgrown and barely visible trail through the woods. Quinn leads the way with Evyan directly behind him, like some combination of guard dog and faithful pet. I bring up the rear, hot with shame at having basically thrown myself at Quinn. I need to be ruled by my head, not my hormones.

We pass by a small log cabin which must once have served as the campground's office. The door is ajar, and I peer inside as we pass by. It's a single room, with a small toilet cubicle just off it. It's been stripped bare of all furniture, equipment and fittings except for a couple of framed posters nailed to the wall. One, of a burnt tree stump waving its scorched arms against a red sky, urges me to keep fire away from our national parks. The other advises me to steer clear of snakes and falling trees.

Great. I feel safer already.

A massive cobweb stretches from the old reception counter clear across to a far corner of the sagging, water-stained ceiling. Dirt, twigs and dry grass, swept in by the wind, litter the floor and collect in piles in the corners. They look like the nests of small animals. Perhaps they are. As we walk on, I keep an eye out for movements in the undergrowth which might signal rats.

Beyond the derelict office is another, bigger log cabin. The male and female signs above its twin entrances tell me that this must be what remains of the old communal restrooms and showers. My memory takes me back to the time before the plague, bringing up memories of facilities just like these, in state parks very similar to this one — images of hiking up mountain trails with my family, striking tents with Dad, waiting impatiently for Mom to thread fat, pastel marshmallows on a long stick so that I could roast them over the embers of a dying fire, listening to the nearby murmur of our parents' voices as they talked and laughed softly in their tent while Robin and I munched our way through secret midnight feasts in ours.

"Toilets and showers over there." Quinn indicates the long cabin.

"Do they still work?" I ask, surprised.

"Yeah, the water is piped directly from the stream up the hill, so it's fresh and clean. But cold, of course, and there are no lights. Nothing like the fine comforts of your own *en suite* at ASTA — think you'll cope?"

I ignore the jibe and stumble over a protruding tree root as I catch sight of what lies ahead.

In the center of a clearing that was probably once a picnic spot, there's a cooking fire surrounded by a circle of logs, and then an outer semicircle of small tents. Standing and waiting for us is a group of a dozen people — male and female, black and white, and about half of whom are wearing red berets. Once again, I'm the youngest by at least a couple of years. One of the red berets, a square-jawed woman whom I estimate to be in her late twenties, steps forward and extends a hand.

"You're Jinx?"

I nod, trying not to flinch under the pressure of her hard handshake and shrewd black gaze.

"I'm Zonia. Not my real name, of course, but it's what you'll call me." Her face is completely serious.

"Right."

"Everyone, this is Jinx."

I give a wave and a small smile, but it fades quickly. No one is looking even the slightest bit enthusiastic about my presence here.

"Make sure you introduce yourselves this afternoon," Zonia instructs them. "Right, let's eat. We'll talk after lunch."

Everyone moves at once, as if in a practiced routine. Two girls, in their late teens or early twenties, position themselves behind a metal trestle table stacked with plastic plates, cups and flatware. Two burly guys in berets — by the look of them brothers and in their mid-thirties — grab large cooking pots off grids balanced over the coals, carry them over and swing them up onto the metal table.

A girl grabs me by the elbow and says, "Hi, I'm Nicky. I'll show you how it works."

She has red hair and is maybe four or five years older than me. At the table, she hands me a plate and spoon, and holds her own out to the girls.

"What's on the menu?" Nicky asks.

"Beef Bourguignon and creamed potatoes," says one of the girls behind the table. "I'm Kirsty," she tells me, "and this is Kate."

They are both wearing red berets, but Kirsty is wearing camo pants and a khaki T, and Kate is wearing khaki pants and a camo vest. Perhaps they divided the matching sets. I quickly stick out my plate for dollops of the food. It doesn't look very appetizing, but I'm aware of the line forming behind Quinn and Evyan, who wait beside me. Just as I'm about to be served, Zonia steps up from the opposite side, and the serving spoons swing across and tip the food onto her plate. No lining up for her, then.

"Sorry," says Kirsty — or is it Kate? — when Zonia moves off, "but we always serve her first. She's our leader."

"She's not our leader. Connor is," says Quinn.

"Yeah. But, like, he's not here, is he?" she says, depositing gloops of meat and white stuff on my plate. "And she was his 2 I.C."

Evyan snorts. "She may not be in command for long."

"And what's that supposed to mean?" asks one of the K-girls.

"Just that there might be better leaders among us." From the way Evyan's eyes flick to Quinn, I can tell who would get her vote.

"Is Connor okay?" I ask Quinn softly, while the girls argue about what makes a true leader.

"They say he's … He just needs some time to get better, but he'll be back soon, I'm sure."

"Good. I heard that one of you got shot on the mission."

"No. It was them — one of them got shot." He doesn't sound pleased about it.

"Yes, a guard, Sofia said."

"Sofia?"

"Yeah, she's been helping me out."

"Good, I like Sofia. I trust her."

I have nothing to say to that.

Quinn has managed to get his food from the girls squabbling with Evyan, and we make our way over to the massive logs positioned around the fire.

"Did he die?" Quinn asks.

"Who?"

"The guard, in the raid."

"Yeah."

"Oh." Quinn sits down on a log. "So someone died all because we had to rescue Connor."

"You blame me for that too, now?" I ask.

"He wouldn't have been there if it wasn't for you."

"Yeah, you're right." I can feel a hot flush of anger rising up my neck. "He would probably have been in the mortuary."

Evyan pushes past me and parks her butt down next to Quinn. I leave him to her, and go find somewhere else to sit.

On the way I pass another huge log on which two pretty girls of around twenty are sitting. They look nothing like how I imagine rebels should. One is wearing a yellow sundress, despite the cool weather, and the other has on a pair of hungry shorts and strappy sandals. They're both wearing makeup and nail polish, and they're wrapped around each other, making out like crazy.

"For God's sake," says Zonia, giving their log a hard kick on her way back to the food table for seconds. "Can't you two stop sucking face long enough to eat something other than each other?"

The girls giggle and go get their lunch. I perch on a log beside Nicky, since she seems the friendliest, and study the people sitting around me.

If I'm the youngest person here, then the oldest is a thin-faced, black guy with glasses and a straggly, graying goatee. He wears a yellow T-shirt with a decal of a grinning rat on the shoulder. Written across the front, in bold black letters, are the words: *Blessed are the rats*. When he turns, I see the back reads: *For they shall inherit the earth*. He perches cross-legged on the sandy ground near me and says, "I'm Neil. Aries."

"Um, hi, Neil."

"I like to be on the level with people, fully honest and upfront. So I need to share with you that I'm concerned about the energy you're bringing to our camp."

"The energy?"

"Yeah, the violent energy. You've killed rats." He shakes his head slowly, like it's the worst crime he could ever imagine.

"Yeah, I have. But they were, you know, infected. And dangerous."

"They were children of the Earth Mother," he says solemnly.

"Yeah. Uh, sorry."

He nods, then turns around to face the fire.

I can feel Nicky's shoulders trembling beside me, and a quick glance confirms she's fighting laughter.

"He thinks we're here to save the rats," she whispers.

I wonder why the rest think they're here. While I eat my food, which turns out to be a canned stew of some kind of tasteless, grayish meat and instant mashed potatoes, I study the band of rebels.

On the log opposite ours, Evyan sits close beside Quinn. She hangs on his every word, agrees with his every opinion and, when he's not looking, tugs down the neckline of her T-shirt to show more of her cleavage. On the other side of her, and angled toward her, sits the driver of the van, who introduces himself as Mark. He watches with a wounded expression in his soulful brown eyes as Evyan laughs at something Quinn says, squeezes his shoulder and picks a leaf out of his hair. I look away, not entirely sure that my expression is any better than Mark's.

While most of the crowd shoot me the odd wary — or at least curious — glance, the loving couple, whom Nicky tell me are called Bree and Candace, sit on the next log along and are completely wrapped up in each other.

Zonia sits in the middle of the longest log, with Kirsty and Kate perched on one side of her, and the two brothers, Ross and Darius, on the other. Ross seems mostly interested in his food, which he shovels in like a starved person, but Darius clearly has all the feels for Zonia.

Everyone has their eyes on someone here, and Zonia is no exception. Her stern gaze is fixed unwaveringly on me. She clears her throat, and silence falls among the rebels.

Here we go.

145

Chapter 23

Suspicions

"So, you're a sniper?" Zonia asks, in a brisk, businesslike way.

I nod, not sure if this is a clarification or an accusation. "I was."

"If you can shoot as well as Quinn says you can, you may yet come in useful."

Evyan gives me the stink-eye, and Neil frowns sadly into his vegetables at this reminder of my violent energies. I notice that his lips move silently. Is he sending up a prayer for the rodents?

I give Zonia a nod. I *could* be useful here. For one thing, I've noticed that no one is standing guard to keep watch for possible plague-infected creatures. Surely there must be some in these woods?

"Quinn says you told him you discovered some stuff?" Zonia asks.

"Yeah. I found out that the suspected terrs and —" I'm not sure what to call them anymore, especially in present company, "— and the alleged dissidents that we darted were brought in for interrogation. Of the worst kind."

"We already knew that," says Darius, adjusting the fit of his beret. Does the headgear mean something?

"So, basically," I continue, "the sniper squad is a black ops unit.

It's used to bring people in, even where there's no real evidence, and then they can be detained without arrest or legal representation."

"Anything else?" Darius asks, rolling his fingers in the air in an impatient demand for something more. His eyes are just the slightest bit squint, which makes his unfriendly gaze intense enough to make me uncomfortable.

"I got the address of the place — the detention center — so you could rescue Connor."

"And just how *did* you get that?" asks Zonia.

All the faces looking at me are deeply suspicious. Even Candace and Bree have stopped their canoodling and are watching me now.

"Well, they didn't just tell me, if that's what you're thinking. I know because I was taken there, too, to be questioned."

I won't allow those memories to come back now. I flick a glance at Quinn, but he's staring at his plate. Evyan scrapes some stew from her plate onto his and gives him an encouraging little elbow nudge, as if urging him to eat.

"They let you see where they were taking you?" asks Darius, his voice full of disbelief.

"No, of course not. They blindfolded me. And anyway, I was out cold for most of the drive."

"Why?" Quinn asks.

"Because a guard hit me upside the head when you escaped, that's why." I touch the row of stitches reflexively.

"Why didn't you run, too?"

Faces turn from me to Quinn and back again, like a circle of Robodogs stuck on the head-shake program.

"There wasn't time." I feel like I've told this part of the story so many times, but I look directly at Quinn, pleading with him to understand, to believe me. "The power was back on, and the electric fence was live — you saw that. And then the guard began moving the spotlight beam to where you were and he would've seen you, may have shot you. So I started shouting — to distract him."

"And I'm supposed to believe you drew attention to yourself to give me a chance to escape? And then you got knocked unconscious for it?" Beside him, Evyan sneers at me.

"Believe what you want." My face grows hot.

"Can we get this back on track, please, people," says Zonia. "If they didn't tell you, and you didn't see where they took you, then how did you know the address of the detention center?"

"I saw it — printed on a waybill for a blood sample to be sent to a laboratory. It was in the doctor's office where I was taken for a medical examination after they … afterwards."

I can feel Quinn's gaze on me now, but I won't look at him. Why is he so angry with me? My story is true — how can it be so impossible to believe?

"And you just noticed it, and then remembered it days later?" says Evyan.

"We're trained to observe and to memorize, Perrier," I say, earning myself a glare from Evyan. "It's what we do."

"When you're not killing rats," Neil murmurs sullenly.

"That's also where I saw the file on Connor and knew what they had planned for him, and when they planned to start."

"And after you were questioned, you went back and signed up for your old duties? And they just happily took you back?" Zonia asks.

"They didn't trust me, wouldn't let me near a gun, but yes, I got myself back on ratting missions. It was the only way I could think of to try to get the message to Quinn about Connor. I remembered his sister saying how they went to the park every day."

"Lucky coincidence they chose to go ratting in that park, and at just the right time," says Darius.

"It wasn't a coincidence," I retort. "Just who do you think got those reports of rats, sighted around 4 pm on weekdays, planted in the system?"

"Not possible," says Quinn. "No way you could've fed that into the system."

"I couldn't, but Sofia could."

"Who's Sofia?" asks Evyan.

"She's this really beautiful and incredibly intelligent cadet in Quinn's unit," I tell Evyan and smile at the scowls she directs back at me.

"Do you have any other useful information for us?" asks Zonia.

"I have some suspicions, based on something Roth said, that ASTA are involved in something more than training."

"No way! We had no idea," says Evyan sarcastically.

"Not a clue," adds Mark in the same tone.

"And" — this is it, the only thing I know, really — "and I just found out that they're killing M&Ms."

Quinn gives me a sharp glance, Darius raises an eyebrow, and Evyan, for once, says nothing.

I force myself to add, "That *we* were killing M&Ms."

"We did suspect, but we've never had any proof. Do you know that for sure?" Zonia leans forward, as if she wants to catch my words before anyone else hears them.

I nod, then tell them about the special cartridges. I speak to the ground, feeling sick with shame, as I explain about the poisons and the imploding bullets and the people I have shot. The memories of my victims beat at the edges of my mind like the wings of avenging angels. I avoid meeting Quinn's gaze. If there's contempt or disgust in his face now, I don't want to see it.

"I reckon they'd get the sniping unit to execute suspects, too, if they didn't need to question them first." I rub at my left eye, which has started twitching again.

For a moment there is silence, except for the scrape of Neil's spoon on his plate as he eats the last of his food. He seems less concerned about the killing of people than animals.

"So you and your squad have been killing innocent civilians?" Zonia asks eventually. Her voice is grim and disapproving.

I nod miserably. The images of the dead break through and flash into my mind's eye once more — the woman with the red shoe, the little boy in the pond, the dreadlocked man, the woman banging her head on the wreck — around and around they spin, like a macabre carousel of pain.

"We didn't know. None of us knew." Even to my own ears, my voice sounds pleading and weak. "I'm still the only one who does. Plus Sofia because she researched the chemical formula. But none of the other guys know, I'm sure."

I scan the faces of the rebels. Many won't meet my eyes, some look critical and others, frankly disbelieving. Quinn looks skeptical.

"That's why I had to run away. I couldn't do it anymore, once I knew," I finish. "And if they found out what I discovered, I'd be in real danger."

"Oh, pul-leeze," says Evyan, rolling her eyes at me. "What would they do to their star sniper? Revoke your T.V. privileges? Send you to bed without dessert?"

"Look, I know I wasn't starved or tortured for three days like Connor was, but I haven't exactly had an easy time of it either!" I say hotly, longing to slap her scorn-filled face.

"Oo-ooh," she mocks. "Did they put you in the corner and give you a really long lecture on how naughty you were?" Darius and Mark snicker at this.

I leap to my feet. I'm not sure what I'm planning to do — perhaps peel off my shirt and show them the burns and scars and yellowing bruises — I only know I want to defend myself. To *make* them — him — believe me. But Evyan is already on her feet, too.

She pushes back her sleeves and takes a threatening step towards me.

"Bring it," I challenge.

"Hey, now." Is that Quinn?

But before anything more can happen, Zonia takes control. "Sit down, both of you!" When I hesitate, still glaring at Evyan, Zonia barks, "Now!"

I plonk my rear back down on the log, gripping my hands together in my lap. My heart is hammering, and my face feels like it's on fire. I breathe deeply, trying to calm myself down. Zonia is saying something to the group, but I'm not paying attention to her. I'm focused on trying to hold back the angry tears burning my eyes. I blow out a frustrated breath. I already know there'd be no point in showing them my wounds. Evyan or Darius would only say there was no proof I'd gotten them during interrogation. And as for Quinn, I want him to believe *me*, to trust me without needing "evidence".

Nicky's voice intrudes on my thoughts.

"Huh?" I say.

"You have blood on your hands." Her voice is soft, her tone gentle, but the words feel brutal.

"I *know*, okay? You don't need to remind me."

"No, I mean literally — look." She points at my hands, which are clenched in my lap. Sure enough, the fingertips and the inside of one wrist are smeared with red. I've been picking at the scabbed cut from the restraints.

I wipe my hands on my jeans, aware of the pair of gray eyes fixed on me from the log opposite, and force myself to focus on Zonia, who is talking forcefully now.

"They're as evil as we thought, and worse. We have to fight them, take them down, by any means possible!" she says to a chorus of agreement from the people on either side of her.

"We first need to make sure the truth gets out, and win the minds and loyalty of the general population," says Quinn. "They're ignorant of what's really happening. We need to educate them."

"Revolution now, education later," says Zonia, thrusting out her lower jaw.

"Revolution *through* education," Quinn counters.

"I agree with Quinn," says Evyan, and immediately the group is plunged into a political argument which splits them down the middle.

Chapter 24

Sleeping arrangements

Zonia's faction includes her admirer, Darius, and his brother, Ross, plus Kate, Kirsty and Nicky. They are all surprisingly aggressive. As far as I understand, they want to start an armed struggle against the government and its allies (like ASTA), and sabotage the pharmaceutical companies. They talk about the need to stockpile weapons, to infiltrate the enemy forces and to identify high-value people in the opposition. It sounds like they're gearing up to fight a war, but still I get the sense that it's more militant hot air than real plans. From their talk of military strategy, I think they know less than I do.

None of Quinn's followers — Evyan, of course, but also Mark, Bree and Candace — wears a red beret. Coincidence? They seem more intent on winning a war of propaganda, and are determined to find out as much as they can about what they call the real war, or the second war, being fought to limit the rights and freedoms of our nation's citizens, and to inform as many people as they can of the truth. Zonia accuses them of being a bunch of do-nothing intellectuals willing to sit by while people's lives are destroyed. Quinn argues that we must be careful that in fighting the enemy, we don't become exactly like them.

Neil seems aligned with neither group. From the few comments that he tosses into the mix, and which are ignored by the rest, I gather that if there were a militia fighting the government over their treatment of rats, rather than people, then that would be the one he'd join.

When there's a lull in the hostilities, I ask Zonia, "So what are you guys doing here? Who are you all?"

All faces turn to her. I guess nobody wants the responsibility of telling me anything important when I may yet turn out to be an enemy spy.

"We're a collection of people who are wanted or suspected or on the run. Some of our homes have been raided, or we have a contact or relative who has been compromised."

"So you're just hiding out here?"

I don't mean it to sound disparaging, but Evyan, Darius and Kirsty make annoyed sounds, and Kate says, "No we are not just hiding out, thank you very much, we're working on *missions*."

I look a question at Zonia, then Quinn, but nobody explains what the missions might be.

"Aren't you worried they'll find you?"

"Look around you," says Evyan, gesturing to the thick woods and brush. "How could anyone find us here?"

"Yeah, we're like in the middle of nowhere," says Mark.

"You've put your tents up in a clearing. They'll be plainly visible from above" — I point up to the open patch of gray sky — "to any passing Securodrone or surveillance chopper. As will the smoke from your fire. You don't think they'll wonder why a bunch of people are camping out in the woods along with the rats?"

Everyone looks upwards. A trio of birds, ravens probably, circle above us, riding the thermals of wind.

There's a long moment of silence, then Zonia says, "Good point. You're proving useful already. Ross, put out that fire at once."

Ross grabs a pail of water and walks to the fire, ready to pour water on the remains of the fire.

"Not like that," I say, "it'll make smoke and steam."

There's a folding shovel lying beside one of the logs, and I use this to dump sand onto the coals, smothering the fire. Ross nods in acknowledgement.

"As soon as we've finished lunch, let's strike camp and set up under the cover of the trees," Zonia orders.

A few of the rebels groan at this, but no one argues with her. Everyone begins clearing up the remains of lunch and packing the provisions into large storage bins. I join the team washing the dishes, which we do in the cracked, rusted basins in the camp restrooms, then I help Nicky strike her tent.

I'm just pulling the last peg out of the soft, mulchy dirt when Evyan says loudly, "So, Zonia, where is our newest addition going to sleep?"

I stand up straight, clutching a fistful of muddy tent pegs. I've been wondering the same thing.

"Well, any volunteers?" Zonia asks the group.

"We're full," says Bree, clutching Candace.

"So are we," says Kate, pointing at Kirsty.

"Us too," says Evyan, with a satisfied smile.

"Sorry," Nicky says softly to me, "there really is room only for two, else I'd offer to share."

"We've already got four in our tent," says Mark, indicating the brothers and Neil, who are striking a larger tent.

I stand and stare at my feet, nudging pine needles into small mounds, while everyone declares that they don't want me. The light rain starts up again.

"Well," says Zonia with a sigh, "I've currently got a tent to myself. I guess you'd better bunk down with me. Plus, that way I can keep an eye on you."

I feel dread at the thought, but don't know how to object. Luckily, Darius beats me to it.

"No way! If anyone moves into your tent and sleeps next to you, it'll be me."

Something almost like the hint of a smile flits across Zonia's face, then she says, "Okay, then. She can take your place in the tent with the other three guys."

Neil looks sulky at the thought of me bringing my violent energies into his sphere; it's like he's been asked to sleep next to a scorpion. "Why can't she sleep in Quinn's tent? He's alone in a two-manner, and anyway, they know each other," he says.

Quinn's mouth tightens, and he fiddles with the ring in his brow. Evyan looks alarmed at the very idea of me sharing with him.

"That's Connor's spot," she says fiercely, as if challenging anyone to dispute it. "He'll be back any day now. And I think it's important, symbolically, that we keep it ready for him. He is still our leader."

I'm ten years old again, standing awkwardly in the gym of Monroe Elementary School. Coach has nominated Abby Gaines and Madison Mason to choose teams, and I wait — heavy with embarrassment and shame — as they call out name after name, but not mine. Everyone knows I'm a dud at dodgeball; nobody wants me on their team. I can catch as well as any of the girls and throw better than most of them, but I don't want to hurt anyone. Whenever I hit someone, it's me who winces. So I tend to throw wide, or low, or soft. I'm always the last person chosen.

"Look," I say now, speaking past the thickness in my throat, "I don't want to put anyone out. Maybe I could just sleep in the van?"

"Not going to happen," says Zonia flatly.

"That's where they lock up the cache of weapons," Nicky explains softly.

They have a cache of weapons? Maybe Zonia isn't just all hot air.

"She'd probably drive off in it," says Kate, "and take it straight back to enemy HQ."

Stalemate. I'm about to offer to sleep in the shower block when Quinn speaks.

"I'll sleep in the van. She can have my tent."

Apparently Zonia trusts Quinn not to make off with the weapons in the night, because she merely says, "Good, that's settled, then."

Quinn helps me put up his tent under a large pine tree, carefully avoiding any eye contact with me, then removes his gear to the van.

That night I lie in the small tent, fighting off memories. Instead of the screams inside my head, I force myself to listen to the cries of night birds, the noise of katydids and crickets, and the rhythm of the rain falling on the tent, while nervously tracking the scuffles and rustles which might indicate the presence of a rat.

Ross is officially on "guard duty" which, as far as I can see, involves lying with his head stuck outside the tent, supposedly keeping an eye open for any threats. I'd be willing to bet good money that he'll be asleep in under an hour. These people are so focused on the political threat of their enemies that they seriously neglect the immediate danger of their environment.

I feel small and very alone, and dense with pain and guilt. I burrow my wet cheeks into the pillow and inhale deeply. Quinn must have taken Connor's sleeping bag and pillow to the van — perhaps he thinks it would be sacrilege for me to lay my disgraceful sniper's head on the leader's pillow — because both the sleeping bag around me and the pillow under my head smell of my pirate.

Chapter 25

Need to know

After breakfast the next day — a stomach-churning combo of scrambled, powdered eggs alongside canned peaches in sweet syrup — Kirsty, Kate and Ross disappear down the trail that leads out of camp and up the mountain. Zonia, with Darius close by her side, huddles together at one end of the circle of logs with Quinn, Candace and Bree. They talk in low voices, and there's no need for anyone to tell me I'm not welcome at their chat. Judging from the hostile glances Kate and Darius occasionally direct in my direction, and Zonia's long, speculative looks, I suspect they are discussing the problems of whether to believe me and what to do with me.

I tug the cuffs of my long-sleeved shirt down over my wrists. I've lost any desire to show them what lies beneath. Screw them. After what I've been through, I don't need to prove myself to anyone.

Feeling conspicuous and at a loose end, I volunteer to help Nicky tidy the camp and take stock of the supplies, which are stored in black plastic storage bins under the two trestle tables. While I count and restack packets of soup and pouches of freeze-dried mac 'n cheese, I notice Neil, Evyan and Mark disappearing into the biggest tent. Mark reemerges holding two coaxial cables, which he connects to extension cables dangling from a nearby tree, their sockets protected by plastic bags. My eyes follow the cables up the trunk to near the top of the branches, where I can just glimpse the circular beige shape of a satellite dish above the thick foliage.

Mark returns to the tent and, with a glare at me, Evyan zips it closed behind him.

"What are they up to?" I ask Nicky.

She follows my gaze from the tent to the dish and back again.

"You can probably guess that we don't have a satellite dish in order to watch T.V.," she smiles. "Neil's some kind of science and I.T. genius, a real computer wizard, and the others are helping him with one of our missions."

"You have computers here?" I'm amazed.

"Just a couple. Neil has rigged them to run off solar panels, and they connect to the deep web via satellite."

"He sounds like someone after my brother's heart."

"You have a brother? Back at home?"

"Yeah, a twin, Robin. He's gotten really into computers and coding." I sit on the lid of the storage bin and push down on the ridged edges to seal it closed, sneaking a glance at Quinn. He's talking to Zonia, counting off the points of some argument on his long fingers. I can hear the musical lilt of his voice from here, but I can't make out the words.

"So what is Neil trying to do?" I ask Nicky.

She nibbles on a cuticle and gives me a long stare, as if deciding whether she can trust me.

"Well, I can't tell you anything specific, even if I did understand — which I don't, not at all — but I think he's trying to build a website which can counteract the lies and propaganda the government puts out. Let people know the truth, you know? Like an underground online newspaper, or something like that old WikiLeaks website."

"But wouldn't they be able to track him?" I start counting the rolls of toilet paper stored in the next bin.

"Yeah, so that's the hard part. He's trying to make it undetectable, and temporary or something, so that it pops up and jumps from server to server before its cyber trail can be traced. And the plan is to connect it to similar sites that people in other sectors are building."

"Wow." The rebels are more organized than I would have guessed.

"They actually got one up and running in the Northeast Sector, but it lasted less than a day before they were traced and captured, and the whole thing was destroyed by the National Cyber Crimes unit. It was bad, really bad, because they found names and contacts and plans on the system and arrested a bunch of our supporters."

I think about Robin, trying to break into high-security systems, and my stomach twists in a knot of worry.

"So Neil has to be super-careful, and it's taking time. I think Zonia's getting impatient. She has other ideas."

"Oh yeah?"

Nicky nods, but this time she doesn't explain further. Unseen by either of us, Quinn has walked up to us, and he looks grim. "She's on a need-to-know only basis, Nicky."

Nicky looks guilty but says, "I don't see how we're supposed to stop her from noticing things."

"Perhaps," I suggest in a tone of false politeness, "you should separate me from the others. Lock me up out of the way somewhere and toss me the odd crust of bread. You could turn the old admin office back there into your own suspect detention center." I use the term deliberately to goad him. "Maybe Neil could give you some zip ties to restrain me." I place my wrists together and hold them out to him.

"Jinx!" Nicky chides, pulling my hands down.

"Maybe we would all be safer that way," Quinn says, his face expressionless. Ouch. "But Zonia has other plans for you."

He stalks off, and I frown down at the bin of toilet paper. I've completely lost count and will have to start again.

"He seems pretty angry with you," Nicky says.

"Yeah, he is."

"Were the two of you an item?"

I look up, taken aback. "What makes you ask that?"

"The air sort of crackles whenever you're together," she says, grinning. "So I figure it was pretty hot and heavy between the two of you at one time."

"Yeah, it was," I sigh. "Then he found out I was a sniper, and then I darted Connor. And that pretty much ended things — for him, at least."

"I can totally see how that would do it. But as guys go, he's one of the good ones. I don't think you should give up on him just yet."

Huh? Is she nuts, can't she see how he clearly feels about me? "He may have liked me once, but he doesn't any longer. I think he doubts I ever cared for him at all. He suspects I was just faking it. It doesn't seem like he believes my version of events, and now that he's confirmed I'm a killer, I think … I think he hates me."

"Oh, I don't think so. He's probably just all kinds of mixed up, you know? Upset about his brother, not sure who to side with or who to trust. And don't forget that he fetched you. Angry as he was, he got Zonia to send the van for you. He didn't leave you out there, stranded. That counts for something, surely?"

It's something to think about, I guess.

"Can I ask another question about what the rebels are doing?" I say, and rush to reassure her, "It's not anything sensitive."

"Sure."

"Why don't you guys just go to the media, and tell them what you know? That way everyone could find out what's actually going on, and there wouldn't be a need for a revolution."

"There is no way we'll achieve lasting change without a revolution," Nicky says firmly, and I'm reminded that she's one of Zonia's supporters. "But that aside, we've tried going to the media, and it didn't work. No editor in the country would run the story. What with the state of emergency, and all its restrictions and embargoes and censorship, they'd be in a heap of trouble. Our suspicions and accusations are just too hot to handle without real, hard proof. One editor is really keen, but he says if he publishes what we've got, they'll arrest him and shut his site down under the Protection of Information Act. They've done it before, particularly in the early days of the plague. He wants proof — video footage, computer code, government memos — before he'll consider it. I don't suppose you managed to lift one of those poison bullets?"

I shake my head. "They keep the weapons and ammo locked in the armory. You sign for everything going out and have to account for every shot when you return your gear."

"Most likely it wouldn't be enough, anyway." Nicky sighs. "There'd be no way to prove where you got it from or how it was being used. It's kinda hopeless. That's why we've shelved that plan and are working on our other mission."

Only on my third day in camp do I discover the nature of the second mission. Zonia must intend for me to find out, because she orders me to accompany Quinn and Evyan when they leave camp, each of us wearing a backpack containing a bottle of water and a packed lunch. Quinn takes the lead up the trail which curves behind the camp and then snakes steeply up the mountain through the pines, maples, oaks and the thick underbrush. It feels good to exercise my body again, and it's amazing to be out in nature. Even in the shade, it's hot on this late summer's day, so when we cross a clear stream trickling over moss-covered rocks in a small ravine, I stop to splash water on my face and arms.

I allow myself a moment of petty glee when I realize that I am way fitter than Evyan. She is so busy trying to catch her breath that she doesn't snipe at me for the whole climb.

When we pause for a quick break, beside a vertical rock face with ferns growing out of cracks in its gray surface, I can't resist offering her my bottle of water. "Dasani, Evyan?"

She ignores me but drinks deeply from her own bottle before we set off again through a densely wooded section. The path is covered with a soft mulch of decomposing wood, leaves and lichen. Our feet slip on the drifts of damp pine needles which release their fresh fragrance as we crush them underfoot, but I'm more worried about the possible dangers lurking in amongst the trees than a twisted ankle.

When Quinn notices me cautiously looking from side to side and periodically checking back over my shoulder, he says, "Expecting trouble? Or are you just paranoid?"

"You guys are careless. Anybody could be watching you."

"No one knows we're here."

"As far as you know. Anyway, there have got to be rats in these woods. They could easily be infected. You should all be much more vigilant about that. You should have an armed guard day and night at the camp, and on these hikes, and when you collect firewood. Just in case."

"Are you volunteering?"

I shrug. "It would make more sense than having me count cans of beans. I'd like to help."

"Or maybe you just miss shooting things. You can take the girl out of the kill-zone ..."

"Oh, get lost." I try to make my tone sound annoyed rather than hurt. If I didn't love him ... Strike that — if I *hadn't* loved him, then the jibes would just be an irritation. As it is, every barbed comment hits home hard. I'm ready to give him a piece of my mind. "You —"

There's a sudden rustle in the bush beside me, and I freeze, paralyzed by fear.

Chapter 26

Surveillance

A blur of tan fur scurrying out from under the bush sends me leaping backwards. I crash into a pine tree, banging my head painfully against its trunk and bringing down a shower of pine needles.

"It's only a squirrel," Evyan snickers, pointing at the long, bushy tail now disappearing up a nearby tree trunk. "You sure scare easy."

"Squirrels can also be infected, you know. Any mammal can," I snap, brushing pine needles off my shoulders and rubbing the tender spot on the back of my head. There'll be a lump there later.

"You okay?" Quinn asks, surprising me.

I nod, which brings down a scatter of needles from the top of my head, and then set off down the path again, cursing the squirrel.

I'm hot and sweaty by the time we reach the top of the small mountain and circle around the back. On this side, the view looks out over a valley in which nestles a vast residential compound surrounded by a take-no-prisoners electric fence. A long, tree-lined drive begins at a set of huge gates, leads past fields and what might once have been horse paddocks, to a large, three-winged lodge. There is a tennis court nearby, plus a large pond, several outbuildings and small cabins, and even what I think might be a small golfing green.

Evyan and Quinn park themselves behind a large, flat-topped boulder and take turns to conduct surveillance of the compound. In spite of my irritation at him, I make a thorough surveillance of Quinn. I'd forgotten how broad his shoulders were and how his thick, dark hair makes a curl at the top of his neck. The fine hairs on his arms are golden in the sun, like a halo against the olive of his skin. My fingers ache to make contact with that skin. It's so beautiful. Everyone in the world should have skin that color.

I lean back against a rock and wince at a sharp prick in my back — more of the irritating pine needles. While I brush myself down again and comb my fingers through my hair, picking out the sharp green needles lodged in its strands, Quinn and Evyan peer over the top of the boulder to observe the buildings below through a pair of binoculars. They note the times and details of every coming and going in a small notebook — no doubt tonight they will report back to Zonia.

"Who're we spying on, Pellegrino?" I ask Evyan.

She grinds her teeth but doesn't respond.

"It must be someone important, by the looks of those security patrols."

Even with my bare eyes, I think I can make out several guards. More silence.

"Never mind, I'm sure I'll find out who it is when they spot us, capture our sorry asses and take us down to meet the owner. I'm surprised they haven't done so already, actually," I say.

"What, now you're going to say there's something wrong with our position again?" says Evyan with a sneer. "In case you haven't noticed, we're behind a rock. *And* we're under the shelter of this pine, so we're not visible from above."

"We don't need to be — we're visible from below."

Evyan snorts dismissively, but Quinn listens while I point out that peering over the top of the big rock creates a perfect silhouette — easy for anyone down below to spot if they happen to look up. The current position of the sun also means that watchers would likely see a telltale light reflection off the binoculars.

"And what you're wearing," I say, pointing at Evyan's orange T-shirt, "hardly blends you into the environment."

I'm wearing my khaki T-shirt again — its long sleeves do nothing to keep me cool on this hot day, but they do cover my bruises.

Evyan gives me a filthy look, but pulls on a black hoodie, despite the heat.

"What would you recommend?" asks Quinn. The way he says the words tells me he doesn't find it easy to ask me for advice.

"We need to create a hide, use the grass and shrubs and mud to make a ghillie suit of sorts."

"A *what*?" asks Evyan.

"A ghillie suit. Camouflaged clothing designed to blend in with the background," I explain. "And we should maybe even move around according to the direction of the sun."

"Lucky for us they taught you how to hide while you were picking people off," says Evyan.

"Yes, wasn't it?" I reply blandly. I will not let her get to me. Or, more accurately, I will not let her *see* how much she gets to me.

Quinn says nothing.

I pick a spot behind a thick bush and remove my brown canvas jacket from where it's tied around my waist. I drape it over the forked branch of another bush growing to one side of the boulder, keeping it in place with a rock. It creates a small, shaded gap through which we can peer through the binocs. I cover it with a combination of long, plucked grass and small, dead branches which I collect from under the trees behind us, and tuck some of the vegetation into my peaked cap and my waistband and let it stick out from my pockets.

Then I pour a little water from my bottle into a section of clay-like dirt, stir it with a stick and smear it patchily onto my face to break up the pale oval that is so easily recognizable as a human face. I offer to do the same for Evyan, but she says, "I'll do my own, thanks," and makes stripes over her cheeks like an Apache warrior in an old western movie.

"Quinn?" I hold out the handful of mud to him.

He stands rigidly still while I smear the mud on his forehead and cheeks, staring away from me out to the side, leaving me free to study his vivid gray eyes, the muscle pulsing in his jaw, the rough stubble of his skin under my fingers. My hand is trembling again. When I make to rub more mud over his exposed forearms, he steps back from me.

"I've got it."

"Here, Quinn," says Evyan in a voice sweet enough to rot teeth, "let me. I've still got a bunch of mud on my hands." And she takes her time rubbing it thoroughly over his arms.

"Make it patchy. You defeat the whole point if it's a one-toned human shape," I say.

She hovers over him, smearing off spots with a fistful of tissues, and makes sure at every moment to keep herself between him and me.

She could spare herself all this effort of dissing me and protecting Quinn from my supposed feminine wiles. He hardly speaks to me, and never to say anything kind. And since that charged moment in the van, he seems determined to prevent his body from physically closing the emotional distance between us.

Nothing of any real interest happens at our surveillance target the whole day. Evyan directs the odd snide remark my way, but Quinn ignores me for the most part, and we trudge back down the mountain in silence. Quinn reports back to Zonia, Mark beckons

Evyan into Neil's tent, and I help Nicky and Ross with dinner — canned hot dogs with rehydrated freeze-dried corn, and instant coffee with long-life milk. I haven't eaten a bite of fresh food since I left home. If the rats don't get me, then scurvy probably will.

The next day, a different team of three rebels heads up the mountain, and Zonia, to Evyan's evident delight, orders me to go clean the restrooms. I suspect this is to get me out the way for another of their 'strategy sessions', because everyone else left in camp huddles together on the logs while I head off, toilet brush in one hand and a bucket of cleaning supplies in the other, to the restroom and shower block. I hang my jacket on a tap, tie back my long hair and begin working. I wipe the basins, scrub the mildewed shower stalls, and mop the muddy floors.

When I fantasized about escaping the confines of home and the smothering attention of Mom, and then the dangerous control of ASTA, I never dreamed that I'd wind up being a rebel janitor. It's funny, I tell myself, not depressing. Funny.

I've almost finished cleaning the last toilet when, for no reason that I can figure, my hands start shaking, my heart skips into a rapid, fluttering beat, and I feel faint. I've been having fewer of the panic attacks in the last few days, but this one is bad.

I slump onto the cold concrete floor with my head between my legs and try to catch my breath. I've found that it helps to stare hard at something and analyze the details of its appearance, because that distracts me from the thoughts that I might actually be having a heart attack or, more probably, that I'm completely losing my mind. So I focus on the bare skin of my arms, noting that the bruises are fading, and the scars and welts are now pale, silvery lines. You wouldn't see them unless you were specifically looking. The nail on my damaged finger is beginning to grow back.

My fingers find their way under the short sleeves of my black

T-shirt and explore the scabby lumps of the electrode burns. A sharp pain tells me I'm picking at the sores again. I force myself to stop, to get up, wash my hands, grab my jacket and leave. At least I'm a bit calmer — though the feeling doesn't last long.

On my way back to camp, I hear a scuttle in the undergrowth and catch a flash of low movement in my peripheral vision. I freeze and train my eyes and ears on a patch of wild azalea about ten meters away from the path, where a watermelon-sized patch of deep brown is just visible between the deep-green leaves. This time it's a rat, I can sense it. If I had a rifle on me, I could confirm the sighting through the telescopic scope and take the threat out with a single shot.

For one short moment I miss my old job, and Cameron — and even Bruce — with a longing so fierce it winds me. But I can't have that back, not without all the other dreadful stuff. There is no going back now.

Moving as slowly and smoothly as I can, I bend to pick up a fist-sized rock and hurl it at the bush. The huge rat flees in a blur of grayish brown and shifting leaves, then it's gone. But it'll be back. The mutant rats were bred to be curious, aggressive and bold. Somehow, I have to make these rebels take the threat of the plague seriously.

Chapter 27

Bull's eye

I march back to camp, where Zonia and the rest of the group are so locked in a heated argument about whether there's a need to source more weapons that they don't even notice my arrival. Not wanting to be accused of eavesdropping on their conversation, I clear my throat loudly, and Darius stops talking mid-sentence.

"What's the matter?" asks Evyan. "Run out of bleach? Get a blister on your mop hand?"

"We have a real problem," I say directly to Zonia.

"With the facilities?"

"No." Is everybody here obsessed with the minor details? "With rats."

Neil looks instantly more alert at this, but everyone else sighs as if bored.

"I saw a mutant beside the path on the way back. And I've heard them near the camp and on the mountain. It's dangerous, and it needs to be attended to."

"What do you mean, attended to?" asks Neil, squaring his thin shoulders and thrusting out his lower lip.

"I don't think we need to worry," says Zonia. "We're very careful to store the food supplies in airtight containers at all times, so we don't attract any animals."

"They're not just after the food, they're after us! That's what they were expressly bred for — to attack people, to bite and spread the virus they carry."

Although I never exactly enjoyed killing rats for the sniper squad, it's the one part of my work for ASTA that I'm not ashamed of. It wasn't enjoyable, but it was necessary.

"The risk posed by rats is greatly overestimated. They are gentle creatures who are more scared of us than we are of them," says Neil.

"No, they're not."

"Yes, they are."

"I'm sorry, but that's just not true. Those mutants are scared of nothing. I've observed them —"

"*Murdered* them!" Neil's beard is trembling with his agitation.

"Have you ever even seen one?" I challenge him.

"No. Which just goes to show how few of them there are."

"It goes to show you're unobservant. They're out here with us, and probably getting bolder and coming closer by the day. I know what they're capable of." I look around from face to face, desperate to make them understand. "It's just stupid to ignore the risk. You people are so focused on bloody bunny-hugging" — I point at Neil — "and vague future targets" — I say this to Zonia — "and grand plans to educate the poor ignorant masses with your precious truths" — this to Quinn — "that you're ignoring the very real and immediate danger under your own noses."

Bull's-eye. I've succeeded in pissing off everyone.

Neil's whole face is suffused with anger now. "Bunny-hugging!" he spits. "You're just a bloodthirsty and ill-informed little girl, who believes all the government propaganda she's fed."

"Yeah, from what Quinn told me, she's good at that," Evyan snipes.

So Quinn told her all about me? Nice.

"Well, thank you for pointing out the error of our ways, Jinx. I'm grateful for your input," says Zonia. She does not sound grateful. "And since you have the vision, you can have the job. So you'll stand guard — against the hordes of dangerous rats out to attack us — for the rest of today and tonight."

"Fine." Someone needs to. "Can I go get a rifle from your store?"

"Well *someone* wants to get their hands on a gun," says Darius, at the same time as Ross snorts in disbelief, Candace says, "No way!" and Neil clenches his hands into fists as if ready to punch me on my bloodthirsty, non-rodent nose.

"No," says Zonia. "You cannot."

"So what exactly am I supposed to do if a rat waltzes into camp? Politely ask it to leave?"

No one answers. One by one they peel away to go about other business.

"Quinn!" I grab his arm to stop him leaving. "Please, tell them. You saw, in intel at ASTA, you saw reports of rats and attacks and deaths. You know they're not cute and fuzzy little pets."

He looks down at my hand on his arm, and I pull it back.

"I can't be sure how many of those poxy reports were accurate and how many were false — planted to pump up public fear and justify the government's repressive controls."

"Are you kidding me? Mutant rats — *plague-carrying* mutant rats — exist! They bite and infect humans and other animals. They are bioengineered terrorist weapons of mass destruction. What do you think our sniper squad went out shooting all those times?"

"Do you really want me to answer that?"

Great, we're back to that.

He walks off, and I call after him. "This is on you. This is on all of you!" Then I slump down against the base of a tree on the periphery of the camp, ready to defend us from deadly mutants with a mop and couple of rocks.

Quinn parks himself on the other side of the camp fireplace with his back to me. It seems to be his favorite place to sit and brood, sending the odd gaze my way as if assessing me, while he practices his new hobby. He throws a pair of sharp knives into selected tree stumps and trunks, yanks them out by the long strings attached to their hilts, and tosses again. Over and over, for hours at a time. I can't figure it. Shooting someone is wrong, but attacking them with a knife wouldn't be?

Then again, perhaps he isn't training himself to hit humans. Perhaps he's preparing to wound trees. Jackass.

Nothing of any real interest happens until my sixth day in camp.

I'm back up the mountain, and this time I'm the one keeping watch while Quinn lies dozing in the midday sun behind the boulder, with Evyan beside him, probably murmuring sweet nothings into his ear. It's a hot day, and the stitches in my scalp itch and tug, reminding me that they should have been removed already.

The compound in the valley below is an odd mix of old and new. The shingle-roofed, stone-and-log lodge and the smaller rustic cabins look like they've been there a while, as do the barns and stables. But other parts — the helipad, the maximum-security perimeter fence and gates, the golf green and basketball court out back — look like they've been added recently.

The binoculars are powerful enough for me to make out details. There's a Televid communication panel mounted on a pole of the tennis court fence; a sunken hot tub on the lodge's deck alongside an outdoor grill with a tall, stone chimney; and beyond the farthest cabins, there's a semicircular area, backed by a split-rail fence, which has lines marked on the ground like a geometry-set protractor.

A man in khaki pants and a green shirt rolls the pool cover off the swimming pool then dusts down the wooden table and chairs on the deck. The windows of the main lodge suddenly brighten — someone inside has just opened the curtains or blinds. I figure they're preparing for visitors, but I say nothing to Quinn or Evyan, one of whom would surely take over surveillance if I pointed out these signs.

I want to see who arrives, because I reckon that the owner is not only rich, but also important. There are at least half a dozen dark-suited guards on duty, and all of them are armed with semi-automatic weapons. I count two guards at the main gate, one at the front and another at the rear door of the lodge, a fifth patrolling the perimeter of the property in a quad bike, and another walking a pair of Doberman pinschers along the paved path which meanders in and out of the shady copse of trees and loops around a large pond. A round Securodrone Rover, about the circumference of a dinner plate, roams randomly over the grounds, presumably transmitting a video feed to a security monitor inside one of the buildings.

I keep watch, lying on my stomach under the rough hide, for about an hour. My lower back and elbows are aching, and I'm about to take a break when a uniformed soldier steps out of the gray stone gatehouse and salutes. The massive gates swing open slowly, and he waves through a convoy of three black vehicles, the middle of which is a stretch limo, and they proceed up the long drive to the lodge.

I stay still and say nothing. A bunch of men and women in dark suits pile out of the front and rear vehicles, and while the others keep their backs to the vehicles and scan the surrounding area, one guard, with a sidearm prominently displayed on her waistband, goes to open the back door of the limo. I adjust the focus on my binoculars. A man climbs out, yawns, stretches his arms, rolls his shoulders, and says something to the guard that makes her smile.

My jaw drops open in utter surprise. I recognize this man.

Chapter 28

I spy with my little eye

The man's square face with its thick, wavy brown hair just greying at the temples is as familiar to me as my own. I've seen it smiling reassuringly on thousands of televised public service announcements, on the sides of dozens of Health and Wellbeing Regulation Fun Buses and billboards, and in online promotions, articles and game pop-ups.

No doubt about it, I am looking at Alex Hawke, president of the Southern Sector.

Next out of the limo is an elegantly dressed woman and two young kids — a boy carrying a teddy bear, and a pigtailed girl in denim shorts holding some kind of device in her hands. The guard at the front door steps forward, shakes the president's hand and gives something to both of the kids. I can't quite make out what the small objects are. Pinwheels? Giant lollipops?

If I had one of the powerful sniper rifle scopes from the ASTA armory, I'd be able to see clearly. I wonder what weapons are in the cache locked up in the van back at camp.

Hawke and his wife disappear inside the house, and his kids follow behind, skipping and waving their new treasures in the air. When the door closes behind the family, two guards — I guess they must be secret service agents — take up position with their backs to the door. I edge backwards out from under the hide and, keeping low on the ground, turn to face Quinn and Evyan, who are stretched out on the grass. His arms are folded across his chest, but her hands are stretched out beside her. The one nearest to Quinn is lying palm upwards as if she's hoping he'll thread his fingers through hers.

"Why are we spying on President Hawke?" I ask baldly.

That gets their attention. Quinn bolts upright, grabs the binoculars and belly-crawls under the hide.

"What did you see? What happened? Why didn't you alert us?" Evyan whispers fiercely.

She creeps up behind Quinn and frantically scribbles notes in the little logbook.

"I thought, when he didn't arrive last night, that he wouldn't be home for the weekend," says Quinn.

"So that's why you're hiding out on this particular mountain — to conduct surveillance on the president at his mountain retreat," I say.

They don't deny it.

"Why are you watching him?"

"None of your business," snaps Evyan, but Quinn says, "Information is useful."

"What information? We can't see or hear inside the house. Are we going to keep a record of what he barbecues and who he beats at tennis?"

Apparently so. The rest of the day is spent logging every movement in the compound. Mrs. Hawke goes for a swim with the kids. A white-aproned man appears carrying a plate of raw steaks and proceeds to broil them on the gas grill. The family eats around the table on the deck. President Hawke drinks two beers and chats to the kids. Mrs. Hawke drinks three large glasses of white wine and reads a book. The boy prefers potato salad to tomatoes. The girl prefers texting on her phone to eating anything or talking to anyone.

About an hour before the end of our watch, Evyan says, "Someone needs to leave now to alert Zonia about Hawke's arrival. She'll want to send a team up to take over from us to do surveillance through the night."

"Want me to go?" Quinn volunteers.

"Or I could," I say. I could do with some exercise to work the kinks out of my muscles.

Evyan hesitates. I can almost see the struggle going on inside her. The person who brings this news to Zonia will surely win some brownie points, and Evyan does *not* want me to get any credit. So she's torn between leaving me alone with Quinn, or spending the remaining hour and the walk back down to camp in my despised company. It's what Sarge would call a lose-lose situation.

"Let Quinn go," I say. "You and I can hang out up here, spend some quality girl time together."

"As if," says Evyan. "Fine, *I'll* go. Just keep your eyes on him. On Hawke," she clarifies, just I case I have my sights set on a different "him".

I can't help it, I give her an evil grin. "Don't worry, Aquafina, we'll cope fine with just the two of us here. Alone."

A few minutes after she stomps off, Hawke comes out of the lodge carrying a shotgun and walks with a pair of guards to the semicircle area beyond the cabins that mystified me earlier — turns out it's a skeet-shooting range. The prez is a lousy shot.

It's the first time Quinn and I have been alone together since I came to the rebel camp, but any lingering hope that he's cold and suspicious towards me only for the benefit of others, and that he might behave differently in private, now evaporates. He doesn't look at me, doesn't utter a word. I find myself wanting to needle him just to hear his voice.

"So, Quinn, are you going to use those intel skills you learned at ASTA to analyze all the info you've written down and come up with some astounding, world-saving conclusion?"

"I'd rather use my skills than yours," he says.

After that, neither of us says anything, but the tension of the unsaid things between us is as loud as a shout. We pack up when Ross, Candace and Bree arrive to relieve us, and walk down through the deepening gloom of the woods in tense silence.

Zonia and Evyan walk up to meet us as we enter camp — Zonia to receive our report, and Evyan, apparently, to check that Quinn has escaped my clutches unmolested. She smooths his hair where it's sticking up and shoots a filthy glance my way. Does she think I've been running my fingers through his locks? Not likely.

"Anything else?" Zonia asks after she's scanned the entries in the surveillance logbook.

I rattle off the details of what I saw — who, how many, what each was wearing, the precise times of arrival at the main gate and at the residence, the number, sex and position of the guards, the model and caliber of their weapons, the exact timing of the different patrols, the registration plates of each of the three vehicles and the fact that, judging from their body language, President and Mrs. Hawke's marriage might be in trouble.

Zonia looks impressed and invites me to join her for a little walk. It's almost dark, so we don't go far, but we're out of earshot of the others when she says, "That was quite some surveillance report. You obviously have exceptional observation and memory skills. And you've already helped our surveillance teams by teaching us about camouflage and ghillie hides."

I don't bother to correct her terminology.

"You've also been useful in highlighting some of our weaknesses in keeping our camp undetected."

I say nothing — I have no idea where she's going with this, and besides, standing out here in the dark woods, I'm more concerned with keeping an ear open for an approaching rat than listening to flattery.

"I think, if we set aside our suspicions and mistrust, we could all learn a lot from you."

"You do?"

"Of course I do. Would you be willing to share your skills with us, Jinx?"

I'm surprised — pleasantly so. This is the first positive approach I've had from any of them.

"Yeah, sure. I *want* to help, in any way I can. When do you want me to begin?"

"Why not tonight? After dinner, perhaps you chat to us all about camouflage and hides and how to observe, and then tomorrow, perhaps we could have a more specialized session with a selected few?"

A couple of the rebels seem interested in hearing what I have to say that night, though Neil pointedly volunteers to go wash the dishes as soon as I begin, and Evyan quickly offers to help him. The next morning Zonia calls Quinn, Nicky, Darius and me, and we set off in a group out of camp and down the faint path that leads to where the van is parked. It's not long before I understand what Zonia meant by a 'specialized session'.

When we get to the van, Zonia unlocks it and slides open the door. Darius climbs inside, kicks aside Quinn's sleeping bag and backpack, and drags a four-by-two-foot, khaki-colored metal locker over to the opening where I stand beside Zonia. When she opens the lid, I catch a glimpse of what's inside: a shotgun, an assault-style semi-automatic pistol, and a brace of handguns.

Well, I'll be danged.

Zonia removes a rifle-shaped nylon bag and several boxes of

ammunition from the locker before carefully closing and locking it again. Then she leads us to a small clearing in a heavily wooded section of the forest and hands me the bag.

"Open it," Zonia says.

I unzip the bag. Inside is an M24 bolt-action sniper rifle, day and night optics and a small cleaning kit. I remove the rifle, and hold it balanced across my arms.

My scalp ripples tight. For an instant I'm back on a roof aiming down at an M&M limping in circles in the alley below.

Stop it. Focus!

I blow out a puff of breath and rub a slightly unsteady hand over my head where the stitches tug.

"What?" I say to Zonia. "Now you *want* me to shoot?"

"I want you to teach us how to shoot."

"Why?"

I'm suspicious. I glance at Quinn, who looks back, stony-faced. What is he thinking?

"Well, Jinx, I've decided that you're right," says Zonia, "We *are* being foolish to ignore the very real threats to our safety. We need to be able to defend ourselves. If a rat ran over my feet right now, I doubt I'd be able to kill it. You've told us more than once we need an armed guard, but it's no good if that person can't shoot the side of a barn. And you can't personally stand guard 24/7."

Finally, she's got it! I actually smile in relief. I don't know when last I smiled — it feels unnatural, like my face might crack from the unfamiliar action of it.

"Sure, of course," I say. "I can teach you, but there's a problem."

"Oh yeah? What's that?" asks Darius. He hasn't warmed to me at all.

"Well, the report when the rifle fires will carry far in this silence, maybe even as far as that lodge on the other side of the mountain. I'm guessing you won't want them to come investigating."

"Won't they just assume it's hunters?" asks Nicky. "There are some diehards who still go hunting in the woods, aren't there?"

"Probably, but I'm pretty sure it's not hunting season until October," I say. I learned a few things about the "sport" while listening to Bruce and Cameron compare notes on our ratting operations. "Besides, the odd crack of a hunter taking down a buck sounds very different to repeated shots from four people in target practice."

"There's a pouch on the side there." Zonia points to the rifle bag. "Inside is a silencer."

"Suppressor," I correct automatically.

"If you use that, surely they won't be able to hear us," says Zonia.

"True enough."

Suppressors don't entirely silence the sound of shots, but the remaining noise won't carry to the other side of the mountain. Also, there are no earplugs or muffs in the bag, so the suppressor will help protect our hearing. I screw the attachment onto the end of the rifle, and Zonia hands me the telescopic scope to fit onto the top.

"You won't really need this," I tell her. "We'll only see the rats when they're relatively close. The scope is for long-distance shots."

"I think we amateurs" — Zonia gestures to herself, Nicky, Darius and Quinn — "can use all the help we can get."

I shrug and mount the scope. It will probably make things easier, and they'll definitely benefit from using the night scope when standing guard for rats after nightfall.

"Then let's get going," I say.

"Don't you first have to tune the gun, or something?" asks Nicky.

I grin. "Or something, yeah."

In a practiced movement, I lift the rifle up to my shoulder and cradle it against my cheek. The smooth curve of the wooden stock against my skin, the weight of the weapon in my hand, the cool steel sickle of the trigger under my finger, all feel like the embrace of a familiar old friend. I click off the safety and squint through the scope, aim the cross of the reticles at a pinecone on the ground about thirty meters away and in the opposite direction of the camp, and gently squeeze the trigger. There's a dull click. I pull back the bolt and peer into the chamber. Empty.

"We're going to need the ammunition."

Silence.

This, apparently, is the moment of truth. Darius looks deeply doubtful about the wisdom of giving me live rounds while I have a rifle in my hands. Zonia not so subtly pulls back her vest to show me the handgun tucked into her waistband. Does she even know how to use it? Even Nicky just studies me silently. Surprisingly, it's Quinn who snags a handful of rounds from the box and hands them to me.

"Thanks," I say softly. My fingers tingle where they touched his.

I open the bolt, load three rounds into the internal magazine and shove the rest into my jeans pocket. Pointing the rifle away from the group, I slide the lever forward and down to chamber a round, then I aim at the pinecone again and pull off a shot. It's a miss.

Darius gives a dismissive little laugh. I ignore him and go systematically through the process of zeroing the rifle — shooting, adjusting the scope, reloading. Soon, I hit the cone. A few more adjustments and practice shots, and I'm hitting tiny targets at three times the distance. With my last two shots, I score snake-eyes — two overlapping holes in the target.

"Impressive," says Zonia, looking very pleased. "How soon will we be able to do that?"

Does she think anyone is capable of becoming an ace marksman with a couple of lessons?

"It takes some practice," I warn, in the understatement of the century.

"Then let's not waste any more time."

Chapter 29

Stone cold

I start the rebel shooting lesson by asking if any of them have ever shot before.

"Never," says Quinn, sounding proud of the fact.

Zonia and Darius shake their heads, but Nicky says, "I've been hunting twice, with my uncle. That was way back, though, before the plague began."

I give an overview of the bare basics of theory — weapon safety, the different parts of the rifle and how it works, how wind, weather, altitude and temperature can affect the speed and trajectory of the round moving through the air. Nicky listens with interest, but Quinn looks uncomfortable. I wonder why Zonia invited him — she must know how he feels about guns and shooting. Maybe that's *why* she did. He's a rival in the leadership stakes, and I've noticed she likes to keep him off-balance. Or maybe she just doesn't want to leave him back at camp while she's away. He might convert some of her followers to his way of thinking.

I draw circles and crosshairs in the dirt with a stick and explain how to use the scope, then take them through the basic differences between shooting stationary and moving targets, and explain how you have to compensate for moving objects, as rats will likely be, by leading the target.

Soon Zonia is yawning, and a bored-looking Darius asks, "Can't we just have a go at shooting?"

"Sure." Let them see for themselves that it's not as easy as they seem to think.

"I'll go first. Jinx, come show me how to hold the rifle," says Zonia, removing her red beret and tossing it to Darius.

I stand behind her and show her the proper grasp. Her movements are too rough and awkward for her to be accurate — her whole hand convulses when she pulls the trigger. Every time the weapon fires, the recoil knocks her back a pace. A dozen shots later she still hasn't come close to hitting anywhere near the closest target — a dense shrub about twenty meters away.

"Here, Darius, you try," she says, holding the rifle out to him. "My shoulder is already aching."

When I try to adjust Darius's hands on the weapon, he says, "Don't touch me. Just tell me how." There's been no thawing of suspicion here.

"Chill," I say, and give him instructions from a yard away.

I suspect he's one of those guys who doesn't like being told what to do by a girl. Especially when that girl is way better at a skill than he is. Especially when that girl is Jinx E. James.

He's not much better than Zonia and gets frustrated easily. He'd be better with the shotgun. Now that I think of it, it would probably be a better weapon for everyone — they'd be much more likely to hit a rat with it. I make a mental note to mention it to Zonia tonight.

Nicky is better than both Zonia and Darius. She stays calm, can stand and lie as still as even a sniper needs to, and has the requisite fine motor control to move the trigger back slowly and gently without simultaneously moving any other part of her body.

"You've got real potential," I tell her.

"You're a great teacher," she replies, grinning in delight and reloading.

Just then I hear a loud rustle in the bushes behind us. I grab the rifle out of Nicky's hands and swing it up to my shoulder as I spin around. Ross's face, seen through my scope, is tight with fright, his eyes wide and round.

"Whoa!" he says, stopping dead on the spot and holding up his hands.

"Sorry," I say, lowering the rifle and easing the safety back on.

"Try not to shoot any of the good guys," Darius says. "Again."

I sigh. I don't know how much more of the sniping the sniper can take. It's exhausting. I'm even losing the spirit to tease Evyan with designer water names.

When Ross reaches us, he tells Zonia that Neil wants her back at camp to see something urgently.

She tosses Quinn the keys for the van and weapons locker and orders me to put him through his shooting paces then leaves with Ross and Darius.

A few moments later, Nicky follows them, telling us, "I think I'm done for the day, too. And I'm on lunch duty." I'm pretty sure she's not. "See you two later." She gives me a quick wink which tells me she hasn't given up her matchmaking hopes.

Quinn and I stand in awkward silence, watching them disappear down the faint path.

"Um," I say eventually, "should we start?"

"Yeah, let's get this over with." Quinn hoists the rifle up as he's seen us do.

"You don't seem too enthusiastic," I say. "We don't have to do this, you know."

"Sure, we do. Zonia's orders an' all."

"Right. Okay. Well, first thing, you need to brace the stock against your cheek here, and move this hand to over here, and hold your finger ready like this."

His skin is hot under my fingers as I move him in minute adjustments. All at once that indefinable something, like an electric charge in the air, is back between us.

He raises the barrel too high. I move to stand right behind him and cover his hands with my own, gently easing it back down.

"And then you close one eye and look through the scope, yeah, like that." My voice sounds breathy, and I'm aware of my chest pressing into his back. "And then you just gently squeeze the trigger — with the pad of your finger, not where it bends."

I release his hands and step back.

He fires. Way wide.

"So this time, don't pull back so hard on the trigger. It's more like a caress than a pinch," I say, and when I hear the words, I feel a blush rising up my neck. It's the same phrase Sarge used back in sniper boot-camp at ASTA. Back then it sounded sensible, maybe the slightest bit amusing. But here, in this quiet place alone with Quinn, it sounds suggestive. I take another step away and to the side of him.

"And breathe. Breathe out just before you squeeze." Now my voice is high.

He fires again, misses by a mile again, rolls his eyes.

"Devil a bit," he mutters.

"Quinn?"

"Yeah?" He meets my gaze. His eyes are the deep bruised gray of a thundercloud. I forget what I was going to say.

"Well?" he asks.

"Um … That bush isn't alive. I mean, you're not going to kill anything by shooting it," I babble on. "And one day you might need to shoot, to save your life or something."

He winces. Then turns and tries a few more times before giving up.

"I can't do this. I don't know how you can."

"If you practice —" I begin, but he interrupts me.

"I don't mean the skill of it. I mean the fact of it. The intention. The coldly calculated aiming at someone and then firing a gun at them."

"Once more for the record: I. Didn't. Know. Okay? I didn't *know* I was killing people!"

"Even if that's true, you knew you were darting people. People who would be hurt."

He spins on his heel and heads back in the direction of the van. I grab the rifle bag and boxes of ammo and run after him.

"I thought they were being brought in for treatment, or questioning. I told you that." I stumble over roots and rocks and branches as I run beside the path, trying to keep pace with him. "I didn't know about the torture until you showed me it that last night!"

"Sure and it didn't stop you darting Connor. Letting him be taken in for torture."

"I've already explained that I —"

"Yeah, I've heard all your explanations, thanks, and I don't want to hear them again." He opens the van, stows the rifle and ammo in the locker, locks up and turns back to me. "It doesn't change the fact that you're a stone-cold killer. If I think about —" He cuts himself off, and his face is almost bleak as he meets my gaze. "Don't you feel any guilt?"

"I feel nothing *but* guilt! All the time. But I can't change what I did in the past. And right now, I'm more concerned about the future. Haven't you noticed that your little band of merry men and women are planning something, Quinn? Did you even see what's in that weapons cache? Here's a clue — it wasn't a damn printing press! Zonia and her red berets are getting ready for war. This is like ASTA all over again. You're prepared to trade in the getting and giving of information, but you wash your hands of the inconvenient consequences of how that information will be used."

He says nothing, merely turns and heads back in the direction of camp. I follow, cursing as I knock my shin on a protruding branch and go sprawling onto the ground. He pauses for a moment, maybe to check I'm okay, maybe because he's tempted to kick me in the head while I'm down in the dirt.

"Besides," I say, getting up, wiping my scraped hands on my jeans and following after him again, "I've watched you practicing with those knives. What's that about if not weapons training?"

"As you just said, I might need to defend my life or something."

"So knives are okay, but guns aren't?"

When he spins to face me, his face is a scary mix of rage and something else. It couldn't be … fear?

"There's a *difference!*" he yells at me. His eyes are silver now. They always go pale when he's angry. "There's a difference between defending yourself, or your … your buddy, in the heat of battle, and sitting somewhere off at a safe distance, waiting for the perfect moment to annihilate an unsuspecting person."

"I thought we were going to shoot rats?"

"Or — *or* dressing up like a little girl so you can get close enough to dart them. One is self-defense, and the other is just … *wrong.*"

"Wow, okay. Thanks for explaining. I might have missed the moral subtleties of taking preventative action versus defensive action, given that they can both be used to *save your ass!* But now I think I understand. Basically, if you or yours do it, it's justifiable self-defense and protection. If I do it, it's 'just wrong' and unforgivable."

He opens his mouth to say something, but this time *I* don't want to hear it. I'm feeling battered and bruised and drained, and the stinging in my eyes tells me I'm about to cry. So I push past him and run back towards camp, diverting to the ladies', where I hide out in a toilet stall, silently yelling at myself to stop crying and have some pride.

191

Chapter 30

Fork in the road

I'm back in the restrooms after breakfast the next morning, trying to cut the stitches out of my scalp with Robin's mini-multitool. I can't see much in the cracked and chipped mirror above the basin, so I'm doing it by sense of touch. I've already jabbed my scalp twice and I'm cursing when Nicky and Kate walk in.

Kate, who is holding a towel and a toiletry bag, ignores me completely and heads for a shower, but Nicky says, "I've been sent to find you. Zonia wants another shooting session."

"Sure. I just need to get these out, they're driving me crazy and should have been out days ago," I say, trying and failing again to wedge the edge of one of the blades under a knot.

Taking pity on me, Nicky offers to help. She moves me over to stand in a puddle of sunshine under a hole in the rusted roof, and clips the knotted stitches with gentle, steady hands. She gives the first stitch a light tug and then a firmer pull.

"Uh-oh," she says. "The skin has grown around the base of the stitches, and I don't think they're going to come out easily. It's going to hurt."

"Don't worry about it, just yank them," I say.

My relationship with pain has changed since it grabbed and

smashed and battered me senseless that night in the interrogation center. Stings and cuts and headaches hardly bother me at all now. It's like they're so tiny compared to what real pain feels like that they barely register on my pain scale.

"Some of them are bleeding a little." Nicky fetches a wad of toilet paper and presses it against my scalp. "Here."

"Thanks, Nicky."

"Anytime."

We step out into the morning sunshine, me dabbing at my head, to find Quinn and Darius waiting. Quinn's gaze flicks to my head, then away.

"Hurry up," Darius snaps. "Zonia already went ahead to set up, and she won't like to be kept waiting."

Nicky and I trail along the path to the van behind him, exchanging glances and suppressing giggles like a pair of naughty school kids following a fuming school principal, and a reluctant-looking Quinn brings up the rear.

When we get to the small clearing we used for shooting practice yesterday, Zonia has already retrieved and loaded the rifle and pinned paper targets at about chest height on several distant tree trunks. Paper targets with the silhouette of a human torso printed on them.

I stop dead and stare at the concentric circles emanating from the two bull's-eyes centered over the middle of the chest area and the forehead. My uneasy feelings from yesterday have coagulated into a heavy lump of suspicion in the pit of my stomach.

"How will practicing with these" — I point to the targets — "help us shoot moving rats, Zonia?"

"I think maybe we overestimated our abilities yesterday. After all, we're rank beginners," says Zonia, laughing lightly, but her cheerfulness seems forced. Her smile is such an unusual occurrence that it looks unnatural, and if I had a dollar for every time I'd ever heard her laugh, I'd have a dollar. "I think we ought to take a step backward and try to hit something easier, don't you? The silhouettes just give us something big and stationary to aim at."

I'm not sure I believe her. Actually, I am sure I *don't* believe her. This is more of her preparation for war. She wants me to turn her band of misfit rebels into soldiers. Or at least shooters.

"Why don't we practice with the shotgun instead? You guys will be much more likely to hit a rat with that, and it would be better at short distances, like in the camp," I suggest.

"Maybe we'll do that tomorrow, but right now, let's stick to one weapon and not confuse ourselves," Zonia says.

Which is a lame excuse, if ever I heard one.

Zonia hands the rifle to Quinn. "You can go first today so I can see if you're any good. Jinx, you can check his grip and whatnot."

Quinn takes the rifle with a sigh and moves a few steps closer to the nearest target, but I stand still, lost in my thoughts. How is it possible that I've run so hard and so far, only to wind up back where I started? Here I am again, doing something I don't want to do and don't believe in, for people I suspect of having questionable motives. I have never wanted to shoot people. Hell, I was never even enthusiastic about shooting the damn rats! And I certainly don't want to teach others how to do it.

"Come on, Jinx, we need your expert assistance."

Ah, so now I'm her *expert assistant*. Sarge called me his *angel of death*. The rebels and ASTA may consider themselves polar opposites, but they have a lot in common. Both are determined to turn me into an agent of destruction.

Zonia places a hand in the small of my back and pushes me over to where Quinn is fiddling with the safety catch.

I stand beside him, on a patch of weeds and grass located precisely halfway between the devil and the deep blue sea. I can't help, and I can't not help. If I train them to be better marksmen, then more police or government forces will be killed. If I don't, and they go in unprepared, more of the rebels might get killed.

Quinn might get killed.

Unenthusiastically, I give Quinn some pointers, telling myself that even if I refused to help, Zonia wouldn't alter her plans.

After the shooting practice, in which no one but Nicky shows any improvement, Zonia surprises me by insisting that Quinn and I accompany her back to the van.

"We're running low on supplies and have a delivery waiting for us with our comrades at the usual spot. You can drive and load," she tells Quinn, then turns to me, "and you will be our protection detail."

"With this?" I hold up the sniper's rifle.

"Take your pick," she says, throwing back the lid of the weapons locker and encouraging me to explore the contents like a kid at a candy store.

I shift aside the shotgun, the high-tech assault weapon, and at least half a dozen Glock pistols, then suppress a low whistle when I see what lies beneath. Anyone would recognize the distinctive shapes of the olive-green hand grenades, but unless I'd paid close attention in the Applied Explosives lecture in sniper training, I wouldn't know what else I was looking at: coils of detonation cord, explosive caps, and several thick blocks of an off-white substance that I know is C-4 plastic explosive.

Just what the hell are they preparing for?

I can feel Quinn's eyes on me, but when I sneak a glance at him, he's looking away.

"Well?"

"Are we expecting the threat to come from close by or far away?" I ask.

"I don't know that we *are* expecting a threat, not a specific one, anyway. I just like to be prepared. Take whichever one will be the best for most eventualities."

I pick up the semi-automatic pistol. It's about the length of a man's forearm, with a slim grip and front and rear sites. It's smaller and lighter than the sniper rifle and feels deadly cold in my hands. I grab two magazines, check they're loaded, and clip one into place. I raise my eyebrows in question at Zonia, still not convinced that she'll allow me a weapon.

"I know," she says. "But I'll be keeping an eye on you." She grabs one of the Glocks and shoves it into the back of her waistband.

"Um, Zonia? You might want to put the safety on if you don't fancy shooting off your butt."

"You're just full of all the good ideas!" She clicks the safety on and stows the weapon as before.

Once she's clicked the padlock shut, she helps Quinn drag the weapons locker out of the van and conceal it under some thick brush nearby.

Then we're off — Quinn driving, Zonia riding shotgun, and me squashed uncomfortably between them, hyperaware of Quinn's arm and leg occasionally brushing against mine. Some way down the track, the dirt road splits, and we take the left fork, which is even more rutted and overgrown. After about fifteen minutes of winding through the thick woods, the trees thin out, and then we're driving through some unfarmed fields. Zonia immediately retrieves a phone from the glove box, plugs it in to charge and starts checking messages and email. With a swift look at me, she angles the phone away from my line of vision.

I shake my head at this foolishness and instead fix my gaze on the bits of Quinn I can see. The old black-and-white sneakers working the brake and gas, the arc of his knee beneath his worn jeans, his long fingers on the wheel. There's a constellation of freckles in the shape of a wave on the back of his right hand. I risk a look at his profile. He looks pissed off, or maybe just worried. A muscle pulses in his jaw, and his eyes are squinted against the sun. He must feel my eyes on him, but he gazes steadfastly ahead. If he ignores me any harder, I'm going to start doubting my own existence.

Far away in the distance to the right of us, I can see the long, low bulk of a stationary freight train — a railway track must run parallel to this dirt road. Is there a highway beyond? I start counting the rail cars, but the train seems to go on forever, and I lose count somewhere after fifty. It ends, or begins I guess, with two locomotives up front, parked at a rail freight platform with a tilted green roof, a couple of small buildings and two parked long-haul trucks parked nearby. Then we're past the train and there's nothing much to look at again until, about ten minutes later, we pull up at a gate in a chain-link fence. The gate is open, though a rusted warning sign dangles from a pole: *Trespassers will be shot. And fed to the pigs. Not necessarily in that order.*

Chapter 31

Spilling the beans

Quinn eases the van down the rutted dirt driveway and pulls up at the back of a run-down farmhouse.

An elderly couple wait on the back porch. She's wearing an apron, and he's wearing denim overalls and a straw hat. It's like a Norman Rockwell painting — except for the high-tech, multi-sectioned stock pen nearby. It looks to be about the size of three basketball courts, and it's enclosed on all sides, including the top, with a fence of the finest wire mesh. I know that the fence will reach a meter underground, too — it's the only way to guarantee keeping the rats out — and a thigh-high, five-wire electric fence circles the outside of the enclosure like a modern-day moat. A bunch of enormous pigs mill and root about inside the sty.

As soon as I get out of the van, the stench hits me. I gag and swallow, and a ball of nausea clogs my throat, threatening to escape if I as much as open my mouth. I keep my lips pinched together, but that means I have to breathe through my nose. The pair on the porch chuckle at me knowingly.

"City girl, eh?"

I nod, swallowing hard.

"It's just some fine-smelling hogs. Y'all get used to it in a few minutes. Come on in, comrades," says the man, who has fished a red beret out of a pocket and stuck it at a jaunty angle on his head. Zonia salutes him as she heads for the house, but as I make to follow, she stops me.

"No, you can't be in on this. You'll need to wait outside."

She makes me lock the semi-automatic in the van. When I protest that I can't protect them without a weapon, she merely orders, "If you see anyone coming, yell. Loudly. And stay in sight," then follows Quinn inside.

It's just me and the livestock and endless miles of nothing here in the back of nowhere. The hogs are massive, with mottled black and brown and pink skin covered in short, spiky hair. And they're noisy — grunting and squealing as they shove each other aside at the feeding trough or writhe ecstatically in wide, wet puddles of mud. One sow with four piglets chasing her teats wanders over to sniff at me where I stand near the fence, then gives a dismissive snort and trots over to smell the butt of a one-eared boar housed in an adjacent pen.

I've never seen pigs in the flesh before, and it's kind of interesting, but I'd trade this experience for just twenty minutes on the internet, hanging out on BackChat with Robin and my friends from back home, catching up on the world out there.

I glance at the fence. It reminds me of the night at ASTA when Quinn escaped, when I was detained and taken to the detention center. The night when the world turned on its axis and became a different place for me. Before I know it, my fingers are scratching at my arms again, and I am staring at the mud, seeing Mr. Smith's face, my body rigid with the memory of blazing, white-hot pain.

I startle back to the present when a particularly noisy hog drops a splattery stench of poop just a few feet away from me. Right now I am here, not there. I am safe. No one is hurting me. I decide to patrol around the farmhouse.

I notice that the outside of the house is studded at regular intervals with small, diamond-shaped security laser transmitters. All the red eyes are glowing. The whole area surrounding the house must be covered with a lattice of crisscrossed laser beams. Did an alarm sound in the house when we passed through the beams?

Around the front of the house, an old, blue Ford pickup sits rusting in the sun. I'm afraid it will trigger flashbacks of that other pickup, so I force my eyes to look beyond. The freight train is on the move again, like a brown Lego-chain low against the wide blue sky. It's traveling — I check the position of the sun in the sky, note the time on my wristwatch — southwest. But southwest of where? If I were traveling on that train, would I be heading back to the Metropole, closer to Robin and Mom, or would I be heading away?

"Jinx?"

Quinn is calling.

"Coming."

He's on the back porch, standing beside piles of stacked boxes and bags. I'm relieved to see some of them contain fresh fruit and vegetables.

"Help me load these up?"

"Sure."

He opens the van and I retrieve the semi-automatic, do a quick 360° scan of the area, then rest it against the side of the van. Quinn looks at it with an expression of strong repulsion, which irks me. I wish he'd just build a bridge and get over it already.

"Is Zonia still inside?" I ask, grabbing two mesh bags of potatoes and lugging them over to the van.

"Yeah, she has some comms to send and receive, and she needs to get the latest orders from High Command."

"What's that? Like a headquarters?"

"Yeah."

I help him lift and carry a few long, flat and surprisingly heavy boxes over to the van. He hops up to shove them across the floor to right behind the seats up front, and I choose this moment when we're out of Zonia's sight to ask the question that's been plaguing me all morning.

"Quinn?"

"Yeah?"

"I'd like to ask you something, and I'd like you to tell me the truth. Please." My hands have found the scabs on my arms and are picking again. "Am I training you guys to shoot rats or to shoot people?"

His shoulders tense, and a muscle pulses in his jaw.

"Does it even matter to you?" he says.

At that, something inside me snaps. I am so sick and tired of being needled and judged and loathed. I can't take it, not for one more moment.

"Of course not," I say. "Rats, people, children — what's the difference for a stone-cold killer like me? I don't care either way, not so?"

"Look, I never said —" he begins, but I hold up a hand to forestall him.

"No, no, you're right. Again." I turn to fetch another box.

"About what?"

"About this. About anything. Everything!" I fling the box inside the van to where Quinn crouches. "You're right and I'm wrong. You're good and innocent and noble, and I'm bad and evil and a bloodthirsty murderer. And I've always been this way. I played The Game just so I could learn how to shoot. So I could leave home, see the world, meet people, and *kill* them! I love killing animals too, but hey, it's the murder of humans that really excites and satisfies me."

I march between the patio and the van, snatching up boxes and hurling them inside, ignoring Quinn when he leaps out and tries to help me with the heavier packages.

"Of course I knew what we were really doing all along, and so did everyone in my unit. Man, I loved sending bullets into sick people, especially that time with the little kid. Wow, I wish I had a trophy to remember that kill!"

"Jinx, I didn't mean —"

I don't let him speak. I *won't* let him explain. I'm beyond angry — I'm incandescent with rage. Everything that I've been pushing down and holding back now surges up and out of me like a molten lava flow of sarcastic rage.

"And darting suspected terrs and dissidents, knowing they would be tortured? Man, it doesn't get better than that. I always wanted to take down Connor. I knew him so well for so long that it was personal, you know? I couldn't wait for him to get his. I volunteered for that mission — because, you know, we were always free to do what we wanted — and what I wanted to do was to dart him. And then you. You both pissed me off. I liked you better once you were tranquilized and … *and* I could get brownie points with my commander for the takedown. I'm only sorry I couldn't get you *both* detained."

I fling a bag onto the floor of the van, and it bursts, sending pinto beans rolling into every corner. I notice my thumb is bleeding — I must have ripped it on a staple or something — but there's no stopping me now.

"Jinxy!"

"I only helped you escape so I could — what was it again? — oh, yeah, so they could follow you right back to your hot little base of innocent rebels here. Only somehow *I* couldn't because I got hit. No wait, you don't need to say it — I know what you're thinking, and you're right — I hit *myself* in the head with a rifle butt and got myself taken to the detention center. Where I tortured myself."

"Tortured?"

"Yes, Quinn, tortured. Oh, did you think they saved the special treatment for your brother alone?"

He's staring at me, gray eyes wide with shock.

"No, rest assured I got my fair share. But I guess I didn't tell them anything because it just turns me on to be hurt and I wanted it to go on and on and on all night!"

I slump in the open doorway of the van. My throat is tight, and my traitor eyes are burning again.

"You … you didn't tell them anything?" Quinn says.

"*No, I didn't!* Not about you or the rebels or their plans, or what you know about the plague. Not even about the note-passing with your little sister."

Quinn blanches at the mention of Kerry. Good. Let him chew on the thought of the damage I could have done.

"Or wait, I don't know — did I? I don't know anymore. I mean, I know what I *think* I did, who I think I am, what *I* think I believe, but clearly you know me better than I do myself, so tell me — did I just spill it all at the first blow? Or the second burn? Or the twentieth shock?"

He's looking stunned and appalled. Maybe even ashamed. He swallows hard and rubs a hand roughly over the back of his neck, but all he says is, "It doesn't matter anyway. We assumed that either you were cooperating with them or that you'd crack, but that either way you'd tell them what they wanted to know. So we scuppered all those plans for Independence Day and such."

"Well, that's just dandy. How awesome to know that I went through all of that for absolutely bloody nothing."

Tears are streaming down my face now. I can't stand how weak they make me feel. I need my anger back.

"But hey, I guess I deserved it anyway, right? All that murder of innocents on my hands, not to mention the precious effing rats."
I force myself up and push past Quinn, who has his hands out,

like he wants to catch me, and continue my rant. "And I guess the reason I went back to ASTA was because I just plain missed the killing. You can take the girl out of the kill zone, but you can't take the kill zone out of the girl, right? And then there's my grand evil scheme to lead them here, or spy on your plans and shoot you all in your sleep, or whatever the hell it is I'm supposed to be doing here. You're right, Quinn. You're right about *everything*."

Another box, another trip to the van.

"I am not just a sixteen-year-old girl who misses her mom and her brother. Who misses *you*. Who is just confused, and scared and lonelier than I have ever been in my life." My voice is a rough croak now. "No, what I am is bad. Through and through. I'm evil and guilty and a stone-cold killer. You're right, I agree. I confess. But would you please just *give me a break* from this. Okay? Please? You win. I am whatever you say, anything you say. I won't argue with you again or defend myself again. But I can't take any more ..."

My last words are a choked whisper. "Please. Just. Stop."

Chapter 32

The journey back

I ride back to camp in the back of the van, telling Zonia this is so that I can hold the supplies in place. She gives me a shrewd glance and doesn't argue. I know my face must be red and puffy — I am not a pretty crier. Quinn, who gave me a long, searching look and a slow nod after my outburst, says nothing.

Back at the camp, Nicky immediately notices I'm upset and draws me away from the others, shooting a scowl over her shoulder at Quinn.

"What happened?" she asks, patting my shoulder.

"Quinn gave me another go, and I just lost it."

"Sorry, Jinxy. I know everyone's been really hard on you."

"I understand where they're coming from, I do. It's just relentless, you know? I'm so tired. And I'm homesick. I miss my mother's food. I miss my comfy bed and my computer. I just want to snuggle into a pile of warm laundry and eat fresh bread."

Nicky laughs. "I know what you mean."

"And mostly I miss my brother. Right now I miss him so bad."

Robin would be able to shake me out of this funk. Robin would know my motives without me trying to justify myself. Robin would pour me a huge glass of sweet tea and give me a hug. Man, but I need a hug. I wrap my arms around myself and hold on tight.

"Tell me about him," Nicky says.

"Robin? He's my twin, and we're really close even though we're quite different. He's funny and really smart, and deep — he writes poems about life and death and stuff. I worry about him. He's gotten into hacking, and he doesn't realize how dangerous it could be for him. He's way intelligent, but not always that smart, you know?"

"He sounds awesome."

"He is, and did I mention that he's better-looking than I am?"

"In that case, we should definitely snatch him and bring him here. Definitely."

I give her a weak smile.

"Just because he could maybe help Neil. No other reason." She grins.

If I had the power to bring Robin here, would I do it? I'd love to see him again, love to have someone on my side who knows and trusts me. But what would happen to Mom if she was all alone? I have a vision of her as she was after Dad's death, quiet and blank-faced and kind of crumpled in on herself, not eating unless I made her, not smiling or coping for months and months. And Robin would not be safe here, none of us are. If I brought him here and something happened to him, it would finish me off.

"Nah, he's safer where he is. At least, I hope he is. You're just going to have to fish in this pool."

Nicky stares unenthusiastically at the males in the camp. "Maybe there's a bear out there I could cuddle up to."

"Hooking up with our animal brethren? Neil would approve."

Nicky chuckles and goes to light the fire as the camp readies for the night. Mark and Evyan are on cooking duty, and Kate and Ross are up the mountain on night surveillance, even though Hawke has left the retreat. Kirsty is guarding the camp, and I'm on duty later tonight. Zonia has drawn up a roster for guard duty but still refuses to arm the person standing guard, so unless rats and government forces are repelled by yells, I figure it's useless — worse than useless, because it lulls the rebels into a false sense of security.

I'm determined to ignore jerk-face Quinn, who is brooding and practicing hurling knives at trees again, and looking brutally handsome, but my eyes have a mind of their own. Twice, when my gaze strays to him, I find him staring at me, but he's too far away for me to read his expression.

Dinner that night includes fresh salad and sweet rosy-fleshed peaches for dessert, and afterwards everyone's in a good mood. Candace and Bree go wash the dishes, Darius sits beside Zonia, his arm around her shoulders, and Nicky sings a song about home in a soft, sweet voice as the fire burns down to embers. I mull over what I'm hoping to accomplish here.

When it's my turn to stand guard duty, I pace around the camp, trying not to make a noise. I shine my flashlight into the woods, scanning high for humans and low for critters. I catch a glimpse of movement, and my heart jumps in the instant before I realize it's Quinn walking down the path to the van. With a sigh, I resume my patrol.

What is Robin doing right at this moment? And Bruce and Cameron? And the folk at ASTA — what are they up to right now?

When, at four am, I finally crawl into my tent, my bed feels more comfortable than usual. I lift a corner of my sleeping bag and feel underneath. Someone has been into my tent and placed a thin rubber camping mattress under my sleeping bag.

Breakfast the next day is remarkable — not only because there is fresh milk and yoghurt and real eggs, but because Quinn, who's serving, gives me a smile and says, "Hi."

My jaw drops, and I stare back dumbly, even though it's not his sexy smile. Quinn has several smiles — happy, charming, bittersweet, dazzling — but it's the sexy one that normally presses fast-forward on my heart and pause on my brain. The smile he gives me over the eggs is … gentle.

"Hi," I say, fixed in place. As he hands me my plate, our fingers touch, and a zing of something tingly shocks up my arm.

"Just move," says Evyan beside me, with an elbow to my ribs. "You're in the way and holding up the line."

"Give her a break," says Quinn, and I stand dazed, not realizing that my grip has loosened on my plate. It tilts, and the eggs slide off into the dirt, splattering ochre yolk in the dirt.

"Here, I got it." It's Quinn, scooping up the mess with a spatula and dumping it in the trash can.

Confused, I walk over to my usual perch on one of the logs and tuck into what's left of my breakfast. Five minutes later, Quinn comes over and hands me a fresh plate of eggs.

"Um, thanks."

"Sure."

I'm taken aback by this change in attitude. There's a pathetic part of me that just wants to cry at the kindness, a bewildered part that wants to ask him what's going on in his head (and his heart), and a wary part that wants to order him to keep his distance from me so I don't get hurt again.

For the next two days, I get more of the same surprising treatment from Quinn. He sends no snide comments my way, and when someone else does (there is no shortage of people to give me a go), he tells them to cut it out. I'm grateful to have a break from the nastiness, but I am not ready to trust him yet. Strangely, now that he's being nice to me, I have an urge to punish him, but he doesn't react to the barbed remarks I direct at him, and merely grins when I dish up the smallest possible portions of food on his plate at mealtimes. It's unsettling.

When he offers to do my dishwashing duty for me one afternoon, I'm so amazed that I keep one eye trained on the forest, half-expecting to catch a glimpse of Sasquatch.

"See," says Nicky, who winks at me every time she notices one of these new thoughtful gestures, "he's coming around."

And despite our history, despite the daunting odds against us, I dare to hope.

Chapter 33

Into the fire

Maybe Nicky's right, maybe I did get to Quinn. Maybe he's coming to his senses. Evyan certainly isn't. I think Quinn's new attitude to me both unnerves and incenses her, and she ups the ante on sheer nastiness when he's not around.

When next we three have a surveillance shift up the mountain, and Evyan is behind the binocs under the hide, Quinn and I stretch out on our backs beside each other in the long grass. Our arms are almost, but not quite, touching. When I turn my head, I can see his square jaw, and straight nose, and my fingers itch to brush his mahogany hair back from his ears. I rest one arm across my chest so that my hand lies over the earring underneath and close my eyes against the sun.

We chat casually about the foods and T.V. shows we most miss. Our words feel tentative and carefully chosen not to spark another fight and, hey, it's no deep discussion about our hopes and fears, let alone our feelings about each other, but it's a fun way to pass the time. And it's such a relief to have a laugh and forget about the painful past and uncertain future — even if only for a short while.

"What would you most like to be eating right now?" I ask.

He mulls it over for a few moments, then says firmly, "Cookies."

"What kind?"

"My mother has this ancient recipe for Christmas cookies. She makes them with almonds and orange zest and a good slug of usquebaugh."

"Uskwee-who?"

"Usquebaugh. The water of life." At my puzzled look, he explains, "That's whisky to you."

"Your mother puts whiskey in your cookies?" I'm impressed.

"Sure. And it's delicious beyond the telling of it. When we were kids, Connor and I would stay out late playing on the street with our football or racing our go-kart, and the only way our mother could get us to come in was to bribe us with a cookie each." He turns his face so that he's looking at me, and there's an intensity in his gaze when he speaks again. "But one piece was never enough, you know? It just gave you the taste of it, and you craved more of that sweet, melting softness in your mouth."

The words are innocent enough, but the way he says them, the way he stares at my lips as he says them, steals away my breath. Then he rolls his head back to face the sky and he's talking normally again, and I'm left wondering if I imagined the moment.

"So we came up with a scheme. I'd climb onto Connor's shoulders — I was taller than him already, but he was stronger — and then we'd stagger around the kitchen like a drunk at closing time, so I could reach the cookie tin on top of the cupboard and nick a few. But Mum must have noticed, and she made a special batch for us, because next time we stole some, they tasted of salt and baking soda."

He laughs. I could listen to that deep, rolling laugh all day, watch how it shakes his shoulders and contracts the muscles of his stomach into ridges under the fabric of his shirt. He doesn't laugh enough. I can feel my inner icicle of resentment at him thawing in the warmth of that laugh.

"So we quit our thieving ways, and soon we were getting our Christmas cookies again."

"You mother sounds like a woman to be reckoned with."

"She is that." He sighs. "Sure and I miss those cookies."

And he misses his family. I can see his affection for them in his smile.

"You know what you haven't said you miss? Colcannon crabbins," I say, remembering how he tricked me into eating a bunch of disgusting stuff when I first arrived at ASTA, by assuring me that they were Irish delicacies.

"Colcannon crubeens," he corrects. "Nah, I never liked Brussels sprouts, disgusting little things."

"I knew it!"

I laugh and kick him gently, and when I leave my leg lying there, just lightly leaning against his, he doesn't pull away. His foot gives mine a little nudge, and I press back. Maybe our feet are doing what the rest of our bodies can't. Yet.

After a lot of talk about sweet tea and cold milk straight from the icebox, and beers in chilled longnecks and the relative merits of Coke versus Pepsi, Quinn announces, "I need to go see a man about a dog," and strolls off into the trees.

Evyan wastes no time in getting her claws out.

"I can see you've said something to Quinn to make him think better of you, but I don't advise you get too used to it. It won't last," Evyan says.

"Oh, yeah?"

I don't meet her gaze. I don't want to see the dislike there. Instead I focus on a cloud of gnats swarming above me, reflecting the sun in sparkling points of light.

"He doesn't really want you here. No one does. You're just an added worry and danger to us all."

"How do you figure that?"

I think that I've helped make this camp safer since I arrived.

"Just by being here," she snaps. "From what I know of the anti-dissident units in the government, and from what I hear of ASTA, they aren't just going to take your running away lying down. They'll be searching for you, mobilizing all their surveillance systems, checking everywhere and everyone. As long as you're still missing, they'll be looking. And that means we all risk being found."

Her expression is so spiteful that I reckon she'd turn me in herself if she could think of a way to do it without jeopardizing the others.

"You all risk being found anyway. It goes with the rebel territory," I say dismissively, but in reality, I'm rattled by her words.

I was careful to lose my ASTA spook before I made contact with the rebels, but since I got here, I haven't thought much about how they would react to my going AWOL. And Evyan's right, they won't take it lying down. Sarge will be mighty pissed, and Roth will be both embarrassed and furious. She won't rest until I'm captured and made an example of. They'll be hunting me, day and night, and of course that raises the risk of discovery for the rebels. Damn. Can I do nothing right, nothing helpful?

But when Quinn emerges from the trees, his hesitant smile is so heart-meltingly sweet that I push aside the hard questions and the sharp fear. He walks beside me back down the slope and lends me a steadying hand when I clamber down one of the steeper drops.

My hope rises still more the next day when, after shooting practice, Quinn walks back to camp with me, leaving Zonia, Nicky and Darius to lock away the weapons.

My shoulder bumps his arm, and our hands brush as we walk side by side along the narrow path. Somehow, somewhere between the oaks and the pines, our fingers lace together. Loosely at first, then tighter. My heart lifts. It feels both full and weightless — a balloon filled with golden happiness, floating on air. With a squeeze of his hand, Quinn draws me off the path and behind the massive trunk of an ancient tree. Without a word, he places his hands on my shoulders and slowly, gently, he pushes me back against the rough bark, and presses the length of his body against mine.

His lips dip downwards to mine, hesitantly, uncertainly, as if he's expecting me to push him away and start yelling. But I want this. My hands tangle in his shirt and his hair, dragging him closer, pulling his face down. His lips are warm and firm as they part over mine. We kiss deeply, urgently, clutching each other as if we might sink into the unsteady earth if we didn't. He tugs my bottom lip into his mouth and sucks on it gently. I'm on fire. The heat that always simmers between us flames into a blaze which draws the breath out of me. I'm burning up, searing into life.

I know there are still things between us, things we need to talk out and understand, but right now our bodies are in harmony, and the discussions can wait until later.

My nerves sing with a sensual awareness of Quinn — the heat of his mouth, the graze of his stubble, the boy-smell of his skin, the strength in the span of his hands around my back, my hips, my butt. He kisses my cheeks, then his lips move down my neck to the hollow of my throat. My head goes dizzy, and my knees melt. I shiver when, with a groan from somewhere deep inside him, he moves his hands up my sides to the curves of my breasts.

"Ah, sweet mercy mine, Jinxy, but you're beautiful. I want you, all of you."

"Quinn, please …" I beg.

My body is swelling, softening, molding into the growing hardness of him. My hands move under his shirt and run over the firm planes of his back. I mew with relief when his mouth slants across my own again. I'm mindless — empty of anything but a pulsing, aching need in the pit of my belly. I want more. I want every part of me to touch every part of him. I start sliding down the trunk. Quinn moves with me, never breaking contact. Our mouths and hands and bodies are locked together.

I can't breathe, but I don't need to. I only need Quinn.

Loud yells from somewhere behind us prize our lips apart.

We're both panting, too short of breath to speak. But we're grinning widely. The universe has clicked back into place, and the two of us are going to be okay. Better than okay — we're going to be together.

Another yell. "They're coming," Quinn says.

"Let's run!"

Laughing, we grab hands and hurtle through the woods, slowing down to a sedate walk a little way out of camp to straighten our clothes, smooth our hair and catch our breath. I'm sitting innocently beside Quinn on a fireside log, still smiling and dying to give Nicky a wink when she, Darius and Zonia walk into camp.

My smile flat-lines, and my eyes widen. Something is terribly wrong.

Chapter 34

Ratter

Zonia and Darius have their arms around Nicky and are helping her limp along. Her face is as pale as ash, and pinched with pain and fear. The left leg of her jeans is rolled up to her calf, and there's blood running down from a small wound above her ankle.

"What happened?" I ask, running up to them.

"Oh, Jinxy," Nicky says in a high, tight voice. "I got bitten. By a rat."

Oh my God.

There are groans and exclamations and curses from the rebels behind me as the news spreads.

I run ahead and grab the bedding from my tent, fold the thin blue mattress into a makeshift seat against a log and ease Nicky down, covering her with my sleeping bag.

Candace is at my side with the first aid kit, handing me disinfectant. Kate hugs Nicky tightly, and Quinn braces her leg to keep it still while I pour disinfectant over the wound. Nicky whimpers in pain when I dab at it with alcohol pads. The bite looks horrible — two ragged lines of perforations — and it's bleeding more heavily than I would have expected. I take the tube of salve Candace hands me. The print on the side says it's antibiotic, antiviral, and anesthetic. I smear a glob onto a large gauze pad, apply it to the wound and wrap a stretch bandage tightly around it to hold it in place.

"Do you think we should make a tourniquet?" Candace asks me, as if I know anything about treating rat bites.

I look around, but nobody else seems to know either, so I shrug and unfasten my belt, loop it around Nicky's calf, and pull it tight.

"It can't hurt," I say.

"Will it help?" Nicky asks, staring down at her leg where the flesh below the tourniquet is growing pale.

Zonia says, in her usual no-nonsense way, "Of course it will. It stops the spread of venom in snakebites, doesn't it?"

Does it? Or is that an urban legend?

"So I don't see why it shouldn't stop the spread of an infection."

If I'm honest, I don't think it will help. Disinfecting and dressing the wound, putting on a tourniquet — these give us something to do, but I don't recall ever hearing any advice on any PSA or medical program which suggested that treating a bite could prevent infection from taking hold. Last I heard, even immediate intravenous antivirals have not been effective. Still, I rummage in the kit, find a pack of antiviral capsules and get Nicky to swallow a double dose.

"Besides, we don't even know whether that rat was a carrier," chips in Neil.

"Was it a mutant rat?" I ask.

Nicky nods, eyes brimming with tears, and pinches her lips tight shut.

I exchange a glance with Quinn. I can tell he's thinking the same as me.

"They aren't all necessarily carriers, you know," Neil continues. "The alternate breeds weren't engineered to be sterile, and the born-frees might not have it."

"The *what*?" I have no patience for Neil right now.

"The born-frees, the ones who weren't bred in a lab but who reproduced naturally out here in Mother Nature. They'll be healthy."

"It's a *virus*, you idiot! It spreads," Quinn snaps, his accent stronger in his anger. "Even if it isn't airborne, d'ya think the mutants haven't been out here swapping spit over their food, biting each other and reproducing? If you can't say or do anything useful, then just bugger off. Go stand guard — and beg your bleeding rats to kindly stay away!"

Neil stalks off in a huff, and Candace and Kate fuss about Nicky, tucking her in, bringing her a cold drink, and reassuring her that things are going to be okay, that she must remember the virus isn't as infectious as the government says, that we probably got to it in time.

Zonia moves to a spot beyond the logs, summoning Darius and Quinn over for a confab. I clean the traces of blood off my hands with a disinfectant wipe and pack away the medical supplies, freezing as I see what lies next to the tube of ointment I have just replaced — a sealed pack of "Second Skin protective hand wear". Shit. I was in such a rush to help Nicky that I didn't stop to think. Too late, I realize that I definitely should have worn latex gloves while I treated the wound. I try to remember if I may have touched my eyes or mouth in the last few minutes. I turn my hands in the air in front of me and examine the scabbed line on my thumb from where I cut it packing the van yesterday. Could the virus have gotten into me, too?

Anger builds inside me as I stare from my thumb to Nicky's panicked face. This is a disaster, and what makes me even madder is that it needn't have happened. None of us should ever have been out in the woods without being super-vigilant and prepared to defend ourselves against rats.

"Zonia!" I yell as I stride over to her. "I need the keys for the van and the weapons locker."

"What for?" asks Darius, belligerent as ever.

"I am going to get the damned rifle, go hunting and kill any rat I find. Do you have a problem with that?" I demand, then spin around to face the others. "Does *anyone* have a problem with that? *Now?*"

Apparently not. Zonia hands over the keys, after first removing the ignition key, and only Quinn volunteers to accompany me.

"Thank you, but no. I'll be safer on my own, if I don't have to watch out for someone else as well."

As I stride out of the camp, I hear Mark tell Evyan, "One hundred dollars says that's the last we ever see of her," and Evyan's reply, "One hundred dollars would be cheap at the price."

Three hours later, I've found and killed two mutant rats. I can't be sure that either of them is the one that bit Nicky — there could be entire colonies living and breeding out here — but it makes me feel better. For the first time ever, I actually enjoy the act of killing. I take real pleasure in locking my sights on the twitching targets and blowing their heads off. Bruce, I think wryly, would be so proud of me.

There's a new rule around camp. Whoever stands guard now does so armed with a weapon, though I don't think any of them except me could hit a reindeer, let alone a rat.

For the first two days, Nicky seems fine. She stays in camp, doesn't eat much and stays away from food preparation, but otherwise, she acts as though nothing major has happened, except that she now sleeps alone — Evyan has moved in with Zonia — and wears a half-face respirator. I watch amazed as, one by one, the others also start wearing masks. So much for the rebels' firm belief that the virus isn't transmitted via the air or contaminated surfaces.

When Quinn hands me a mask and insists I put it on, I can't resist saying, "What — we'll say there ain't no heaven but we'll pray there ain't no hell?"

"It's just to be safe," he says, shrugging and giving me a quick mask-to-mask kiss, like he did in our early days at ASTA.

Nicky smiles and winks at me, delighted that Quinn and I are together. I smile back at her, hoping with every fiber of my being that she has indeed dodged the plague bullet.

Chapter 35

Entreaty

But when Nicky wakes up on the morning of the third day after being bitten, it's clear that she is very sick.

"My head is splitting," she says, pressing her palms hard against her temples, and cueing a memory of the M&M in the one red shoe who did the same. "And I ache all over."

My heart plummets, a lead weight sinking through dark waters.

She looks reluctantly at the glass of water and Tylenol tablets that Candace hands her. "My throat is so sore, I can hardly swallow. And I don't want the water."

I pass a pair of gloves to Candace and nod when she raises her eyebrows at me, then pull a pair onto my own hands.

"C'mon," urges Candace, "you'll feel better once the pain meds kick in." She tucks a thick blanket around Nicky who, despite the heat of the day, is shivering with the chills. "You've probably just got a bad dose of flu."

Yeah, rat flu. I'm certain of it. Nicky's symptoms are an absolute match for the progression of Mononegavirales Zoonotic Viral Hemorrhagic fever, the terrorist-engineered, genetically blended strains of Ebola, Bolivian hemorrhagic fever, rabies and God knows what else.

After I discovered the horrific truth of how my father died, I read up all about the plague, so I know that if Nicky has contracted the plague, she'll be dead in under two weeks.

Nicky forces the tablets down, but then chokes and starts coughing into a fistful of Kleenex. Candace pats her back gently until the fit subsides and Nicky slumps back against her pillows, gasping for breath. I hold out a plastic bag, and when she drops the tissues into it, flecks of red are clearly visible against the white.

I take it to show Zonia. "Nicky has the plague."

"You can't be sure."

"I am. Within days she'll start hemorrhaging blood out of her nose, eyes, mouth — everywhere. She'll be a lethal viral bomb. We need to decide what must be done."

"If you're right, there is nothing to be done," says Darius.

"At the very least, we need to move her away from the main camp. I thought maybe in that little reception office? And we need to get strong meds to make her more comfortable. Do you have anything serious, or can you get any?"

Zonia nods. "I can source some. We can isolate her in that office, but I'm not sure you should be the one nursing her. Let someone else do it. You're too val —"

I interrupt her, not wanting to hear more of my faults. "Candace and I have been taking care of her so far. I think we should continue. There's no need for anyone else to come into contact with her."

Quinn looks ready to protest, but Zonia says, "Alright, then. Do what you need to do."

Within an hour, Candace and I have struck my tent and re-erected it near the small log cabin which once served as camp reception. We sweep the abandoned office with a leafy branch torn off a nearby tree, and dust it as best we can. We move Nicky's bedding there, hang the plastic groundsheet from my tent over the doorway, then half-support, half-carry Nicky to her new bed and try to make her as comfortable as we can.

In the afternoon, Quinn calls from outside, and we find he has left supplies for us against the base of a tree a little way from the office — soft food, water, protective wear, a package of medication vials together with a dozen disposable syringes and, surprisingly, one of the Glocks with two full magazines of ammunition.

"Let's make this the drop-off spot. Let me know if you need anything else," he says. "And wear your respirator."

"Okay, okay. Just you stay well back," I reply.

"I don't like this, Jinxy. It's too dangerous for you."

"I'll be as careful as I can," I reassure him.

"I'll stay with you."

"No! There's nothing you can do. Now go."

He hesitates, backs up a few steps, and then walks reluctantly off, his shoulders tense and his hands thrust deep into his jeans pockets.

Candace reads the medication insert and gives Nicky a shot of the pain killer. When Nicky sighs and slips into a restless, twitchy sleep, I pull back the blanket and lift her T-shirt to inspect her chest. For a long moment, Candace and I stare at the sprinkle of fine red spots that extends across her torso, then we tuck her in again and go outside to sit up against the outside wall of the office.

"Will we get it?" Candace asks.

"I don't think so." I pick at a loose thread on the knee of my jeans. "But I guess we'll know soon enough."

For the next few days, Candace and I take turns nursing Nicky and resting in the tent. We do our best to maintain the quarantine and infection-control practices — pulling disposable PPE suits on over our shorts and T's, switching to full-face respirators, wearing double pairs of gloves whenever we're with Nicky, setting up our own biohazard disposal bin and practically bathing in disinfectant. We use the male restroom, and everyone else now uses the females'. We keep our own dishes and collect food from where Quinn leaves it at the drop-off spot.

When I again refuse to allow Quinn to join us, he sources a hammock from somewhere and hangs it between two trees just behind the drop-off spot. He spends his days there, watching us, throwing knives, talking to me when I come to collect supplies. It's a comfort to have him nearby — it's like he's keeping vigil with us.

"I think you should fix the door of the office," he says when we collect the next set of supplies, which includes a screwdriver, a hammer and some screws.

I nod. It's probably a good idea, because Nicky is growing increasingly agitated — seeing things that aren't there, and sometimes resisting our attempts to help her, especially when we try to get her to drink water. Twice she's wandered out of the office. Soon we'll need to start locking her inside. Like a prisoner. Or an animal.

"No more pain meds?" I ask Quinn when next I see him. "We're running low."

"Sorry, we'll keep trying."

"Okay."

"Hey Jinxy," he calls, when I turn to head back to the office.

"Yeah?"

"I miss you."

"Yeah, I miss you, too."

Nicky gets worse by the hour. She has regular nosebleeds and fits of violent shaking. Pinpricks of red speckle her eyes, her fever spikes despite the medication, and she has crippling bouts of diarrhea on the toilet off the small office. She coughs up black blood, and cries from the pain when the meds wear off. The rash spreads from her chest and back to her arms and legs, and darkens to purple blotches.

"I feel like I'm suffocating," she says, drawing a deep breath which bubbles wetly in her throat.

I don't know what to say, so I wipe her burning forehead with a cool cloth.

"I don't have the flu, do I?" she asks me, poking at one of the bruise-like marks from which a pink fluid seeps.

"No, Nicky, you don't." I won't lie to her. "I am so, so sorry."

She sighs. "How long do I have?" Her voice is weak and thready. Resigned.

"Maybe a week." Maybe less. Grief chokes my voice, tightens my chest and burns at the back of my eyes.

"Okay." Suddenly she grabs my gloved hand and squeezes hard. "Promise me, Jinxy," she says, her eyes burning with fever and fear, "promise me that when it gets too bad, when I … you know, lose it, that you'll take care of me."

"I'll take care of you right to the end," I reassure her, pushing sweat-soaked strands of hair back off her face with my free hand.

"You know what I mean!" she says fiercely, and I understand what she's trying to say.

"No, Nicky." No-no-no-no-no. "You can't ask me to do that." It's unthinkable.

"It has to be you — you're the only one who knows how to use a gun." Her tight smile is a grimace of bleeding gums and red teeth. "Any of the others would probably shoot me in the foot."

"No! I won't kill you." I've damned my soul enough.

"You've done it before. For others. For *strangers*," she wheezes.

"That was different."

"How?"

"I didn't know what I was doing!"

"Don't you think it's even more important now you do? Please, Jinx, do it for me. You know what's coming. Spare me that."

I do know what's coming. I watched video footage of my father disintegrating into a demented, pulpy, suffering mass. I've seen M&Ms with their skin bubbling over their dissolving tissue, pulling out their hair and tearing at their flesh. And I *have* killed them. But never have I taken the responsibility of making the decision to end someone's life, even if only to put them out of their suffering.

I don't know what to do. I don't know what's right or wrong anymore. *Nothing's* right, nothing's clear. So what is less wrong? What is more kind?

"Please, Jinxy," Nicky begs, her grip slackening as if she has exhausted her strength. "Promise me."

And, God help me, I do.

Chapter 36

Tears of blood

That night, Nicky has her first convulsion. Her eyes roll back into her head, and her body goes rigid. When the thrashing of her arms and legs eventually subsides, her fingers continue to twitch, and spasms ripple across her face. She comes around several minutes later, asking, "Is he here? Is *he* here?"

"Who, Nicky?"

"I don't want him here. But he'll come, if he knows," she whimpers. "Please, keep him away, don't let him come. Don't let him!"

"We won't," I reassure her. "We'll keep him away."

Nicky coughs, and Candace and I move her onto her side just in time. A gout of black vomit streams out of her. It smells putrid, and contains thick, dark chunks of what might be blood clots. It takes an hour to clean it up and dispose of the cleaning materials.

"It's only going to get worse," Candace whispers. "What are we going to do?"

That question again.

"I don't like the green. It's wet. And it's so big!" Nicky yells suddenly, her crimson eyes bulging. "Get it off me, get it off!"

She scratches at her pulpy face, drawing blood, and yanks out hair from the disintegrating skin of her scalp. She growls and snaps her teeth at Candace and me when we bind her arms to her sides with a stretch bandage to stop her doing more damage. That night, for the first time, we lock her in the room.

The next morning, when I open the door to check on Nicky, she springs out of a coiled crouch in the far corner, slams her shoulder into me and sends me stumbling backwards. In an instant, she's on me, her hands locked around my throat and squeezing hard. Before I can think, my arms have swung up and out and broken her hold, then knocked her down onto her stomach. Thank God for Charlie's lessons in how to interrupt an attack, and disable an opponent.

"Help!" I yell, sitting on Nicky's back to hold her down while she thrashes and scrabbles on the ground.

Candace comes running.

"She must have chewed through the bandage," says Candace, pointing to a small pile of bloodstained dressings lying in the corner.

"Let go let go let go let go *let go!*" Nicky screams beneath me.

Candace and I restrain her as best we can with the supplies we have and lock her in the room. Nicky howls wordlessly and ceaselessly from inside. The wails echo off the trees like the cries of a trapped wolf, raising goosebumps on the skin of my arms.

"What do you think?" Candace asks.

I sigh. I am not going to be allowed to duck out of my promise.

"I think it's time," I say.

I go early to the drop-off spot and twist a piece of long grass into knots while I wait for Quinn, but this morning it's Evyan who brings the supplies. I glance at Quinn's hammock. It's empty, though his backpack still leans up against the tree trunk.

"Where's Quinn?" I ask Evyan.

"He's on surveillance duty with Kate and Mark. He does have

more important duties than keeping an eye on you, you know."

Perhaps it's better that he's not present. It's going to be hard enough saying what needs to be said without looking Quinn in the eye as I say it.

"Please tell Zonia that I would like everyone to come here for a meeting as soon as possible."

"Oh, you would, would you?"

I don't have the energy to get angry. "Yes I would. Tell her it's about Nicky."

When everyone except Quinn, Kate and Mark are gathered together beyond the drop-off spot, I begin.

"Nicky has started hemorrhaging blood from everywhere. She's completely out of it and suffering badly. We've run out of pain meds. And it's now dangerous to nurse her."

A line of grave faces stares back at me.

"Before she— When she still knew what she was saying, Nicky begged me to help her when she reached this stage."

"Help her?" asks Evyan. "What exactly does that mean — *help her*?"

I don't know how to say this any way but straight out. "She asked me to end her life."

A few of the rebels exchange glances, but nobody says anything.

"I would like to know what you all think."

After a long pause, Zonia asks, "How would you do it?"

"I would have preferred to have given her an overdose of the pain meds and let her slip away." Actually, I would have preferred to have nothing to do with it at all. "But that's not possible now. She would have to be ... shot."

Bree, Kirsty and Neil flinch. Zonia's expression doesn't change. Darius looks suspicious again. Does he honestly still believe I'm just looking for a chance to shoot someone?

"If anyone else would like to volunteer to do the necessary, you're most welcome," I say, yanking the Glock out of my waistband and holding it out to them on the palm of my hand.

There are no takers. Big surprise.

"I would like to know that everyone agrees that this is what we should do. We can take a vote." No response from anyone. "Zonia?"

She just stares back at me, doesn't even nod. This is all going to be on me.

"Are there any *objections*, then?"

Still nothing. They are such a bunch of cowards.

"Right."

I spin on my heel and stalk back to the cabin, feeling all their eyes on my back. Candace comes with me but stops outside the cabin, saying, with a guilty grimace, "I'll wait out here. I'm sorry to leave it to you, Jinx, but I just can't."

I can't either. That's the point nobody else seems to get. Nothing in my life has prepared me for shooting a friend in the head. I can't.

But I must.

I open the door tentatively, half-hoping that Nicky will attack me again. It would be so much easier if I could do this in self-defense. But when I open the door, the only thing that hits me is a fetid stench, as solid and breathtaking as a blow to the solar plexus.

Nicky sits in a corner, hunched over a pool of blood and dark, lumpy fluid, crooning, "No green, no him, no green, no him," over and over again. As she chants, she rocks back and forth, reminding me irresistibly of my father, when he was dying. Nothing about this is going to be easy.

"Nicky?"

She looks up at me. Her eyes are leaking tears of blood.

"There's no green, Nicky, it's gone."

She looks at me raptly with eyes that seem fixed on a different reality.

"And there's no him. He's gone. It's all gone."

"All gone?"

"Yes, all gone." I try to make my voice gentle and soothing. "It's time to sleep now, Nicky."

I risk getting close to her, placing my feet carefully to the side of the mess on the floor and crouching down. I reach out a hand and gently brush the blood-matted hair off her forehead.

"Do you want to sleep now, Nicky, hmm? Do you just want to go to sleep?" I say softly.

Something like a flicker of awareness lights her eyes. Or perhaps I'm just imagining it, desperately wanting her to have some part in this. Her chin jerks. Is it a nod, or an involuntary spasm?

"Just close your eyes, Nicky." I brush my hand over her eyes, closing the lids. "And go to sleep."

She groans, but her blood-rimmed eyes stay closed.

Then I lift the pistol and place it against her temple.

And I fire.

Chapter 37

Pyre

I sit in the late afternoon sun, slumped against the outside wall of the office, exhausted and empty. I can't move except to tremble, and that I can't stop. My hands shake continuously, and shudders ripple down the length of my body. I feel cold and nauseated.

Is it rat fever?

I can't allow myself to think or feel, because that will crack me open down the middle, so I stare hard at a pokeweed plant growing nearby. Between its vivid green leaves, sprays of inky-purple berries droop down on magenta stems. They remind me of Roberta Roth's hair. A flat brown millipede moves down to the end of one spray, then turns around and heads back up the stem.

In a month, what berries the catbirds and thrushes haven't eaten on their way south for the winter will begin to shrivel and dry. The leaves of these oaks and maples and sourwoods will flame amber and gold and crimson. Fall.

Back home it will be Halloween, with T.V. specials about vampires and zombies. My friends will be all over the social media sites, virtual trick-or-treating, and sending drone deliveries of candy in the shapes of fangs and veined eyeballs and blood-filled jelly rats. I can't think, now, why I ever thought any of that was amusing.

"Jinxy?" It's Quinn's voice.

I look up, not sure what his response to my actions here today will be.

He's carrying a battered red gas can, and he's walked beyond the drop-off point.

"Wait." I scramble to my feet and hold out a hand to stop him. "Don't come any closer."

He stops and says my name again, and his voice is full of compassion. He reaches out a hand as if to squeeze mine across the space between us. "I heard. I'm so sorry."

Tears overflow, and I want nothing more than to hide myself in his arms, but when he takes a step toward me, I make myself say, "Stop! I mean it, not another step."

He sighs, puts down the gas can, and places a box of matches on top of it. "It's gas. For the cabin."

I nod. "Okay. Now back up."

He takes a few paces back, and I retrieve the gas and matches. Candace throws all the bags of contaminated dressings, cleaning materials and equipment into the cabin, while I splash the gas around the base and up over log sides and what I can reach of the roof. We both peel off our PPE suits, gloves, masks and booties, and toss them through the doorway. I feel oddly exposed in just my shorts and tank top, as if I'm standing naked in the growing shadows. The air is cool on my bare skin.

I use the last of the gas to trail a thin line in the sand away from the cabin and hurl the gas can away. Then I pause, holding the matches. This is the only funeral Nicky will get; we should say something.

I think of her kindness to me when everyone else was unfriendly, her trust when it came to sharing information about the rebels, her encouragement about Quinn.

"Thank you, Nicky. Goodbye." It's about all I can choke out.

Beside me, Candace recites the Lord's Prayer.

Then I strike a match and toss it onto the gas trail. The fire races along the ground and then envelops the log cabin with a "whmphf". Flames devour the wooden walls and roof. The front window bursts outward in a shatter of glass shards. We stand and watch the pyre, a blazing sunset against the dimming light of the shady forest.

Above the roar of the fire, I hear a deep voice behind me. Quinn is singing Amazing Grace.

That saved a wretch like me.

Candace joins in, but my throat is too tight to let any sound escape.

… bright shining as the sun …

The front wall of the cabin collapses backward in the pyre of flames, the roof caves in and the structure falls in on itself. Still it burns ferociously, consuming Nicky, destroying the virus.

… Was blind, but now I see.

Chapter 38

Regrets

We let the fire burn right down to ashes, and then I shovel dirt over the remains. The mound gets higher and higher, but I can't seem to stop digging and dropping, digging and dropping. A warm hand closes over mine, and I'm jolted from my daze.

"Quinn! What …? You shouldn't be here!"

He tugs me gently away from the mound, and I notice that a two-man tent has been erected at the drop-off point.

"That's for Candace. I've moved yours a bit further away into the trees, so we can have some privacy."

"*We?* Quinn, I might not be safe. You aren't even wearing a mask. You need to stay away."

"No, I need to stay with you."

I'm too tired to argue. Too lonely to insist.

Our tent is glowing golden in the darkness — Quinn has lit a lantern and hung it from an inside hook. I crawl through the opening and lie down on one of the sleeping bags, wishing I could just sink into a dreamless sleep myself. Quinn stretches out beside me and props his face up on one hand, studying me.

"I had to," I whisper. "Do you see? I *had* to do it." Please let him understand.

"Shhh, there, sweet Jinxy. Of course you had to." He strokes my cheek with the backs of his fingers. "I'm so sorry it fell to you. I know how you cared about her. Here, don't cry." He moves closer to kiss the tears at my temples.

"Sorry," I say, wiping away the tears that won't stop coming. "You must think I'm so weak."

"Hush. You're not crying because you're weak. You're crying because you've been strong for too long."

His kindness completely undoes me. Where all the accusations and fights and insults have toughened me up and sewn me shut tight, Quinn's gentleness and understanding unstitches me, and I unravel.

He lies on his back and pulls my head onto his shoulder, and I begin talking. His warm hands rub my arms and hold me tight against him. Our closeness in the tent seems to invite confidences. I can't see his face, and I'm glad — it's easier to talk this way. And once I begin, I can't stop. Between sobs and hiccups, I tell him everything. I tell him how I felt about him, what I knew and didn't know, the details of what happened on that last mission — why I darted his brother and then him.

He strokes my bare arm and I feel many things in his touch — tenderness and gentleness and compassion. His fingers pause when they reach the lumpy scab on my upper arm.

"What is this?" he asks.

"It's a scab. It's not getting better because I keep picking at it."

"A scab? From what?"

"Never mind," I say, but he's pushed himself back up onto an elbow and is studying the burn.

A deep frown crinkles the skin between his slanted brows as his thumbs move up to gently circle the ugly scab and puckered skin on my upper arm. He checks my other arm and finds the more inflamed sore.

He raises his gaze to mine, and there is puzzlement and something like anger in the depths of his gray eyes.

"How did you get these, Jinxy?"

"Do you really want to know?"

He tilts his head, gives me an *are-you-kidding-me* look, and says, "Of course."

I expel the breath I've been holding since his fingers touched the sores. Where to even begin? With the facts, I guess.

"They're burns."

"Perfectly circular burns, on the exact same spot on both arms?"

"They're burns from the electrodes. From where they shocked me."

He still looks confused.

"In the interrogation, Quinn. When they tortured me?" I try to say it lightly, but even I can hear the tense bitterness which sours my voice.

"Sweet Jesus." His voice is a whisper.

He sits up, grabs the lantern and holds it over me, then leans over and inspects every inch of my arms, tracing the faint scar lines with his fingers and running the pads of his thumbs over the fading marks which encircle my wrists.

"What did they do to you, Jinxy?"

He peels up my tank top to inspect me and lays his hand, soft as a blessing, over the yellow bruise which still stains my ribs. That's a souvenir of the combat training, not the interrogation, but before I can set the record straight, he's examining the scar on my head. I feel a touch, light as a butterfly's rest, on my scalp, and I realize he's just kissed the scar.

"I'm so sorry for this," he says.

His lips move down, and then he's kissing my face where a thin, pale line marks the spot where the shattered glass of his room's window back at ASTA cut my cheek. "And this," he murmurs.

His lips brush my shoulder, then move to kiss my burn sore. I try to pull away, it's too ugly, but he bows his head so that his lips touch the scab. His forehead rests against my shoulder and he whispers, "So, so sorry. This should never have happened to you. Never." His lips move down my arms to my wrists, anointing me with kisses and contrition.

"Ah, Jinxy," he says when he eventually lifts his head. "Why didn't you tell me everything as soon as you arrived?"

"I don't know. You were so cold and so mad at me. I was scared you wouldn't believe me. And I wanted you to believe me, Quinn. *Me.*" I press a hand to my chest. "Not the evidence of burns and bruises. I felt like you shouldn't need proof. Like my word should be good enough."

He nods. "It was. When you gave me hell, when you told me what happened to you, it woke me up. You made me listen and think. And I believed you. But to actually see …"

I'm overwhelmed with emotions I can't even name. I can't speak, so I lift his hand — still wrapped around my own — to my mouth and press a kiss on his knuckles. His eyes, when he meets my gaze, are full of regret. His black lashes are wet.

"I'm so sorry for what they did to you. It's my fault for getting you into this mess in the first place. If I hadn't told you about the rebels, if I hadn't shown you that footage, they'd have left you alone. You'd still be safe and sound at ASTA."

"Yeah, if you hadn't opened my eyes, if you hadn't taught me to question what I'm told, I'd still be at ASTA — killing people without even knowing it. I've done so much wrong, Quinn, and I don't know how to make it right."

"You're not the worst person on the planet, Jinxy. We've all done things that are wrong. We all have to live with ourselves. You're not the only one with regrets."

I tilt my face up to look at him. What is he saying?

"Keep talking, Jinxy, get it all out," he urges, kissing me on the tip of my nose.

I tell him about the horror of discovering I'd been killing plague victims, my fury at Roth and Sarge's deceit, my determination to try to help, and my confusion over how the hell I should go about doing that.

His hand cups my shoulder then slips inside my shirt, where his fingers play with the silver earring on my bra-strap, turning it around and around as I explain how ambivalent I feel about the rebels.

"I don't trust Zonia," I say.

"Me either."

"I think she wants a war — a real one with battles and stuff — and she wants me as one of her soldiers. She thinks I'm a killer, but I'm not, Quinn. I don't want to kill, I never wanted to kill." I sigh, heavy with the weight of what I know, what I've done. "It does something to you, it changes something inside when you kill someone."

"I know," he says, so softly I barely catch the words.

"You don't. You can't know what it's like."

"I do."

I pull myself up and look down at him. He opens the clasp of the earring and removes it.

"You're probably not going to want to wear this anymore."

"Why?" I ask, suddenly wary.

"Jinxy, when I said I was sorry — it wasn't just for what happened to you. I'm also sorry for how I've treated you since."

"You were *so* angry."

"Yeah, but mostly at myself."

He was angry at himself? Why?

"I've been an asshole, Jinx. Mean and angry and judgmental."

"Well, yes," I say, with a smile. But from what I can see of Quinn's face in the dim moonlight, he isn't smiling. He looks grim.

"And hypocritical. I think I felt so guilty that it made me crazy, and I projected that guilt, that anger, onto you."

"Guilty? For what?"

"Ah, God, Jinxy." He takes a deep breath and blows it out in a gust. "That night, when we hit the detention center to rescue Connor, it was chaos. Zonia and Darius took the guards at the front security desk hostage, and we made our way to where you said Connor was being held. But there was a guard outside his cell, armed with this huge gun. Zonia threatened to kill her hostage unless the guard opened the door. And she would have done it, too — she had a knife to his throat, and she pressed it in hard enough to draw blood. I wanted to stop her, but Connor was behind that door."

I sit up, pulling my knees to my chest. Quinn speaks to the roof of the tent.

"The guard laid his gun down on the floor and unlocked the cell door. Ross pushed him inside the cell and pulled out Connor — or what was left of him. He was half-dead, Jinxy, covered in blood and bruises and hardly able to stand. And his one eye!" Quinn cups a hand over his right eye, as if holding a swollen bulge. "When I saw him, when I saw what they'd done to him, I was furious! I wanted to kill them with my own bare hands. Darius and Ross were carrying Connor between them. I tried to help, but Zonia ordered me to lock the guards in the cell, get the weapon and bring up the rear. So I did. And we almost made it. We were out the doors and halfway to the van when we ran into a patrol."

"What happened?"

"They ordered us to stop, to drop our knives. I was behind the others, and they didn't see I had a gun. Then Zonia refused, and the guards lifted their weapons, and I knew that they were about to shoot. And I had that damn thing in my hands. And I couldn't just let them kill Connor, or the others?" He says it like a question, like a plea.

Quinn scrubs a hand across his face and says harshly, "So I pointed it at them and pulled the trigger. And in that moment, I knew exactly what I was doing. I made a decision to do what I've given you such hell for doing. I wasn't aiming to kill — hell, I wasn't even aiming, didn't know how to — but the shots hit one guard in his chest. Just … punched bits out of him and he went down and I … I don't know exactly what happened after that. Next thing we were in the van taking Connor to the safe house."

"Oh, Quinn."

"When you rocked up here, I didn't know what to think or feel. Then you told me that the guard died, and it was definite — I'd shot and killed a man. Deliberately. And somehow it was just easier to blame you than deal with my own guilt — especially when I saw that filthy gun in the locker, in your hands."

"It's the same weapon? The semi-automatic?"

Quinn nods and then looks me in the eye. "I'm sorry, Jinxy. Sorry for judging you. Sorry for ever getting you into this. Can you forgive me?" His voice is raw with emotion, and his eyes glitter.

I think about it, putting together the pieces, trying to understand the whole bloody mess of it more fully now that I understand him better. This war makes traitors of us all. Traitors to our nation, to truth, to love and hope. To ourselves.

"Yes," I say eventually. "I forgive you. But, Quinn?"

"Yeah?" His voice is a mixture of relief and trepidation.

"If you ever leave me again, we're done."

"I will never leave you again." He takes the earring, which he has been gripping in his fist, and threads it through the lobe of my ear. "I vow it."

Something, a hard mass of panicky uncertainty inside me,

dissolves.

"I guess we've got some building up of trust to do, you and me," I say and lie down again on my side. He turns onto his side behind me and curves his body up against mine. I can feel the warmth of his breath on my neck when he speaks.

"I trust you, Jinxy. Implicitly. You're the best person here."

"How can you say that after today?"

"You're honest," he says. "Your heart is good, and you're the bravest person I know. You did what no one else could, or would."

The tears start up again. "I killed a friend."

"Death isn't always the worst thing. Sometimes it's the lesser of two evils. I had never seen the plague close up before, and it's … beyond words. What you did for Nicky was a mercy. And what you did to the M&Ms, well, I still think it's not right —"

"So do I!"

"— and they have no right to be executing infected people, let alone conning teenagers into doing it for them, but, Jinxy, it ended those poor people's suffering, too."

He hugs me close against him, and we lie together like that — his heart beating against my back, his lips pressed to my neck — in the dark forest, spooned together in our sadness and our love, while outside a soft rain begins to fall, dulling the sounds of creatures rustling in the dark forest.

Just before I fall asleep, I hear him murmur, "I love you. I got in first."

Chapter 39

Recoil

For the next two weeks, Quinn and I spend every moment that we can together, talking, working side by side, and touching — exploring, kissing, or just holding each other — because we both have a sense that we're in the precious calm before the storm, that danger and conflict are headed our way. We move my tent back to the end of the line of tents around the camp and spend the nights there together, but we take it slow because this thing between us feels new and fragile. We open and close every day with an, "I love you," competing to see who can get in first in the morning and last at night.

He holds me tight when I cry over the loss of Nicky, and when I get nightmares and flashbacks — the images of her last days, of that last moment, are especially vivid and disturbing. He cheers me up by telling me funny stories about Kerry and his parents, who sound like a feisty pair not easily impressed by anything. It's evident how much he loves his family. I'm surprised when Quinn informs me, as we prepare lunch alongside Evyan one Thursday, that I won over his father when I sent the note about Connor in the park that day.

"And your mother?"

"Ah, she's less easy to please. Connor got his eyes from Dad, but his suspicious nature from Mom. Sure, and I miss him something fierce."

"Your father?"

"No, Connor. I'm sure he's due back soon, but Zonia won't tell me."

Yeah, I've noticed that she likes to keep her cards close to her chest. It's part of her power game.

"And you? Are you missing Robin and your mother?"

"I do worry about my mother — that she'll go dark again — but I miss Robin more. Although" — I tear open a packet of freeze-dried soy "meat" chunks and tip the contents into a bowl of boiling water — "I really do miss my mom's cooking." I watch with fascinated disgust as the shrunken chunks suck up the moisture and swell into gray, spongy blobs. This cannot be healthy. "And I worry about Robin, too — I don't know what I'd do if anything bad happened to him."

"Yeah," says Quinn, and I look up at him sharply, realizing that something pretty bad happened to his brother. How well is he coping, I wonder?

We've spoken about Connor very little, but I've heard enough for me to realize that Quinn deeply admires and respects, maybe even idolizes, his brother. From some of the things he says, or rather the way he says them, I get the sense he grew up in Connor's shadow, and that he feels he still needs to win his brother's approval. It's clear he loves Connor, and it must have gutted Quinn to see him in such a bad way after the interrogation.

"Try not to turn that into mush," Evyan snaps at me, pointing to where my hands have been absently mashing the lumps of soya. "It's not alive, so you don't need to kill it."

She's been full of these sorts of digs at me since Nicky died. In my head, I know it's because she's jealous of the growing relationship between Quinn and me. But my heart clenches like a stabbed anemone every time she reminds me in some or other way of what I did.

The mood around camp has been somber since Nicky's death. The rebels have been sincerely upset, but it irks me to no end that Zonia and her crew act like they have no responsibility whatsoever in their comrade's death. There's a convenient amnesia about the fact that I warned them about the rats and they chose to ignore me.

And they do *not* like me for being right. Although none of them would help Nicky in the only way that was possible there at the end, and although I acted so that they didn't have to get blood on their hands, they still resent me for doing it. I killed her, so it's like *I'm* responsible for her death. Me — not the plague, or their lax attitudes, or Zonia's refusal to post armed guards. Which she now does, without fail, on a 24-hour basis.

I feel like the ancient mariner in that poem we studied in English last year — I killed the albatross, and they want me to wear my guilt like a dead bird around my neck, because I'm cursed. I'm the ominous reminder of a reality which includes bad luck and death, and they mutter and whisper about me when they think I can't hear, and wish me gone. All except Zonia, who totally wants me to stay. Because she has a plan for me.

Zonia is not there to eat the spongy soya stew at lunch. She's been out of camp all day.

"I hope she gets some fresh fruit and vegetables. I'd kill for an apple," I say to Quinn as we dish up lunch to the moving line of rebels.

"And here I was thinking you'd kill for the sheer pleasure of it," says Evyan.

"Give it a rest, Evyan," Quinn says.

Zonia arrives just before sunset, looking, as Quinn phrases it, "fair to bursting with news."

There's a lot of whispering between her and Darius and the rest of her red-bereted cronies, and they cast long, evaluative looks my way as I sit beside Quinn after supper. It's unnerving. Quinn has been teaching me how to throw knives, and I'm not half bad, though he's still better. I think of all the lethal things I've been trained to do and wonder if one day someone will teach me something completely benign. Knitting, perhaps, or flower-arranging.

"Time to relieve Mark," I say, pressing a kiss against Quinn's jaw. "See you later."

But when I get to the "guard post" — a dead tree stump on the outer perimeter of the campground — and make to take the weapon from Mark, Zonia pops up beside me and says, "Not tonight, Jinx, I need to talk to you."

"I'm on guard duty."

"Evyan!" Zonia calls. "Come stand guard tonight instead of Jinxy."

Great. Now Evyan has another reason to sneer and give me filthy looks.

Zonia clamps a hand over my elbow and steers me back towards the camp. Quinn looks up in surprise as we approach, but Zonia holds up a hand to indicate he should stay where he is, beckons Darius to join us, and keeps walking.

"You know why we're here?" Zonia says, sweeping a hand to indicate the forest as we make our way down the path that leads to the old camp office and the van beyond.

"Yeah," I say, uncertain as to where this conversation is headed. "To keep an eye on Hawke."

"We have been keeping an eye on him. And together with our operatives in key points, we've collected a wealth of information on him and his retreat. We know, for example, that there are bunkers under that lodge. Bunkers stocked with weapons and explosives and equipped with a massive communications center using both analog and digital technology, as well as provisions and an extensive living compound."

"Wow, who knew."

"We did, Jinx. We make it our business to know."

"If he needed to, Hawke could retreat belowground to protect his scared ass, and he could run his government securely from there. Indefinitely," Darius chips in.

"And we can't allow that. We are determined to prevent that," says Zonia. "In fact, High Command has tasked us with the mission of destroying that possibility."

"Yeah?" I say, not sure what they're getting at.

We arrive in the small clearing around the charred remains of the old camp office. I keep my eyes off the heap of burned black logs and gray ashes, but images of Nicky flood through my mind anyway. Especially that last one.

"Jinx. *Jinx.*"

Zonia is speaking to me. I turn my back on the ruin and try to bring my mind back to the here and now. "Sorry, yeah?"

"You've seen the explosives in the weapons locker?"

I had wondered what they were for. Now I think I can guess. "You want to blow up the president's retreat?"

"That was the plan," says Darius.

"Originally," says Zonia. "But we had no real idea of how to get past all the security and make it inside to get the job done. And we're not demolitions experts. But then you came along, and I realized there might be another way. A much neater way."

"What do you mean?" I've got that feeling again, the one that tells me something bad is coming.

"Tomorrow is Friday, the twentieth of September," Zonia says.

I stare at her blankly. What does the date have to do with

anything?

"It's the Day of the Fallen."

"Oh, right."

It's a new holiday — this will be only the second time it will have come around. It's the day we're meant to remember and commemorate all the civilians who have died in terror-attacks, especially the millions who have perished from the plague. Last year, Robin and I sat with Mom in front of the T.V., watching President Hawke as he made speeches and laid a massive wreath against the Fallen Memorial. His tribute to the dead reduced me to tears, and even Robin looked moved. Mom sat stony-faced through his address, but when one of the presidential guards lifted his bugle and started playing Taps, she pushed herself off the sofa and hurried to her room, staying there for the rest of the day.

"It's a long weekend, and we've had word that President Hawke will be coming to his retreat. We'll have three full days," says Darius from beside Zonia.

Huh? Three full days for what? "You want me to stand surveillance again?"

I'd be happy to stretch my legs and get out of camp for a while. In recent days, Zonia has tended to post me on guard duty pretty continuously — there haven't even been any more shooting lessons.

"No. Not surveillance. I want you to use your specialist skills and do what you've been trained to do best," Zonia says, looking at me intently.

"You want me to …?" Not again. Not. Again.

"Yes."

"*No!*" I shout. Everything in me recoils at the very idea of what she is suggesting.

Chapter 40

Refuse

Zonia ignores me and continues speaking in her brisk, businesslike way. "Hawke will go fishing for sure, at that little pond, or skeet shooting on the range. And we know he only takes one or two of the guards with him when he does. He'll be out in the open and completely vulnerable. It should be easy for you."

"No, Zonia! I refuse to do it."

I don't want to shoot anyone ever again. And I especially don't want to shoot the president. Apart from the minor fact that it would be murder and treason, I'm kind of fond of the guy. I know the rebels think he's bad through and through, but I've always respected him, even liked him, and the thought of him dead upsets me. My feelings aren't as positive as they used to be, now that I know more about what the government is up to, but I'm a long way off from wishing him dead, let alone wanting to be the one who assassinates him.

"I'd do it myself," continues Zonia, "but I know I'm hopeless, and Darius's no sniper either. Nicky was our best bet, really, but she's out of the running now."

"She's dead!" I say, horrified at her callousness.

I shut my eyes tight for a second, as if that could repel the image that flashes across my mind — my gun against her head. My finger pulling the trigger. Her body slumping at my feet.

"Yes, yes, very sad. But the revolution must continue, even when it means individual rebels have to sacrifice their lives."

"She didn't sacrifice her life — she was bitten by a rat! I warned you that could happen."

"What's this all about?" asks Quinn. He strides up the path towards us, tucking a knife into the sheath he now wears on his belt.

"And Quinn doesn't have the *cojones* to do it," Zonia says.

"Do what, exactly?" asks Quinn.

"Just because Quinn thinks sniping is morally wrong doesn't mean he's a coward. There are all kinds of courage!" I snap.

"Can someone please explain what you guys are talking about?" says Quinn.

"We are one of two rebel teams who have been given the mission to take out President Hawke. And I plan on us being the team that succeeds." She makes it sound like a fun game of capture-the-flag. "And our sniper specialist here is going to help us with that."

"No I am not," I insist. "I will not assassinate the president!"

"*What?*" says Quinn.

I spin to face him. "Did you know about this?" I demand. "Did you know this is what they had planned for me?"

"No!"

Zonia carries on talking calmly, as if I haven't just point-blank refused. "You're a gift, Jinx, a gift that just fell into our laps. This is a vital task for the revolution. If Hawke is removed from the equation, it'll save many lives down the line. He's a menace and a threat to our nation, and more powerful and dangerous than any rat."

"He's like a mutant who needs to be euthanized so that others aren't infected," says Darius with a smirk.

"Listen to yourselves!" I can't believe this is happening.

"Zonia," says Quinn. "We need to discuss this."

"And that's what you were trained for, not so? To take out threats to humanity?" she says to me, ignoring Quinn. "You're already skilled and primed."

"Locked and loaded," adds Darius.

"Zonia, this is wrong. You can't —" Quinn begins.

"I can and I will," she says, her eyes cold and her jaw set. "We are losing this war. *Losing!* We need to turn things around by removing high-value targets if we want a better future for this nation."

"Not this way!"

"The end justifies the means." She says it with a note of finality, like it's the end of the discussion.

But I am far from finished.

"That's exactly what *they* say! How do you even tell yourself apart from them anymore? Even your language is the same — *take down, euthanize, remove high-value targets* — you're talking about assassination, the cold-blooded murder of the President!" I turn to Quinn again. His face is twisted into a grimace of concern and anger. "I thought this was a political movement to expose what the government and its agencies are doing, not an armed resistance. I never signed up for civil war against my fellow Americans."

"Neither did I," says Quinn.

"Besides, as soon as he's shot, they'll know what direction it came from, and this whole mountain will be swarming with special forces on the ground and in the air. Have you thought about that?" I ask Zonia, hoping to deter her from this course with practical considerations, since the ethical ones don't seem to matter to her.

"I have," she says. Though I wonder. "From tonight we'll all be packed and on standby to bug out at a moment's notice."

"Zonia, let's just talk about this," Quinn pleads.

"We're beyond talking. The order has come from High Command," she says.

"I. Won't. Do it," I say, enunciating every word.

"If you won't follow orders," Zonia says, her voice cold and flat, "then we need to reconsider if you are any use to this group. If you are even loyal to the rebel cause."

"What, now you're going to court-martial and execute me?" I take a step towards her.

"Stop! Just stop this," Quinn says, grabbing my shoulder and tugging me back. "Zonia, just cool it. You can't *make* Jinxy shoot Hawke."

"Oh, can't I? Just try me," she says, closing the gap between us. "Besides" — she gives me a contemptuous look — "I don't know what you're making such a big deal about. You shot Nicky easily enough."

I fly at her, striking the side of her face with all my strength. She gasps, outraged, and Darius pulls back a fist, ready to send me flying, but Quinn steps between us, and the blow lands solidly against his chest. Quinn manages to land a punch on Darius's jaw before Ross tackles him to the ground. Darius and Ross climb into him, landing fists and feet against his stomach and shoulders. Zonia steps around her protectors, drawing the Glock from the waistband of her pants and pointing it at me. Swiveling from my hips, I strike her arm, sending the weapon flying. In less than a second, I've grabbed her wrist and flipped her hard, face-first into the dirt, where she lies, winded. I reach over to where Quinn lies curled on the ground, protecting his face with his arms and kicking out at his attackers, and snatch the knife from his belt. I pull Zonia's head back by the hair and hold the blade to her throat. She's gasping, trying to catch her breath.

"Stop!" I yell at the pair working over Quinn. "Back off, now!"

Darius and Ross freeze, then step a few paces back.

"You okay?" I ask Quinn as he rolls, groaning, onto all fours. His bottom lip is split and bleeding.

"I'll live."

"Glad to hear it," comes an unfamiliar, deep voice from behind me.

I let go of Zonia's hair, and her face thuds into the dirt. I spin around, knife outstretched to defend against the new threat.

The man drops two big, black duffel bags and holds out his hands placatingly. He has brown hair and is thin, stooped, and hollow-eyed. He's young, I know he is, but he looks old.

Connor O'Riley has returned.

Chapter 41

Blood and water

"Connor!" Quinn leaps up and runs over to his brother, locking him into a tight bear hug.

"Quinn." Connor's voice is muffled from where his face is mashed against Quinn's shoulder.

I knew Quinn was taller than his elder brother, but Connor seems smaller even than I remember. I notice the fingers of the hand which holds Quinn close. They are red and swollen and stick out at strange angles, like they've been smashed, broken and set wrong.

"Connor!" Quinn says again when they break apart, but this time his voice is shaded with concern rather than relief.

And I can see why. Connor looks like a wreck of the man I saw on the O'Rileys' porch back in May, and on the sidewalk just six weeks ago. His shirt hangs loosely on his hunched frame, his cheekbones stand out sharply in his thin face and there are shadows — dark as bruises — under his eyes. There's a deadness to his face.

"I thought the O'Riley boys always fought together, or not at all," Connor says with a tight upward turn of his lips, a forced smile that doesn't touch his dark, burning eyes. He turns to face the rest of the rebels, who have come running up the path and are hailing him like a returning hero.

"Welcome back, man," says Mark.

"We really missed you," adds Evyan.

Ross and Darius stand on either side of Zonia, and none of that trio looks enthusiastic at their leader's sudden reappearance.

Rotating on the spot, Connor greets his fellow rebels one by one until at last he faces me again. He frowns at me, perplexed, for a second, and then recognition hits.

"You!" His voice is heavy with loathing. The last time he saw me, I was facing him square on, shooting a tranq-dart into his neck.

Quinn steps up beside me and takes my hand. His hand is warm and large and firm. It calms and steadies me. I could do anything if Quinn was with me, holding my hand. I could take on the whole world.

"Connor, I'd like you to meet Jinxy James," Quinn says.

I stick out my right hand to shake his, but drop it when Connor looks at it like it's a dead rat and says, "The ASTA operative who shot me and got me taken to the detention center?"

"The rebel who gave us the information to spring you free," Quinn corrects. I give his hand a grateful squeeze.

Connor shoots a dark look at our entwined hands, and then says to Quinn, "So you're with her, now?"

"I am."

"And you trust her?"

"I do."

"Well, that makes one of us." Behind Connor, Evyan sniggers. "Faith, and here I was thinking blood was thicker'n water."

I glance up at Quinn. He looks like a kicked puppy, but before he can respond, Connor has stepped past him to greet Zonia.

"Welcome back," she says, without warmth. Her face, I'm happy to see, is smudged all over with dirt, and there's blood on her chin.

"I come bearing gifts," Connor says, withdrawing some folded pieces of paper from an inner pocket of his jacket. "These are from High Command."

"Ah." Zonia opens and reads the first one, then says to me, "Congratulations — you're on your way to hitting America's Most Wanted list."

"What?"

"Sought for questioning in connection with suspected involvement in a string of terrorist attacks across the nation," she reads the phrase.

"No way!"

"Seems the whole of the Southern Sector is out looking for you, young lady. APB's to all police stations, the armed forces, probably even the president's own guard."

I hold a hand out for the paper — I want to know exactly what it says — but Zonia gives me an *as-if* look and stuffs it into a pocket.

"Speaking of the devil, is he here?" asks Connor.

"He will be, if the intel was good," says Darius. "We have a three-day window of opportunity starting tomorrow."

"Perhaps we can put my second gift to good use, then." Connor squats down on his haunches and unzips one of the big duffel bags.

"Suh-weet!" says Darius, and Zonia smiles wider than I've ever seen her do.

Inside the bag are several semi-automatics and ammo magazines.

"This is a surprise," says Zonia. "I would have expected you to bring some pamphlets or information posters, or something."

"That was the old Connor."

"There's a new Connor?" Quinn asks. He looks worried.

"When you go through what I went through in that place, you learn a few things about yourself. And the true nature of your enemy."

Zonia looks at him curiously, but there's a smile building behind the questions in her eyes.

"I'm beginning to think you were right, Zonia. I no longer think *words* are going to cut it."

"Yeah!" She holds up a hand for a high five, but it's awkward because Connor has to use his undamaged left hand to slap hers.

"So, do you think we can get close enough to Hawke to eliminate him with these?" Connor asks, standing again.

"We don't need to," Zonia replies. "We now have a better plan. Safer, neater and sure to have fewer casualties on our side than a full-on, face-to-face firefight."

"Oh, yeah?" A flicker of excitement animates Connor's face.

"Come on, I'll tell you about it. Ross, stow these in the weapons locker, will you?"

The rest of us head back down the path to the campground.

Zonia leads the way, walking beside Connor. Quinn follows close behind his brother, reaching out a hand to squeeze Connor's shoulder or ruffle his hair every so often, as if to reassure himself that Connor is truly here, alive and well. More or less. Quinn still holds my hand, so I keep pace with him, which allows me to hear Zonia's conversation with Connor — as she no doubt intends me to.

"So what's this new plan for taking down Hawke?"

"As you may have noticed, we just happen to have an honest-to-God expert sniper in amongst our collection of rebels, and a sniper's rifle in our collection of weapons."

"You're going to get *her* to shoot Hawke?"

No, she is not. I grind my teeth together to keep from speaking, but I keep listening.

"You bet I am. She's not keen — she's suddenly developed a bunch a scruples now that she's being asked to shoot the enemy rather than innocent civilians — but she'll come around. I've seen her shoot, Connor — she could take down Hawke with a single bullet. 'One shot, one kill', isn't that their motto?"

"So *you* trust her, too?"

"It's not a question of trust — way I see it, she doesn't have much of a choice. If she stays, then she needs to follow orders, same as everyone else. And if she leaves — hell, where would she go? Not back to ASTA, not home to her family. You read the intel memo — they're searching for her everywhere, no place is safe for our Miss Jinx E. James."

When we get to the camp, Quinn grabs the other duffel bag from his brother. "Here, I got that. Let's get you settled. We moved the tents to back in the trees, this way."

I figure this means Connor gets his tent back now, and I'll need to move. Will Quinn share with him again? I have no right to feel put out. Connor was here first, and he's family, I remind myself as I tag along behind them, listening.

"How are Mum and Da?" asks Quinn. "Have you seen them? Are they okay?"

"No." At Quinn's look of alarm, Connor clarifies, "I mean, no I haven't seen them, but they're fine, apparently. They were questioned, but not interrogated. I guess the authorities think they don't know much, which isn't far from the truth."

"That's a relief."

"I've got a letter for you from Mom, and a message from Kerry. She says to tell you she loves you, and her new front tooth is coming in."

Quinn's face softens into a smile, and he exhales a relieved sigh. I can see how much his family means to him, how much he misses them, and how his fear for them all — especially Connor — has been weighing on him.

"Faith, but it's good to have you back." Quinn's Irish lilt is stronger when he talks to his brother.

"It's good to be here. I don't mind telling you that there were moments when I didn't think I'd make it," says Connor.

Maybe this reminds him of me, because he spins around and gives me a dark glare.

"Was there something you wanted?" he asks. His eyes are cold, judging.

"Uhm." I swallow hard. "I need to get my bag and stuff from your tent."

"Oh, right, yeah," says Quinn. "Sorry, Jinx, do you mind? I'd love to catch up on all the news."

"It's no problem. I'll move in with one of the others, or move to the van or something."

No way will Zonia allow me to bunk down with the weapons cache. I'll have to move in with Evyan.

In Nicky's old spot.

I grab my backpack and the few of my things which lie loose in the tent and walk off, leaving Quinn and Connor together, wondering if this is a sign of things to come.

Chapter 42

Snake eyes

It's an unseasonably chilly night, and I don't have my own bedding. Quinn pops in to see me before bedtime and offers me his sleeping bag, but I refuse. He manages to scavenge some blankets from the others, and I sleep under these, with my backpack as a pillow. Evyan does her best to make me feel utterly unwelcome, and seizes the opportunity to get in a few more digs.

"What — no room for you at the O'Riley inn? After Connor's had a nice long chat with his kid brother, Quinn won't want you at all, not even as his camp skank."

I wake up in the middle of the night, shivering with cold, to find both my blankets lying outside the tent, gathering dew. Thanks, Evyan.

Next morning, after breakfast, Zonia calls for a minute's silence to commemorate all the victims who have died in this war — the victims of the plague and, she insists, especially of the corrupt government.

"I am pleased to tell you," she announces, "that sometime during the next three days — today, tomorrow or Sunday — we will complete our vital mission here and move on."

Everyone cheers, except Connor, whose face remains immobile,

Quinn, who looks troubled, and me. I wonder if my face looks as mutinous as I feel.

"I want us ready to bug out at a moment's notice," Zonia continues. "Everyone is to pack all their belongings, roll their bedding and attach it to their bags and backpacks, and pile it all under that tree." She points at the pine nearest the fire pit. "After each meal, the team on duty is to pack all provision boxes and collapse the tables. When the time is finalized, I'll give the order, and most of our rebel unit can move out in advance. The operative, and one or two others" — her eyes stray to Quinn — "will stay to complete the mission. They can rejoin us afterwards."

In that moment, I understand her true intention. I'm disposable. So is Quinn, probably. He's way too much of a pacifist for her liking. She means to get the two of us to climb the mountain and assassinate Hawke while she and the rest of the rebels make their escape. If, after completing our "mission", we manage to evade our pursuers and catch up with them, she will have lost nothing. But if we're killed or captured, then it will merely look like I, Jinx E. James, wanted dissident and fugitive, went off the rails and together with my lover took vengeance on the sector's president for my treatment in the detention center.

Zonia knows what I've been through, that I'll do almost anything rather than surrender myself up to that again. So Quinn and I will be conveniently killed in the crossfire, and the government will have caught its assassin with no need to look any further. She plans to kill the president and get rid of me and Quinn, who is now her chief opposition, in one fell swoop. Talk about snake-eyes.

I look at Quinn to see if this train of thought has occurred to him, but he's too busy urging Connor to eat all his breakfast to analyze Zonia's motives.

"Kate, Ross and Kirsty, you're on surveillance detail. Connor, Darius, let's go," commands Zonia. "You, too, Jinx."

"I'm not killing the president. Not now, not ever," I state.

"I was just going to ask you to demonstrate your skills for Connor here — he has some doubts. Surely you don't object to shooting at a piece of paper."

I'm so relieved that she's not planning on dragging me up the mountain to murder the president right at this moment, that I find myself nodding.

"I'm coming with," insists Quinn.

"Of course, I know the two of you are a unit," says Zonia, prickling my suspicions again.

In the clearing where we've practiced shooting, I plug a dozen rounds in a close cluster into the center of the head of the target silhouette.

Connor, who scans the area constantly and jumps at any loud sound, remains unimpressed. "She'd be shooting across a distance of close on a mile."

I want to defend my skill, to tell him that snipers have taken out targets at distances of over one and a half miles, but I stay silent.

Zonia takes the rifle, points it through a gap in the trees in the direction of the pig farm in the valley and peers through the scope. "There. See that massive oak that's turned completely red? There's a dead tree to the left of it, with some kind of a bird's nest in the V of the branches. Hit that."

"I'm not shooting a bird's nest," I protest.

"For God's sake, you're as bad as Neil. Shoot the branch below it, then."

I take back the rifle and find the dead tree through the powerful scope. I don't see any birds, but there might be eggs in the nest. I estimate that it's about a mile away. I bend down, grasp a handful of dirt and let it trickle through my fingers. There's a very slight crosswind, and I'll be shooting from a high angle, down the mountain. It won't be an easy shot. And the one targeting Hawke would be even harder.

I grab the sandbag from the rifle case, lay it on top of a nearby boulder and rest the barrel of my rifle on it. I dope my scope for windage and elevation and then settle myself for the shot, aiming the intersection of my reticles at a bulge in the branch below the nest. I still my mind, loosen my shoulders, and take a few deep, calming breaths.

Then I let my breath trickle out one last time against the stock pressed to my cheek, and gently squeeze the trigger.

I hear the muffled crack of the rifle before the shot hits the branch.

"Damn," I say, clambering back to my feet and handing Zonia the rifle.

"You missed?" says Connor.

"No, I didn't miss. But the impact knocked the nest off anyway."

Zonia and Connor take turns checking through the scope. I go to sit with Quinn. For once he's not throwing knives — he's staring at his brother with deep concern. I follow his gaze. Zonia is holding forth passionately, probably about the need to commit murder and treason, and Connor nods in agreement as he returns the rifle to its bag.

"I thought when he got back, there would be a fight for leadership, but it looks like they're on the same page now," I say.

Quinn nods sadly. "He's changed. I mean, I understand that he's really angry and bitter and wants revenge, but even so, he's not the same as he was before. It's like something broke inside him. I just feel so guilty."

"You? *You* feel guilty?"

I figure the guilt is pretty much all mine, and I've been lugging it about since I first saw the state Connor is in. I may not have been the one to torture him, but there's no getting away from the fact that I helped capture him. If I hadn't darted him, maybe he and

Quinn would have got away. Probably not. But maybe.

"Yeah. Because *I* escaped. With your help, I got away scot-free. I didn't have to go through what he did. I wish I could have saved him."

"You did," I point out.

"Yeah, but not soon enough."

Yeah. Not soon enough.

Zonia sends Quinn to return the rifle to the locker. Most of the rebels prefer to have the shotgun when they stand guard duty. Only Neil and I use the rifle. Me, because I stand an excellent chance of hitting rats with it while they are still at a safe distance, and he because, I suspect, he wants to miss.

Zonia and her new BFF approach me with expectant faces.

"Well?" she asks me. "It's obviously doable."

"But not by me. I don't know how to say this in words that you'll understand: I am not going to assassinate the president. There is nothing you can say that will change my mind."

"You think so?" she says lightly. "That's a pity. A damned shame."

Her words make it sound like she's accepted my refusal, but I don't trust this sudden capitulation.

"Well, I was obviously deeply mistaken in you," Zonia says. "I thought you snipers were selected for your courage and nerve, not just your skill."

"I'm not *scared* to do it!"

"Then why won't you?" says Connor, turning those cold eyes, that masklike face on me.

"Because it's *wrong*. On principle. You should both know that."

"It's bizarre to hear an effing sniper say it's wrong to shoot someone. It'd be funny if it weren't so hypocritical," says Connor.

"I won't shoot someone in cold blood — that's the freaking reason why I left ASTA."

"But there are circumstances in which you would be prepared to shoot?" says Zonia. She is toying with an old, dry pine cone, cracking back the scales and peeling them off, one by one.

I nod. "Of course. If, say, we were under attack, I'd be prepared to return fire in self-defense."

"Mmmm, yes, I see. To defend yourself, or perhaps Quinn, or your friends amongst the rebels here," she nods thoughtfully. "Or … your family?"

"My family?" Where did that come from?

"Yes. Say, for example, your brother — Robin, isn't that his name? — was in danger, then would you be prepared to shoot? To keep him safe?"

I stand perfectly still, hyperaware of the icy pit that is my stomach.

"Robin?" I ask.

"Yes. I heard all about him. Poor Nicky, I think she hoped to meet him one day." *Crack.* She peels another scale off and tosses it away. "From what she told me, he's been getting into all sorts of things he shouldn't. Hacking is such a dangerous game. It's so easy to get caught. A tip-off on the See-Say line is all it would take." Her voice is light, almost playful.

"You wouldn't!" I say. My voice is breathy with fear.

"Believe me, there is nothing I wouldn't do."

I appeal to Connor. "You can't think this is right? Blackmailing me through my brother, someone who's never done anyone any harm?"

But his eyes are implacable in his dead face. "Tomorrow, after breakfast, you will go up that mountain. And you will not come down until Hawke is terminated."

Chapter 43

Piggy in the middle

The next morning blows in on a cold snap of strong, gusting winds and driving rain. Saved by the weather. No way can they expect me to pull off a million-dollar shot in these conditions. Besides, Hawke will probably stay indoors by the fire all day anyway. I'm relieved at the respite, but I know it's temporary. Tomorrow is Sunday — Hawke's last day at the retreat, and the pressure will be all on me.

Everyone except the surveillance team hangs around camp, edgy and irritable. I head for the showers, wishing that by some miracle hot water would come out of the pipes to unwind the knot of tension in my back and neck. But the water is icy.

I'm just coming out of the shower when there's a double rap on the corrugated steel door. I wrap my towel around me and take a hesitant step towards the door.

"Jinx? You in there?" A voice calls sharply. Connor.

"Yeah."

I stay where I am, shivering in the chilly air, my wet hair trickling a puddle onto the cold floor at my feet.

"The forecast for tomorrow is cloudy, but no rain or wind. Hawke's sure to be out on the grounds. Be ready to leave at dawn."

"Wait! Connor, please."

I run, dripping and barefooted, past the showers and toilet cubicles out of the door and slam right into Quinn.

"Did you hear? Did you see that?"

"I see this," he says, his voice rough and deep.

He's looking down between us. The towel has come loose. One end is wedged precariously between our bodies, the other hangs down into the mud. The whole top half of my body is bare, and very little covers the bottom. I can feel a cold breeze and splashes of rain on my butt.

"Oh!" Heat rushes into my face as I squirm against him, trying to retrieve the wayward end of the towel without exposing the rest of myself.

Quinn groans at the wriggling full body contact. "Did you know you blush here, too?" he asks, running his hands down the sides of my neck, over my chest, and lower, around the curves of my boobs.

"I..." Wait, what did he ask? I can't think, can't breathe.

And then I don't have to. His mouth closes over mine, and we're kissing, and instead of oxygen, I'm breathing *him* in. He holds me up with a strong arm tight around my waist, pulling me against his length. His mouth slants across mine, driving out all thought, all fear, all doubt. My hands steal behind his head, tug at the hair on his neck. My chest is crushed against his, but still one big, warm hand edges in and cups a breast. I'm gasping. I need air, I need Quinn, I need more. Now. My teeth tug at his bottom lip. He shudders and kisses me deeper. There's a desperation in our mouths, in our exploring hands. As if our bodies know that time is running out.

The sarcastic clearing of a throat nearby snaps my head back. Connor is standing a few yards away, watching us.

"Quinn, your brother," I whisper fiercely.

He turns around, and I snatch the towel before it drops, wrapping it securely back around me while hiding behind the protection of Quinn's broad shoulders.

"Can I have a word, little bro?" Connor asks.

"Right now?" I'm glad to hear the irritation in Quinn's voice.

"Sorry. But I'm not doing so well today — I could use a shoulder …?"

"Of course, yeah. I'm there," Quinn says, rubbing both those beautiful hands over his face as if to scrub away the lingering trace of our kiss. Of me. "Jinxy — later, yeah?" he says to me.

"Yeah, later." But I say it to his back, because he's already walking away, following his brother.

I stand shivering and barefooted in the mud and watch them go. This feels like how it's going to be from here on out — Quinn reconnecting with his damaged brother, out of love and concern. And guilt.

And me left standing alone.

I'm about to turn and head back into the restroom when Connor turns and looks over his shoulder at me. If that hollow, immobile face was still capable of smiling, it would be grinning widely now. The dark eyes are not blank — they're gloating.

Connor sticks by his brother's side all morning, and it's not until afternoon, when I spy Connor leaving their two-man tent, that I have a chance to confront Quinn with what Zonia said yesterday.

I stick my head inside the opening. Quinn is lying on his back, one arm behind his head, staring at the roof of the tent. His other hand rests on his chest, holding a small piece of blue paper.

"Can I come in?" I'm not confident enough to just climb inside anymore.

"Jinx! Of course, come here." There is pure delight and welcome in his voice. There is.

"Can I talk to you about something?"

"Since when do you need an invitation?"

He tosses aside the paper and pulls me to his side, to my favorite spot in the world — tucked under his arm, with my head on his chest.

I get to the point immediately. "They've threatened to turn in Robin unless I shoot Hawke."

"They? Who?"

"Zonia. And Connor."

"They said that? *Connor* said that?"

"Not in as many words, but the threat was clear."

"Nah, d'ya think you could've misunderstood, Jinxy? They were probably just joking, or maybe trying to scare you. But they would never do that, especially Connor. No way." He tucks a stray curl of hair behind my ear, and traces a finger down my neck. It's distracting, but there are things we need to discuss.

"You said he'd changed."

"Not that much." His chest shakes under me as he laughs gently. "We're the *good* guys, Jinxy."

Maybe. Though I'm beginning to wonder if purely *good guys* actually exist. "But bottom line, if I stay here, if I'm a rebel, then sooner or later they're going to make me shoot Hawke. And it's wrong."

No response.

"Well, what do you think I should do?"

"My brother and I have been chatting today, and it's made me think. Connor seems to think that there's more to Hawke, that he's deeply corrupt and up to something really bad, and that the country would be better off without him."

"Do you agree?"

"Of course. Connor's dead right about Hawke needing to go, about this nation needing a change of government."

"So you think I should shoot him?" I can't believe this.

Quinn pauses. "Connor thinks we should, and he's in with Resistance High Command. He's been in this since the beginning, he knows lots. I respect his opinion."

Connor this and Connor that!

"I know you love your brother and admire him, but what do *you* think, Quinn?"

I know I'm making him piggy-in-the-middle, that in asking him to nail his colors to the mast, I'm asking him to choose between Connor and me. Super — more guilt.

I feel again like I did that day of the mission at ASTA when I had to make an impossible choice, one which would lose me Quinn either way. If I go ahead and kill Hawke, I become the very stone-cold killer that I don't want to be, I become the thing that Quinn has always hated, I betray myself and become as bad as the people I want to defeat. But if I don't, the rebels will believe I'm betraying them, and perhaps they'll turn Robin in. Perhaps they'll turn me out.

If they did, would Quinn come with me — turn his back on his broken brother, and his family and the rebel cause just so I wouldn't be alone? And would I — should I — even want him to? It would put him in enormous danger to be out there with one of the sector's most wanted fugitives. He'd be safer staying here, or wherever Zonia and Connor plan on taking the group after tomorrow.

"Time to take a stand for what you believe, Quinn. Do you think I should assassinate the president? Yes or no?"

It takes him only a moment to answer. "No. Of course not. It would be wrong, it's against everything I believe."

I sigh. There are actual tears of relief in my eyes.

"But I also think you and I are in a minority about that, and Zonia's going to put a lot of pressure on you, on us, because she's had the order from High Command. And time is ticking down on

Hawke's stay at the retreat."

"And so?"

"I'll talk to Connor tonight, make him see sense. Whatever they did to him at that place has twisted him up inside, he's not himself. I'll bring him round."

But I don't think so. I know some of what went on in that room and can guess at the rest. I think about the hell of my single torture session and try to imagine what it must have done to Connor to endure that for almost three days, in addition to having to suffer starvation and dehydration. It's unimaginable. No wonder he hates me. And he does — I've seen it in the icy darkness of his eyes and the severe set of his mouth when he looks at me. And he hates them — ASTA, the government and President Hawke — with the fiery passion of a newly converted zealot.

I don't think he's going to change his mind anytime soon, let alone before tomorrow morning. Not so as to spare the scruples of the girl who got him captured, and not to save the life of the man who, ultimately, was responsible for having him tortured.

I want to tell Quinn about my theory that Zonia's planning to burn us, but his breathing slows and deepens, and his hand slips off my arm. It'll have to wait until later. In the meantime, I'm not above snooping. Moving slowly and carefully, so as not to wake him, I reach over and retrieve the blue paper. As soon as I unfold it, I see it's a letter to Quinn, from his mother. Although I know I should respect his privacy, I begin reading, my heart sinking lower with every word.

Dearest Quinn,

Thank you, thank you for saving Connor! In this mad world, family is the only thing that matters. It's the only thing we have. I couldn't bear to lose one of my children, and we came so close. I suppose your brother must be in a very bad way after those bastards had their go at him. You've always been so strong, Quinn, you need to help him. Promise me you'll stay with him and look after him. And promise me you'll try to stay safe and not go looking for trouble. I'm relying on you.

May the road rise up to meet you. May the wind be always at your back. May the sun shine warm upon your face, and until we meet again, may God hold you in the palm of His hand.

All my love,

Mum

Ah, crap.

Chapter 44

Countdown

I nap alongside Quinn until Connor comes to prize his brother away from my clutches again.

"Rise and shine, sunshine, it's suppertime."

After we've eaten and the light is beginning to fade, Connor calls for silence.

"Listen up, you lot. Zonia would like a word."

She tells us to get a good night's sleep and to strike camp before dawn tomorrow.

"Another transport will be here by seven am, and I want us rolling out as soon as possible after that." She eyes me where I stand apart from the others. "We'll send the van back for you and Quinn."

Sure she will.

"Who's standing guard duty tonight?"

"I'm on from six 'til twelve," says Quinn.

"And I'm on from midnight until six am," says Neil.

"Quinn, do you want the rifle or the shotgun?"

He shrugs. He's never bought into the idea that any of them could hit a rat anyway.

"Well then, we may as well take the shotgun back now and get the rifle. Neil prefers it, and we'll need it first thing in the morning anyway. Darius — would you get it?" Zonia hands him the keys to the van. "Jinx, make sure you get to bed early — we need your eyes sharp and your hands steady tomorrow."

She's obviously decided to pay no attention to my flat refusal to cooperate. What will she do at dawn? Have Connor and Darius drag me up the mountain, then hold a gun to my head? It's not beyond her. Nothing is.

And what would Quinn do if they tried — defend me against his own brother? What if the situation turned violent, if either Quinn or Connor got hurt, or worse? And do I even have the right to ask Quinn to side with me, if that means breaking his mother's heart and abandoning his brother?

What am I going to do? My old nemesis of a question is back with a vengeance. I wipe my sweaty hands against my denims.

Back at home, above the oven where Mom bakes us brownies, there's an old, round, wooden clock which Dad always swore came from Atlanta's original Union Station — from back before General Sherman rode into town — and had been passed down through the generations until he inherited it. It's as big as a manhole cover, and you can hear it ticking loudly when the T.V. is off. Right now, my heart beats hard in my chest, like the second hand of that clock, counting down the seconds to Zonia and Connor's deadline.

Quinn cricks his neck and stalks off to the guard tree. I follow slowly. I hear the thud of metal striking wood before I reach him. Quinn is sitting against the tree trunk, rifle laid beside him, tossing his knives. I pause, heart clenching when I see the expression on his face. It's bleak. There's no good decision for him either, I realize, no choice that won't hurt someone he loves. I'm about to join him when I see that Connor, approaching from the opposite direction, has beaten me to it. He crouches down on his haunches beside Quinn and talks earnestly, occasionally touching his brother's shoulder as if for emphasis. I watch them forlornly. Quinn doesn't quit tossing the knives, but he doesn't stop listening, either. And Connor doesn't stop talking.

Restless, anxious, desperate not to think, not to have to make a decision, I return to camp. It's almost deserted.

"Where are all the girls?" I ask Mark.

He nods his head in the direction of the shower blocks. "Washing dishes," he says.

"All of them?"

That's a first. It's not like it's generally a preferred activity.

Mark shrugs. Maybe I should join them, volunteer my help. There will probably be extra work packing up supplies and equipment before the departure in the morning.

Oh my God — the morning. The dread inside grows colder, heavier.

I can hear the clatter of mugs and plates in the basins as I draw near to the restrooms. The door is ajar, and I stretch out a hand to pull it open but stop in my tracks when I hear my own name being spoken. The girls inside are gossiping loudly. About me.

"… can't understand why they allow her to stay." I think that's Kirsty.

"They won't — after tomorrow." That satisfied voice is definitely Evyan's. "They only need her for her shooting skills. Once the mission is over, she'll be out on her ass."

"Here's hoping!" The high-pitched giggle that follows is Bree's.

"I don't think they should have allowed her to stay this long. She's a bad influence on morale." Kirsty again. "And I think she brought us bad luck."

"If you ask me, I don't think we can trust her. I mean, like, not at all," Kate chips in. "I think she could still be working for ASTA. She's probably spying on us right now. And if she is collecting information on us, then when Zonia boots her out, she'll just go running back to them to spill the beans."

"And if she isn't working for them, then we're in even worse danger."

"How do you figure that?"

"Because," says Kate, "then they really will be on an all-out hunt for her. To take her in or to take her down. It's a threat to all of us just having her here."

"She's not wanted, she should just go." Kirsty.

"I feel sorry for her." Candace?

"Say *what?*"

"Sorry for her? Why?"

"She's not a bad person. She did an amazing job taking care of Nicky." Yes, that's Candace. She, at least, has come to my defense.

"Yeah, until she, like, *shot* her!"

"Oh, get real — Nicky was dying already. Jinx just ended it a bit sooner, is all. It took courage." Yeah, it did. You tell 'em, Candace. "But," she continues, "I agree that it's a bad idea to have her here with the rest of us. Darius told me that she's wanted across all three sectors now, that there's a massive search on for her. That's got to make it more likely that they'll find us."

So even Candace thinks I'm just a danger to the group.

"She jeopardizes all of us, even Quinn!" Evyan again. "If she loves him so much, then why is she risking his life? Just tell me that! Why is she tearing his family apart? Connor hates her — she tried to kill him. He'll never let Quinn stay with her."

I'm so tired of fighting, of trying to do the right thing, of failing to convince people that I'm a good person. Is there anything I could say to this group that would change their minds about me? It's hopeless. What's worse, they're dead right about me being a danger to them and to Quinn. And though it almost kills me to acknowledge it, Evyan's right that I'm tearing him in two.

I'm about to slip away when the door is yanked open from

inside. Kirsty, Kate and Bree stare back at me, silently condemning. Evyan takes a step towards me and says belligerently, "Can we help you with something?"

I shake my head, turn around and walk away. They can't help me with what I need. And I can't, or rather won't, help the rebels with what they want most from me.

I take a long, meandering route through the woods back to camp, snagging my solar-cell flashlight from my pocket and shining the thin beam at the dripping trees and wet undergrowth, trying to sort out my thoughts and fears. The moon is rising in the sky, between pockets of cloud, casting a silver light on the glistening leaves and rocks. I feel as trapped here, in the wilderness, as I ever did at home or at ASTA.

I don't belong, I don't fit, and it's intolerable that I'm causing pain to Quinn. And danger to Robin.

Chapter 45

Lesser of two evils

By the time I'm back in camp, I know I need to confront Connor.

I need to apologize and ask for his forgiveness. He doesn't have to like or approve of me — hell, I know he never will — but if he can agree to put the past behind us, then it will be so much easier for Quinn. But I need to get him alone, and he stays glued to Quinn's side until midnight when Neil shambles over to take over guard duty. Quinn notices me sitting by the almost-dead embers of the fire and comes over to give me a tight hug and a kiss on the top of my head.

"Ah, you smell good," he sighs, burying his nose into my hair.

"Yeah, I washed my hair."

"Yeah, I remember," he says with a wicked grin, and just like that, I'm blushing again. No one can set me off as quickly as he can. "So why are you still up? Can't sleep?"

I nod. "Too much to think about. You know, tomorrow morning and all."

"I've spoken with Connor tonight. And I think I got through to him."

"Really?" My heart lifts with hope.

"Yeah, he said he'd think about it. Just let him sleep on it and tomorrow he'll think differently, I'm sure of it."

He dips his head to give me a long kiss.

"Faith, but I'm exhausted. I need to sleep. But we'll spend the whole of tomorrow together, yeah?"

"I'd like that."

"Goodnight, wench. Love you."

"Goodnight, pirate. Love you, too. I got in last."

He stumbles through the darkness to his tent, emerges to brush his teeth, and then disappears again. I look into the dark trees and spy Connor sitting near the pile of bags and backpacks, searching his duffel bag for something. This is probably the best opportunity I'll get.

A twig snaps under my foot as I approach, and Connor startles at the sound.

"Oh, it's you," he says flatly and goes back to digging in his bag.

"Yeah, just me."

He ignores me for a long time then finally stops what he's doing and looks up at me with those dark eyes, that expressionless face.

"If you have something to say, spit it out."

"Connor, I — Can I sit down?"

"Suit yourself." He shrugs.

"I want to apologize. I'm so very sorry about darting you, and about what happened to you afterwards because I did. I didn't want to do it, but I didn't really have a choice."

He tilts his head a fraction of an inch, but says nothing. I hurry on to explain, to defend myself.

"I wanted nothing more to do with them — I'd already handed in my resignation. But they insisted on me doing one last mission. I had no freaking idea it was going to be you, I swear. I wouldn't have hurt you for the world — you're Quinn's brother."

"Then why did you?"

"They had a backup sniper, posted a block behind you. He was armed with a real rifle and live ammo. And when I hesitated, he said that if I didn't dart you, he'd shoot. And I believed him."

"So you darted me to save yourself?"

"No! No. It wasn't *me* he was threatening to shoot. It was you. I did it to save you and Quinn. I chose what I thought was the lesser of two evils. To keep you both alive. I still don't see what else I could've done, but I'm so, so sorry. I know I have no right to expect your forgiveness —"

"Aye, you're right there," he says.

I bite my lip to stop myself from saying anything more, and there's another long silence while he studies me impassively. His left hand rubs at his right, massaging the twisted fingers. Do they ache?

At last, he speaks. "And if you'd had live ammo, Jinx, would you have shot me then?"

I stare down wretchedly at my own hands, remembering the scene — Quinn pleading with me, Bruce shouting threats, my confusion rising. Would I have? I force myself to meet his gaze. His dark eyes are nothing like Quinn's gray ones, but there's a similarity in their faces, around the mouth. It makes it harder to say the next words.

"I don't know. I hope not," I say miserably. "But, honestly, if it meant saving Quinn? … Maybe."

He nods slowly a few times. "I appreciate your honesty. Let me be honest with you in return."

"Yes, okay. That's good." We're getting somewhere now.

"I will never forget what happened, and I will never forgive. And if it's the last thing I do, I'll open my brother's eyes so that he sees the real you. And cuts you loose. I'll be with you both on that mountain tomorrow, but I'll be protecting *him*. You will take down Hawke — and please believe me when I say I'll make sure you do it — and then I'll get my brother to safety and have nothing further to do with you. Except to make it my life's mission to keep him away from you." He stands up. "And now I need to be somewhere else. Anywhere else."

He strides off, leaving me sitting, stunned, bent over my pain, beside the heap of bags.

What am I doing here? Between Zonia and Connor and the rebels, it's never going to work. I'm not wanted, and unless I agree to kill Hawke, I'm not needed. I'm worse than useless — I'm a danger to them all, especially Quinn. I should just go.

I could.

No one is around, no one is watching me. I could just grab my bag and walk out of here. Thwart their plans to use me. Zonia would be furious — a win — and the rest would be relieved. Except Quinn.

I'd be hurting him badly. But I'd be hurting him if I stayed, too. If I leave, he'll be heartbroken for a while, but he'll be safer. And he can honor his mother's plea and help Connor, and maybe one day when this is over, he can return safely to his family. But only if I leave, before tomorrow.

So I do.

I grab a long duffel bag from under the pine and tip out its contents, then I snatch up my backpack and fit it over my shoulders, take out my flashlight and strike off into the woods, passing the guard duty tree on my way. Neil is sprawled against the tree, fast asleep already. I lift the rifle out of his loose grip, stow it in the duffel bag, and keep walking — through the trees, to the path that leads to the van and the dirt road beyond. My feet move faster and faster, until I'm running at full speed down the shadow-rippled road, my backpack thumping against my hips.

Less than a year ago, I was a little girl playing a computer game. Now I'm a wanted suspect hunted by the government, rejected by the people I wanted to help, leaving the man I love too deeply to stay with, and unable to go home for fear of endangering my family.

I trip over something in the road and sprawl into the dirt, grazing my hands and banging my elbow. I push myself up and start again. I keep running, though my lungs burn in the cool night air. There's a raw, bloody taste in my mouth, and tears cool my cheeks.

But I'll keep running — like a wraith in the moonlight, down the back road, left at the fork, through and out of the forest, and all the way to the railway siding. I'll climb onto one of those railway cars headed southwest and lie low until I'm far away. Then I'll jump off and find a disposable phone somewhere. I'll call Robin to warn him, tell him to erase his tracks and clean his PC.

And then I'll run and run until I disappear.

Part Four

Chapter 46

Running away

Gross. A hair twists through the bread dough I'm kneading, and I can tell it's one of mine — brown with ruby-red dip-dyed ends and just the faintest trace of blond regrowth at the root.

I try to extract it from the dough without snapping it and leaving half behind.

"You're killing me, kid," Tallulah says, looking at my efforts in amused disgust.

I flinch at the word. Last week she called me a bread-killer because I'd destroyed the yeast by adding water that was too hot. It was my second batch of the day — I'd ruined the first by adding a tablespoon instead of a teaspoon of salt.

Rattled by the word "killer", I've watched her carefully to see if she knows or suspects anything, but I'm pretty sure she has no clue who, or what, I am. No one here at the Inner City Teen Shelter does.

"Jared. Jared!" Tallulah raises her voice to get the attention of the sixteen-year-old lanky boy who is sitting on a stool at the workbench, peeling carrots, moving in time to the music playing through his headphones. "Please take out the trash; that bin is overflowing."

She points to the trashcan, then jerks a thumb in the direction of the alley beyond the back door of the kitchen, where the garbage dumpsters lie. I'm glad she asks him and not me. I try not to set a foot outside, not even into the service alley. I feel safer inside, away from surveillance cameras and police patrols and the watchful eyes of good citizens.

I've been here two weeks, licking my wounds and trying to lay low while I figure out what the heck to do with my life. In a twist of irony, the goods train that I stowed away on, that was supposed to take me far away, just brought me straight back into the heart of the Metropole. I'm less than twenty miles from home and very tempted to go back and check on Mom and Robin. But I know they'll still be under surveillance. I need to stay the hell away if I want to keep them safe.

When I jumped off the train, the morning was gray with clouds and drizzle and doubts. I wondered what would be happening back at the state park. Zonia would be furious. Would she try to get Hawke some other way? Evyan and most of the other rebels would be thrilled at my departure. Connor would be smugly satisfied, no doubt consoling Quinn, reassuring him that he was better off without me.

Ah, Quinn. He would be confused, angry, hurt. Every time I thought of him, my chest tightened, my eyes leaked and my brain blurred with images of his face, his hands, his smile. I couldn't allow myself to go there. It would reduce me to a helpless puddle of misery, and there were things I had to do.

With my hair stuffed up into a beanie and my collar turned up high to hide some of my face, I made my way through City Central station. Very few people travelled by train anymore, but the station was still a place where people came to buy from the *Smart Vendor* machines which took both credit and prepaid cash cards. I examined the contents of the machines.

On offer were the usual products for desperate appetites — porn magazines, cigarettes, booze, weed, junk food and headache tablets. For those wanting divine assistance, there were medallions of St Agricola of Avignon to ward off the plague, collect-a-set prayer cards of the Fourteen Holy Helpers, and — presumably to hedge your bets — Wiccan Sticks ("herbal incense to defeat the miasma of the plague"). Those who put their faith in science could purchase Second Skin respirator and latex glove packs, sanitizer gel and wipes, and bottles of ImmunyChews ("boost your immune system with super-strength vitamin C, zinc, ginger and echinacea"). But I was more interested in the facility for buying items from the *Smart Vendor* online site.

Using a false name and one of my cash cards, I placed an order. Ninety minutes later, a drone delivered my package to the address I'd supplied — an intersection a couple of blocks away, rather than to the station itself, because I didn't want any intel agent to be able to connect the order to what I was about to do.

I walked back to the station and headed for the ladies' restroom. I opened the package, removed the scissors and, gritting my teeth, hacked away at my long hair. I liked my hair, I really did. I hadn't cut it for years, but it was probably the most distinctive thing about me and it needed to go. When I was finished, I had a head of short, raggedly cut blond hair. It was nothing like the cute pixie-cut I'd been aiming for, but it would have to do.

"WTF, man!" said a rail-thin girl who came in to use the toilet while I was cutting. "If I had hair like that, I'd keep it."

"Yeah, well, I'm tired of the way I look. I need a change, you know?"

"I do, man, I do," she said, staring glumly into a mirror.

She looked like a junkie — hollow cheeks, sores pocking her face and a tremor in her hands. Pulling down her mask and lighting up a joint, she apologized, "I'd offer you, man, but, like, the rat germs and stuff. And I've got nothing better."

"No problem."

I gathered up the blond hair from the basin, the hair that Quinn had loved to run his fingers through, and flushed it down the toilet, then followed the instructions in the box of hair dye to turn my blond hair *golden-chestnut brown* with *sexy cherry-red* ends.

"S'gonna look good, kid," the girl said, leaning up against the basin while she smoked the joint and stared at me.

A thought occurred to me. "Hey, do you know of a place nearby where I could hang out for a while? Like a homeless shelter, or something?"

She picked a piece of tobacco off her tongue and stared at it for a moment, then ate it. "Yeah, I guess. You could go to Tallulah's. Though it's not that nearby."

"Tallulah's?"

"Yeah, it's officially called Teen City Shelter or something. But everyone knows it as Tallulah's. Over on the corner of North and Long. But she won't let you stay unless you're clean, man." Another drag on the joint. "Won't even allow booze on the property."

"I'm clean."

"Your loss," she grunted and meandered out of the restroom.

My eyebrows looked too light for my hair, so I retrieved a black eyeliner from my backpack and darkened them with a few feathery strokes, and then circled my eyes with thick, black rings for good measure. What the hell, I might as well go all in. I outlined and colored in my lips with the black eyeliner and stared at myself in the mirror. I looked surly, tough, wild. Nothing like myself. A black leather rocker's jacket would have completed the disguise nicely, but my gray hoodie would have to do.

I hung the new face mask around my neck then peeled the backing off the temporary henna tattoos I'd chosen and applied them to the backs of my hands. A dove of peace for the left hand, and a circular yin-yang symbol for the right. They would last for a couple of months, and they looked like the real deal — an identifying feature that surely any alert for Jinx E. James would mention, if she had them.

Then I locked myself in a toilet stall and removed the remaining item from the package. I fired up the cheap phone, searched for the address the junkie had given me on Google Maps, and memorized the route.

My final task was to warn Robin. It had to be the last thing I did before leaving, because they would still be monitoring his and Mom's lines. As soon as I contacted him, I'd ping on some surveillance system somewhere, and I'd need to bug out of here fast before they could trace the call and send an extract team to capture me.

I keyed in Robin's number, then hesitated, debating whether to call or text. I decided on the latter. I'd have to be super quick, and I didn't think, once I got him on the line, that I'd be able to keep it brief. Once I heard Robin's voice, I'd want to hear all his news, and it might take precious betraying seconds to explain. Also, the sound of him might set me off crying again, as I did all last night and most of this morning.

I paused before typing the message, wondering how best to code the warning so as not to tip off the intel interceptors.

Do a Mr. Johnson on the Maisy of your new hobby.

The Johnsons were our neighbors, and Maisy had been their gentle dog. Back before I left home to join ASTA, Maisy died, and Mr. Johnson buried her in their garden. I hoped Robin would understand that I meant he should bury the evidence of his hacking. I didn't sign the message. He'd know it was from me.

I hit send on the text, then stamped on the phone with my boot, crushing it into small pieces. Flushing the bits down the toilet reminded me irresistibly of the time I'd done the same to Quinn's phone. No, I would not think about him, would not remember the teasing glint which lit his eyes, his warm, firm lips, his *I love you*'s. He was better off without me, safer and less conflicted. I believed that. I hoped there would be a time in the future when we could reconnect. Right now, it was simply too dangerous.

Pulling up my mask, I set off through the drizzling rain for the homeless shelter, but I hadn't gotten five blocks before I was stopped by a passing police patrol.

"You okay, kid?" one of the officers asked, lowering his window just enough to check me out.

"I'm fine."

I kept walking, eyes on the ground, heart hammering. I lifted the hand closest to them up to my backpack straps, so that the tattoo would be clearly visible. My hood was down so my new hair was on show. *Don't panic, you look nothing like yourself*, I told myself silently, *nothing*.

"Where are you headed?" The cop car crawled along beside me.

"Tallulah's."

"Okay, then. Tell her Jim said hi." I nodded, and the car peeled off down the road.

By the time I got to the Inner City Teen Shelter, it was late afternoon and still raining. Sodden, cold, hungry and a single kind comment away from breaking down and bawling like a little kid, I pressed the buzzer. The woman who opened the door was enormous — tall, big-boned and weighty, with the kind of maternal bosom that would have been good for crying on, but I settled for the usual elbow-bump greeting.

She gave me a careful once-over and then said, "You're looking for a place to stay?"

"Yes, please. If I may. I can pay."

"A homeless teenager with good manners and money. That's a

first."

Damn, I needed to disguise more than just my appearance if I wasn't to give myself away.

"Well, come on in, child. You'll catch your death standing outside in the rain like that."

Thirty minutes later I was installed in my room, my tummy full, my clothes unpacked, and my rifle wrapped in a dark sweater and hidden behind the narrow wooden closet. The room was tiny and basic, but the bed looked clean, and my spirits lifted as I sank into a full, hot bath in one of the shared bathrooms.

Tallulah hadn't questioned the name I'd entered in the register book — Kerry Robins, the first name I'd been able to come up with — but she had asked, in a brusque though kind tone, "You running away from something, child, or someone?"

I'd shrugged and fiddled with my earring. "Isn't everyone here?"

"I guess we are at that," she said, and asked nothing further.

Over the next few days, I learned there were about thirty kids staying at Tallulah's, all between the ages of twelve and twenty-one. Some had casual jobs — sorting trash at the recycling center, or working cleaning shifts at the nearby Purification Center Disposal Unit where infected corpses and biohazard material were incinerated — but most hung out all day at the shelter. Tallulah had taken the trouble to set up some skills training modules, so the kids could, if they wanted, learn how to cook or bake, or sign up for computer-based training in programming and systems design.

From what I could see, though, the favorite activity of most of those living here was putting on a pair of virtual reality goggles, sitting at one of the computers in the common room, and playing The Game. A good quarter of them liked to play as snipers. Even now, ASTA would be collecting data on these players, assessing skill levels, selecting potential future cadets. It turned my stomach. I hadn't played The Game for months now, and I never intended to again. I wanted nothing more to do with it or its devious makers.

Every day, I tried to put thoughts of Quinn out of my mind. Every night I allowed them to flood back in once I was in bed and could cry in peace, with one hand on my earring and my face mashed into the pillow. Where was he now? Was he missing me at all? Was Connor filling his mind with lies about me, was Evyan closing in for the kill? There was a hollow in the middle of me, an emptiness which was full of the absence of him. My arms felt cold and bare without his embrace, my face muscles stiff without the smiles he drew from me, and my ears were constantly pricked for the lilt of his voice or the deep rumble of his laugh.

It helped a little — a very little — to keep busy. Today, like every morning, I'd walked straight past the common room, ignoring the harsh sounds of The Game's explosions, shouted commands and ringing shots, and the excited yells of the players, and walked straight on into the kitchen.

And here I am, making bread. Although I'm not very good at it, I am determined. Besides, it's soothing to plunge my hands into the warm, elastic mass of dough, pushing in with my dove hand and pulling back with my yin-yang one, kneading the dough into a satiny-smooth ball.

Tallulah moves her massive frame over to my side of the work bench and pinches out the length of dough containing the hair.

"Sorry," I say. "Should I toss this batch, too?" I must cost her a small fortune in wasted ingredients.

"What the eye don't see, the stomach don't grieve over," she says, examining the root end of the hair for a brief moment before flinging it into the trash can and giving me a conspirator's smile.

I smile back. I'm glad to be here, under her wing. I don't feel safe, precisely. I don't think I'll ever feel safe again. But I feel welcome, and that's a refreshing change.

Chapter 47

Hawke and dove

"Jared," Tallulah says loudly to the kid peeling carrots at the kitchen workbench, "that's more'n enough, boy. Stop peeling and start chopping. Nice and small, mind, like I taught you. Sweet Lord, but it's hot in here!" She opens the back door a few inches, and a breath of cold air drifts in, along with the stench of rotting trash from the alley. "I know I shouldn't leave the door open because of rats, but my brain is overheating."

"If there are rats in the alley, you should report them. They'll send out a team to destroy them. They have specialist teams for that, you know," I say glumly, dividing my big ball of dough into roll-sized portions.

"Honey, if I've reported the vermin once, I've done it a dozen times. And they've never sent a soul to get the rats. No 'specialist teams' come to this part of the city."

Quinn once told me that the government chooses the areas it sends assistance to — making concerted efforts to keep infected rats out of middle-class suburbia, because that's where their voting base lives, while allowing rats — fevered and otherwise — to thrive in areas where the poor, and illegal immigrants and other undesirables live. He called it a form of social engineering. Looks like he was right about that, too.

I set the flattened balls of dough on a baking tray above the massive stove for their second rising.

"Oh no, oh no, this is breaking my heart." Tallulah waves one of her big hands at the T.V. balanced precariously on top of the refrigerator in the corner of the kitchen. It's playing one of the dramatic soapies to which she is addicted. The lead actress has just died a tragically beautiful and completely unrealistic death from rat fever, reducing Tallulah to tears of deeply satisfied misery.

"There now." She sniffs and wipes her eyes with a dishcloth. "But it's an ill wind that blows nobody any good. Now at least Rock will be free to love Storm."

Over the rolling titles, three sharp pips sound out, and then the Southern Sector Government logo appears, followed by the face of President Hawke. He still has that thick, wavy brown hair and square face, but for some reason he no longer strikes me as a huggable teddy bear of a man. Maybe because I came as close as chaos to being forced to kill him, he now seems like just another person to me — an ordinary politician, probably not to be trusted with anyone's wallet or vote.

Mom never liked him. I wonder what she and Robin are doing right now.

Wait, Hawke is saying something about an assassination attempt. Was it the rebels? I snag the remote to turn up the volume.

"But I am pleased to say that rumors of my death have been greatly exaggerated." Hawke grins widely, showing teeth so white they almost have a blue tinge.

"Smarmy son of a bitch," says Tallulah, who has also stopped to watch the Prez.

"The attempt was foiled, and we have arrested several dissidents whom we will be questioning to ascertain information which will help us in the apprehension of even more terrorists."

Several dissidents? Who? Was Quinn captured? I know what that "questioning" entails, and I wouldn't wish it on my worst enemy. Well, perhaps just on Roberta Roth. But maybe the story isn't true, maybe it's just more propaganda. Surely Zonia wouldn't have attempted the assassination without a trained sniper or even a rifle? Unless they reverted to the original bombing plan.

But Quinn is safe. I ran away so that he would be, so he damn well has to be.

"Remember, if you see something, say something!"

I expect to hear the familiar jingle which ends all government PSAs, but instead a serious female voice announces, "These are the faces of the Southern Sector's most dangerous dissidents and terrorists, all of whom are wanted in connection with serious crimes."

A succession of photographs flashes slowly on the screen. Men and women, old and young, some of them standing behind electronically numbered boards, as if for mug shots.

"Under no circumstances should you try to apprehend one of these dangerous offenders," warns the voice. "You should immediately report any sighting to the authorities using the number displayed at the bottom of your screen."

And then I am looking at my own face displayed on the screen. It's the photo from my ASTA ID, when my hair was long and blond with cobalt-blue streaks, and my face looked young and eager. It feels like my image is up there for minutes, hours, as I stand rigidly still, trying to keep my face expressionless while my heart races inside my chest, like a fugitive desperate to escape a prison cell. Will Jared or Tallulah recognize me? Not possible — I look nothing like myself. *Nothing.*

Another face flashes, then another, and I can breathe again.

"You okay there, Kerry?" Tallulah says, giving me a cagey glance. "You look like you just seen a ghost."

"Yeah, no, I'm fine. I … I think I just have low blood sugar."

Is it my imagination, or is she studying me too carefully?

She hands me a fresh-baked cinnamon cookie. "Then eat something. You're already thin enough to be blown over by a breeze."

The last of the onscreen faces is replaced by the See-Say logo, but before the jingle can play, Tallulah snatches the remote out of my hands and kills the power.

"I can't stand that man Hawke and his messages," she says, slamming a cleaver clean through the backbone of a raw chicken spread out on the chopping board in front of her.

"You do?"

"He's a slime-ball." She brings the cleaver down hard, jointing off legs and thighs and breasts. "It amazes me that people don't see it. Most of the kids here seem to think he's the best thing since flavor-change gum. Hey, Jared?" She elbows him, and he lifts up an earphone to hear her better. "What do you think about President Hawke?"

"Hawke? He's cool. I'd vote for him — like, if I could vote. And if you'd ever let me stop with the vegetables."

Tallulah rolls her eyes at me in a see-what-I-mean expression and tosses the bones and scraps of chicken into an enormous stockpot bubbling away on the stovetop. There'll be old-fashioned chicken soup with fresh-baked rolls for lunch — if, by some miracle, my bread turns out edible.

"It's funny. I really used to like him, but I don't think I feel the same about him anymore."

"Yeah? Why's that?"

"Don't know," I say, shrugging.

"I've been meaning to ask you, Kerry —" Tallulah begins.

"I smell cinnamon." Carlos, the youngest kid in the Center, strolls into the kitchen.

He's a roly-poly pudding of a boy with huge, soulful brown eyes, which he turns on 'Tallulah' now. As always, she melts under the power of those puppy eyes.

"Give me a love, first," she insists, folding him into her ample softness.

The kid endures the embrace stoically, keeping his eyes on the prize — the tray of cinnamon cookies cooling on a rack in the breeze beside the back door.

"There, now. Go help yourself to a cookie. No more than two, you hear?"

Carlos nods solemnly and closes in on the cookies. Behind her back, he sneaks one under his mask and pops it whole into his mouth. He slides two cookies into each of his pants pockets before grabbing the permitted two. I grin. Eyes of a choirboy, soul of a conman.

Then Carlos chokes, coughs, backs up several paces, and screams.

The back door of the kitchen, already ajar, now swings open wide, and the four of us stare in horror at what stumbles into the kitchen, bleeding, snarling, growling.

It's an M&M.

Chapter 48

Lost and found

I yank Carlos back by the collar and push him behind me. Tallulah grabs Jared by an arm and yanks him off the stool.

"What the —" His eyes bulge when he takes in the scene.

The M&M is an emaciated old man, with balding gray hair and a single tooth which he bares when he growls at me. He's wearing the tattered remains of a pair of gray suit pants, stained with dark patches. The skin of his chest is stretched tight over the sharp arches of his ribs and cratered with clusters of oozing, putrefying sores. He smells of decay and death.

"Get out of here!" I yell at Jared, Carlos and Tallulah, snatching up a broom to hold the M&M at bay.

The man pulls his cracked lips over his bloody gums and growls a rasping, "Yake-yake-yake-yake." Is he trying to laugh?

He seizes the head of the broom. I think he means to yank it out of my grasp, but instead he rubs the rough bristles against his chest, shredding the thin skin, drawing blood.

"Don't!" I say, even though I know it's futile.

"Sweet Jesus have mercy!" Tallulah whispers behind me, then she hustles Jared and Carlos out into the hallway, and the door bangs shut behind her.

"Yake!" the old man says. His eyes are on me, and I swear that in their crazed, bloody depths, I see a pleading desperation. "I-yake."

"You ache," I say, as comprehension dawns. "I'm sorry."

He begins scratching with the bristles again, grunting. I relinquish the broom and slip out into the hallway, locking the door behind me. Banging and growling noises come from the kitchen. In the hallway, Tallulah and the boys stare at me, white-faced.

"Jared, take Carlos to the common room and stay there. Lock the door and don't come out until we say it's safe. Do nothing else, call no one." I cannot have a response unit swarming all over this place, wanting to interview us, checking up on my identity. "I'll take care of it, okay? Tallulah, you stay here and make sure the M&M doesn't get through that door, and that none of the kids comes near."

She nods, watches me run for the stairs.

"I'll be back in a minute."

"To do what?" she asks.

"To take care of the situation," I call back, bounding up the stairs two at a time.

In my room on the second floor, I retrieve my rifle from behind the closet, check it's loaded, screw on the suppressor and remove the safety catch.

Back downstairs, Tallulah's eyes widen when she sees what I'm holding.

"What in the hell? You brought a long-ass gun into my place?"

"Yeah, sorry about that."

I unlock the kitchen door, crack it open an inch and peer inside. The old man's back is to me — his spine a tight knobbled line of vertebrae beneath his disintegrating skin — and he is banging his head against the wall. Why do they always do that? It brings back a rush of bad memories — of other M&Ms, of sniping "targets", of

Nicky. Of my father.

"Close this door and lock it again as soon as I'm through. And don't open it until I give the all-clear. No matter what you hear, understand me?" I order Tallulah.

"Wait —" she begins, but I'm through the door and inside the kitchen before she can protest and after a moment, I hear the door close and the lock click behind me.

I lift the rifle into position and aim it at the back of the man's head. For once, I won't have to look into my victim's eyes as I pull the trigger. A detached part of me observes the stock against my cheek, my eye lining up the sights, my finger already easing back on the cool crescent of the trigger. For the first time, I am about to shoot another human being, an innocently dangerous old man, without there being any doubts in my mind. I know what I'm doing; I know it's the right thing to do. I'm clear on that. And I can find no guilt or shame or hesitancy inside myself. My hands are steady, my breathing slow and relaxed.

Should I be concerned about the ease with which I am about to kill this man?

I fire.

The man collapses, hitting the ground with a wet, mushy thud.

"Kerry?" Tallulah calls from the other side of the door.

"I'm fine. Stay where you are."

I lay the rifle on the workbench, step over to the kitchen sink to grab a pair of thick rubber gloves, and slide my hands into them. I grab the poor old man by the wrists and drag him out the back door and several hundred yards down the alley, laying him down behind a dumpster overflowing with garbage. He cannot be found near the shelter. Nothing must connect the rifle slug in his head to the sixteen-year-old girl now residing at Tallulah's.

"Sorry," I tell the crumpled heap of ragged cloth and flesh that was once a human being. "Hope you're in a better place now."

I cover the body with a flattened appliance box extracted from the trash and step back to check it's not visible from the alley.

Back in the kitchen, I mop up the blood and gore from the wall and floor, then wipe down every last surface with bleach. I carry the mop, bucket and cloths downstairs to the basement and hurl them into the incinerator, along with my gloves, and stand and stare at the fire for a few minutes. The flames spark and blaze sulphur-yellow, warming my face and giving off toxic plastic fumes which catch in my throat. I close the iron door with the poker and hook the catch. Done.

I stuff my rifle into a clean black garbage bag and bang on the door that leads to the hallway. Tallulah opens it, staring around in suspicious amazement at the clean, empty kitchen.

"What in the name of all that's holy happened in here?" she demands.

"Nothing happened in here. Nothing at all. An M&M wandered in, I clanged pot lids together, and it got scared and ran off down the alley."

She narrows her eyes, studying me for long moments.

"I took care of it, okay?"

"Go tell Jared it's safe to come out now," she says. "I'm off to my office. I need to … have a drink."

I spend the rest of the day in my room, avoiding Tallulah and any difficult questions she might have for me. Surely there must be many secrets in a place like this? I can only hope that she's good at keeping them.

It's early evening when there's a soft knock at my door.

"Yeah?"

Carlos sticks his head around the door and beckons me with one crooked finger.

"Suppertime?" I ask.

He smiles cherubically. The boy sure does like his food.

Tallulah is at the foot of the stairs, waiting for me.

"You go on to the dining room, Carlos. But you, young lady, are coming with me."

My heart kicks into high gear as she clamps a broad hand over my forearm. Her voice is grave when she says, "There's a man here to see you. He's in my office — the rest of them are waiting outside."

"What?" Understanding hits. She's turned me in. "No!"

"Oh, yes. You've been puzzling me since you got here, but when I saw you with that rifle today, I finally put two and two together." She pulls me down the hallway. "That hair sure had me fooled — I was on the lookout for a girl with long blond hair and no tattoos, not some raccoon-eyed, dip-dyed brunette. But today, in that PSA, I saw it. Your eyes are the eyes of that girl on the most wanted list. It don't surprise me you can keep a calm head and shoot to kill. And they did say you'd likely have a weapon with you, and would be prepared to use it."

"No, Tallulah, please. You don't understand — I can explain," I plead, tugging against the iron grasp on my arm.

"As soon as I saw you with that gun, the dots in my old brain connected up. I'd already had the alerts, so I knew what I had to do. And I made the call," she says, dragging me inexorably down the hall to her office. Where a member of the extract team waits. Or perhaps Sarge himself, eager to get the restraints on Blue and drag her sorry ass back to the detention center for another go-round.

I can't. I cannot endure that again.

"And now they're here, relieved to have found you, and ready to fetch you away."

"Please, please, Tallulah! I'm not what they say, I'm not a terrorist." I grab at a door handle on the way, try to brace my feet in the jam, but she jerks me free and walks on. "I'm begging you, just let me go. I'll leave, tonight, I'll just get lost and disappear."

We're at the end of the hall, outside her door.

"I reckon that's precisely what they're afraid of. But now he's got you, he ain't gonna want to lose you again." Tallulah reaches out a hand, twists the doorknob and pushes me inside her dimly lit office, slamming the door shut behind me.

For a moment I'm so shocked and confused that my mind can't compute what my eyes are seeing.

"Finally," says the unmasked man getting up from the chair in the shadows beyond the lamp light. "I've found you."

Chapter 49

Vow

Quinn. Quinn? *Quinn!*

It must be him. Who else would fold me in his arms and hold me tight? Who else would stroke my hair while he mutters, "Jinxy, my Jinxy. You're safe. Ah, my wench. You're a sight for sore eyes."

"Quinn?" I pull back to stare into gray eyes brimming with moisture.

He tugs down my mask and kisses me softly on the lips once. And again.

"It's me, Jinxy. Faith," he exclaims, pulling me back into his embrace, "but you had me tied up in knots. I thought for sure you'd … that they'd … but you're safe."

"What are you doing here?" I'm still half-dazed by the shock.

"I've come to fetch you, of course. Why did you run off like that? You made me vow never to leave you, then upped sticks and ran away from me!" Anger replaces the relief in his voice.

"I *had* to go."

"No, you didn't — not alone. I know what you think, that I was being torn between my loyalties to Connor and to you. Why didn't you ask me to go with you, let me make my own decision?"

"How could I ask you to make that choice?"

"By leaving, you made the choice for me. And you don't get to decide for me, Jinxy. I know what I'm letting myself in for, and I have a right to make up my own mind about it."

"But it's your life at stake."

"That's right, it's *my* life. So it's my decision."

"I'm sorry, I am. I didn't know what to do. I couldn't kill Hawke, and I was scared that they'd make me. And I knew I was bringing danger to everyone and heartbreak to you, Quinn. I knew you wanted to be with your brother."

"Aye, I did at that." He sighs, cups his hand behind my neck and brings my forehead to rest against his. His skin is warm against mine. "Look at your hair," he murmurs, running his hands through my short, dark hair, rubbing the red tips between his fingers. "Faith, but I love you." He smiles. "I got in first."

I don't want to move. Can't move. But I force myself to speak.

"So … Connor?"

"I couldn't make him see, Jinxy. I tried reasoning with him, but he's set on his path, and I can't go with him down that road. We've parted ways."

"You *left* him? Left the rebels?"

"Yeah, I figured I had to. A few came with me, though." Evyan, I'll bet. And where Evyan goes, Mark would be sure to follow. "We're what you might call a rebel splinter group, and our first mission was finding you."

"How did you?"

"Tallulah. She's a key informant on the underground rebel network. Keeps her eyes and ears open and gives us a safe place when one of us needs to hide out. She was one of our supporters that Zonia alerted when you disappeared. Of course, Zonia just wanted to get you back for her plans."

"*Was* there an attack on Hawke?"

"Nah, I think they caught a hint that something was planned, and he went underground — literally."

"In the bunker?"

Quinn nods. "I was desperate to know you were safe, I've been wanting to follow after you ever since you left, so I volunteered to man the comms. That way I would be the first to see any incoming messages like the one Tallulah sent today."

Once an intel, always an intel. "And Zonia let you?"

"I acted like I was mad with you. Faith, I *was* mad! Running away like that." He places his hands on my shoulders and gives me a slow, gentle shake. "But I told Connor and Zonia that I was finished with you, and I guess they believed me. I looked upset enough, and" — he traces a finger over the curve of my ear and softly flicks the earring — "I may have shed some tears."

"I'm sorry, Quinn." I catch his hand, squeeze it hard. "It pretty much broke me in half to leave you. It just seemed like the best — the only thing, really — to do."

He kisses me on the lips with infinite tenderness. "Say you'll never leave me again, Jinxy, promise it."

There's a catch in my voice when I speak the words I know I have to. "You can't stay with me, Quinn, it's too dangerous. I'm on the most wanted list. They're showing my freaking face on T.V. Sooner or later they're bound to catch up with me."

"Sooner or later they're bound to catch up with all of us. Until then, we'll be together, every moment. Swear it."

I want to. I want nothing more than to stay beside him, for always. I'm tired of running away from the people I love.

"Okay," I whisper.

"Say the words," he insists.

"I swear that I, Jinx E. James, will never again leave you, Quinn O'Riley."

"Damn straight!" There is pure love in his eyes, and it fills my chest with joy and stitches my heart back together.

We kiss to seal the deal.

After a long moment, I surface, corral my thoughts, and ask, "So, what happened when Tallulah contacted you?"

"I alerted the others who'd told me they also wanted out, and soon as Zonia and her crew weren't looking, we bugged out and came straight here."

"Like there was no time to lose," I say, smiling.

But his face is suddenly dead serious. "There isn't any time to lose. Jinxy, I'm sorry."

"What?"

It takes only five words to send me from elated to frenzied.

"It's Robin. They've got him."

Chapter 50

Circles never end

"*Robin*? Who's got him? When?" I demand.

"Two days ago. But the message only came in from Sofia last night."

"Sofia? What's she got to do with it?"

"He's being held at ASTA, well, at the PlayState programming unit next door."

"He got caught hacking," I say. It's not a question. A part of me has been dreading this would happen ever since Robin told me of his new passion.

"Yeah. He hacked into The Game — can you believe that? But it must've triggered some alarms."

"Or Zonia ratted him out," I say bitterly.

"Either way, they tracked him down and hauled him off."

Mom! She must be falling to pieces. And Robin — what are they doing to him, even now? My own knees are weak. I sink into one of the chairs, and Quinn takes the other, swings it to face me and holds my hands tight in his warm ones.

"But not to the detention center?" I check.

"No. Well, not yet. Seems they wanted the techies to interview him first, try to find out how he managed to get round their firewalls and break into the system, so they could figure out where and how to fix the weak spots in the security. Apparently they didn't get much in the way of evidence off his machine, he'd wiped it clean or something."

Good. He must have taken precautions when he got my message, even though he continued to hack. Crazy!

But two words of what Quinn said stick in my brain.

"You said, 'not yet'?"

"Sofia says he's scheduled for interrogation, because they want to know exactly what he saw and how much of it he understood. They plan on moving him to the interrogation center as soon as the coding geeks have gleaned what they can from him. Which," he answers my unasked question, "will probably be in the next week."

"How does Sofia know about it?"

"She saw the news when it came through on the intel system and realized it was your brother. She suggested to her commanding officer that a representative from the intel unit go sit in on the interviews with the hacker, to establish whether their own systems might be vulnerable, and she volunteered to be that person."

"She's seen Robin, met with him?"

"Yeah. She says he's doing okay. So far, they've treated him well."

So far. "How did she contact you?"

"It's complicated. Point is, if we plan on rescuing him, it needs to be before they transfer him to the detention center, because once he's there, it'll be impossible to break him out. We've been told that they've beefed up the security majorly since we snatched Connor."

I nod. "You said *them*? Rescue *them*?"

"Sofia wants out, too. She knows it's only a matter of time before they discover her leak and unauthorized searches. It's not safe for her to stay."

"Right. So … we're going to go back to ASTA to break into the very place where I escaped from less than two months ago?" It seems to me that I've spent most of the last year running away — from home, from my job, from the truth, from ASTA, from Quinn.

Now I'm running back, running *to*.

"The irony hasn't escaped me," Quinn says with a wry smile. "And it's going to be dangerous as all hell, Jinxy. There's a good chance that we'll get captured, or worse."

"In that case, I love you, Quinn, and I got in last."

He smiles, but says earnestly, "Are you sure you want in?"

"Am I sure I want in on the mission to save Robin? Of course. Besides, you'll need me to have even the slightest chance of success."

"No argument there. Can we leave now?"

"Just give me a minute to grab a few things."

"You still have the rifle?"

"Yeah."

"Bring it."

Oh, I'll bring it, alright.

I'll bring all of me, my outrage and anger at ASTA, my determination to save Robin and protect Quinn, my steady hands, and my perfect aim with my weapon. They trained me, they deceived me, they pissed me off. They've looked for me, and now they're going to get me.

I'm back downstairs in minutes, my backpack on my shoulders, my rifle in my hands. Tallulah pulls me against her bosom for a goodbye hug.

"Good luck, child. May the angels watch over you."

Amen to that — I'll need all the luck and any heavenly assistance I can get.

"Thank you, Tallulah. For everything."

Quinn is waiting at the open door. "Ready?" he asks with a wild grin, his pirate eyes sparkling in the faint light.

With him on my side, with him *at* my side, I can go anywhere. I can do anything.

I feel strong and tough. Roth was right about one thing, I'm not a little girl anymore. I am a rebel, armed and dangerous. *They* don't rate me as weak or ineffectual or insignificant. If they want me so badly, if they're so determined to capture me, then it must be because they fear me and want to control me.

I'm a threat.

My back straightens. No more running, then. It's time to take the fight to them. It's beyond time that I accept — hell, that I *embrace* — who I am. And who I am is strong, expertly skilled and resolutely determined.

I sling my rifle over my shoulder and pull Quinn close to give him one last fierce kiss.

"I'm ready. Let's go."

"Together," he says. It's not a question.

He takes my hand firmly in his own, and I hold on tight.

"Together."

◆ end ◆

Jinxy and Quinn's story continues in Book 3 of the series, *Rebel*, due for release in October 2016.

Would you like to be notified of my new releases and special offers? My newsletter goes out once a month (at most) and is also a great way to get book recommendations, a behind-the-scenes look at my writing and publishing processes, as well as advance notice of giveaways and free review copies. You can sign up for my author's newsletter at my website: www.joannemacgregor.com

Writers like me live and die by our reviews, so if you loved this book, please consider leaving a review on your favorite online site. Feel free to contact me via my website (www.joannemacgregor.com), Facebook (@JoanneMacg), or Twitter (@JoanneMacg)!

ACKNOWLEDGEMENTS

I would like to thank all my wonderful beta-readers for their invaluable help and feedback, and express my special gratitude to James Bristow of Magnum Shooting Academy for his patient advice on weapons and shooting — any inaccuracies are on me!

www.ingramcontent.com/pod-product-compliance
Lightning Source LLC
Chambersburg PA
CBHW021104110726

47900CB00007B/2017